Lock it Up, Don't Burn it Down!

Copyright© R. J. Vitti 2022

All rights reserved

ISBN-13: 979-8-218-10005-6

Cover design by: R. J. Vitti
Cover art by: Greg Alt (RIP)
Printed in the United States of America

Dedication

This novel is a labor of love dedicated to my lovely wife and best friend, Naomi Rose Vitti. Without getting too sappy, if you took all the best attributes of all the women you have known and roll them into one, you would have Naomi.

Naomi comes from hearty Maine stock with all the smarts, common sense and determination we all wish we possessed. Without her constant support, companionship, and no-nonsense feedback, this book would still be sitting, unfinished, in an envelope at the bottom of the file cabinet.

Naomi, this one's for you!

Foreword

I t's been said by some successful authors and critics that every book needs a reason to exist. If you look back to the very origin of books, you will find that books were and are written to convey a message, a missive, a parable a political or philosophical position, to educate and entertain.

Some early books were little more than reports. During the Franco-Prussian war, Highly Illustrated German war chronicles were published to help the people understand and support the war. At the end of the War, one illustrious publisher-historian collected a copy of each chronicle and turned them into a book, what we might call today a "coffee table book."

So, why write a book that's not about war, or romance, or murder? Because history books come in all sizes and flavors, and are always written by the winners. Rarely is a book written to simply describe life as it was without the sensationalism of a world crisis.

This book was written to merely entertain, educate, and perhaps move the reader to action. Not to any specific task or mission, but just to go get it done.

This book is not intended as a chronological autobiography. Those are reserved for important folks, like dead presidents, kings and queens, rock and roll bands, overpaid professional sportsmen and serial killers.

But wait! There's more. As you start into the book, you'll find that there's a book within the book. The author makes a real effort to describe what it takes to become a writer, especially in difficult political and financial times.   You may find some "preachy" wording, or a concept that bothers you. You may even come across a few "ugly" words. The author has no desire to insult or belittle anyone. But life has ugly words and concepts not everyone agrees with. That shouldn't keep you from enjoying the stories.

As you get into reading, you'll quickly realize that this is a collection of short stories. But the book was never intended to be chronological.

Finally, a couple more thoughts. This is FICTION! Any resemblance to persons alive or dead is purely coincidence or a product of your imagination. Second, since the author chose not to conform strictly with the arbitrary and capricious "rules" of writing and publishing (e.g., No "professional" editor at $5 a page!) You will probably find a small number of errors. Jut let them go. It's not worth your time to grind over a missing comma or paragraph indent. Just enjoy the stories, and fill in the blanks where you need to. Remember, life is messy, deal with it!

With the Warmest Regards, Kona and Maggie

Introduction

Meet Bob, the grandson of Italian immigrants who arrived in New York through Ellis Island just before the turn of the the 20th century. He is the third child of Mike and Angelina and has seven siblings. Bob's family was considered by some to be the poor working class. But that was never the way Bob saw himself. He only saw opportunity, excellence and potential. At a very young age, he believed he was a hero in the making.He was about 11 when his Mother, who was seven months pregnant, slipped and fell in the kitchen. As Mom was screaming and unable to get off the floor, Bob kept his composure enough to call the police. A hero without a cape, but a hero nonetheless. Eventually.

His book chronicles the stories of his life. Bob reveals his humble beginnings, his various and interesting jobs as a kid, and some unsettling stories about being relentlessly bullied in middle school. He also shares some of his stories from his years in the Army. He writes about teaching golf and coaching high school and Special Olympics. The bottom line is, it's written to be an enjoyable collection of stories with a bit of insight into life in the 20th century.

He wrote the first draft on New Year's Eve, 50 years earlier, his life kept him so busy that he never had the time or energy to go back to writing. So, there he sat, decades later, trying to finish his "Great American

Novel." Fifty years of work, kids, grandkids, foster kids, financial disaster, careers success and career failure, loyalty and betrayal, love found and love lost had transpired since the start of his book. All the stuff needed for the "Great American Novel."

Finally, throughout his years, Bob could never quite figure out why it was always cold in that house on Hoyt St. The explanation had eluded him as a kid, and escaped his analysis as an adult. Perhaps that answer will reveal itself before Bob departs this mortal coil. Perhaps.

Table of Contents

Chapter 1~The Novelist

Bob didn't wake up one day and say to himself, "That's it! I'm going to be a writer." His interest in writing came slowly by way of his yearn for reading. As a youngster, he would sit for hours on the front porch of the old farmhouse on Hoyt St. reading his library books. Each summer, he would join the public library kids reading program, where they would earn stickers for each book they read. In his tenth summer, he managed to read 174 books in ten weeks! He filled up his dinosaur sticker book three times, plus.

His first act of writing, beyond school book reports, was his "journal." Girls had diaries, but boys wrote journals. At first he was fastidious at his daily entry, recording anything of import from the day, and capturing his financial inflows and outflows in the journal. He always tracked every penny earned and spent in writing. While he often got lazy and missed a day, he never questioned why he was doing it. He just knew it might be significant some day.

Bob had plenty of writing assignments in Seminary school, including great success with the two movie documentaries he wrote, filmed, produced and narrated; a one man video production. The first one in Junior year was on Thoreau and his philosophy of simplicity and civil protest, and a second in Senior year on Dante and his Inferno. Although he hadn't written a script before, they turned out well enough, along with the 8mm film and audio track, to garner a grade of "A" from   the English teacher both times.   He always managed to get top grades in his English classes since he began grade school. Writing came naturally to him.

His journal entries stopped completely after high school. But his writing continued as an English major in college. He had plenty of opportunities to write on a variety of topics, usually assigned by the professor.

Unfortunately, as with most colleges, one professor was a total prick! His "creative writing" professor in Sophomore year was a self-appointed literary Einstein, long, greasy hair, yellow gapped teeth and all. And while he never found the courage to tell anyone, he was a card-carrying left-wing socialist. Bob didn't recognize that at the time, since he was naïve on so many real-world topics. He only figured it out when he found consistently poor grades any time he wrote about Vietnam. He couldn't, at first, figure out why anything he wrote about war never got more than a "C" grade. He lacked the wisdom to change course and write on topics more to the personal liking of his wannabe Walt Whitman "professor." He might have learned the lesson had he been taking a Poly-Sci course, but not an English creative writing course!

His first foray in to non-school assignment story telling was his vain effort to write a novel about his first girlfriend, Cheryl He began writing on New Years Eve, 1970, just a couple of weeks after she kicked him to the curb for a drug-addled rich boy who lived just a few doors away from her and was headed to the same college. Bob completed about 30 pages on his yellow, portable Olivetti. He worked well into the night, falling asleep sometime in the wee hours of the new year! He read it once the next afternoon, stuffed it in with all his other original works inside his school notebook. They didn't see the light of day for decades. But, it was a start. Unfortunately, he never got the traction that true creative passion generates.

While he did, on occasion, read through his writings in later years, it was usually when the family was moving or cleaning out stuff and, like a puppy at the kennel, the dusty works just found him. But it would be decades before he got back to creative writing, no thanks to that egomaniacal English professor, and his demeaning critique of the stuff Bob had written for class.

On one such occasion, he came across a large, manilla envelope. In it were several hand-written short stories, essays and poems. Then he noticed the cranky lettering of the old Olivetti portable. He pulled out the few faded, yellowed pages and began to read his first attempt at the "Great American Novel."

His writing throughout his technical career was met by positive feedback, which he carried throughout his professional life. In one of his early Army assignments, he was assigned to write articles for the Post newspaper, as well as the narrative for a video intended to instruct recruits on the post-Vietnam Army policies on Drug and Alcohol Abuse. That twenty minute snorefest was foisted on every new trainee class coming through Ft. Leonard Wood for years to come. Not his best work, those poor bastards.

As an officer, his daily routine was filled with written reports, orders, and training curriculum. No Pulitzer material, but good experience. In later years, as he was assigned to the advanced courses in Fort Gordon, Fort Ben Harrison, and Fort Riley, his writing skills were constantly put to the test, and excelled. Time and time again, he would pump out one or another technical report or tactical and logistics plan. This type of writing was not entertaining or enjoyable by any measure, but all required to "get his twenty years."

After he was out of uniform and into a civilian job, his writing skills were continually pushed. Writing contract proposals for the government was a never-ending endeavor, with a multitude of volume managers, technical content contributors, graphic artists, Red teams, Blue Teams and Murder Boards. A real circus to keep folks busy outside their normal duty assignments, and mostly a waste of talent. The real writing challenge was to clearly describe how your solution was better than the other guy's, which in most military contracts, wasn't much more than a taxpayer-funded popularity contest.

He never found the time or the incentive to write for fun until he was retired, decades later. Even then, his motivation was lacking. In fact, his motivation for about anything creative was lacking. He had married the most imaginative and creative person on earth, and spent countless hours over the years working crafts for fun, and sometimes a small profit. But now, with most of his life behind him, he didn't really want to waste valuable time doing anything that didn't bring him joy. That was the real challenge. While he usually enjoyed reading what he wrote, getting to the finished product was a chore. The literary term is "blocked", but it was worse than that. Bob had sunk to the level of "What the hell? What's the point? Do folks even read books anymore?" Especially a book by him about him? That would make it an autobiography, something he didn't feel worthy writing. Autobiographies are written by kings, presidents, statesmen, industrialists, and most recently, by sports and Hollywood "celebrities." Not Bob. He just wanted to tell stories about growing up that others might enjoy, hell, maybe they even learn something! But not an autobiography.

A local published author Bob played golf with offered the advice to "write the ending first." That way, you'd be writing to that end, with a goal in view." Good advice that Bob couldn't execute for obvious reasons. After all, who wants to write of his own demise, his own obituary? So, naturally, he started at the beginning. Finally, he became the writer.

Chapter 2~41 Hoyt Street~The Origin of This Species

I t was always cold in that house. Not just in the frozen death grip of your quintessential Nor'easter, when the wind, the sleet, the devil's ice would rape across Long Island Sound and plunder the Connecticut coastline forcing the large, blurred panes of glass of the vintage farmhouse to rattle in their frames, allowing blast after blast of cold, wet air into the bedroom. So cold was the air that it easily overwhelmed the coal furnace two floors below. Ice would form on the inside of the glass, especially if anyone was breathing nearby, creating random crystalline displays that crept slowly across each pane.

It didn't take much for a child to imagine that he was caught in the middle of a Three Little Pigs cartoon. The wind would blow with such force that the very walls would appear to be moving in and out with each violent gust. The best Bob could do was to put on long johns and an extra shirt, and pull the threadbare blue blanket up over his head. That way, at least, his breath wouldn't be wasted on painting the windows.

It was a small, two story farmhouse with Victorian accents situated on a 60 by 90 foot downtown lot in the town of Northfield, CT. Unlike more modern houses, this one was built strong.

The main support beams went all the way from foundation to attic. The floors were hardwood tongue and groove, stained then painted over the years. The only weakness in the old house was the lack of insulation against the New England winters. Construction techniques of the day used plaster over lathe for the walls, with only a bit of old newspaper between the lathe and the exterior sheathing. It's no surprise the walls would breathe!

In the early days, a basement was used for little more than root cellar and coal storage. There were no rec rooms or wet bars. Just dirty, cold and damp spaces under the floorboards. A set of standard interior stairs rose along the west wall to a door that entered the playroom. There was a full door at the top of these stairs, which served to cut the drafts, minimize the musty odors, and keep the kids from falling down the basement steps!

At some point in its early life, the house was fitted with a coal furnace in the basement.   Its full circumference exceeded twenty feet, with huge, round ducts leading from the firebox to the first floor. But only the first floor. Any heat that reached the second floor bedrooms rose almost accidentally through one, double-sided grate connecting the dining room ceiling to the boys' bedroom floor. A huge, steel grate was planted in the playroom floor and fed the "fresh" air back to the basement monster. A very inefficient system which became totally useless on those horribly cold nights when no amount of coal could keep the house above 50 degrees.

The roof had three peaks, each with its own window. The large attic windows had cross frames of stiles, each intersecting the wrinkled glass and creating several mini-windows. The attic space was always dry and sunny, thanks to the abundance of windows. Years of dust had accumulated, spreading an even coating of musty, silent history across the less-than-tight floorboards. At the back of the attic the brick chimney hugged the wall and exited out through the roof to the sky. There wasn't even a hint of insulation in the attic. The chimney originally served the wood stove in the kitchen and most probably a central hearth in the dining room. The chimney was later adapted to vent the basement furnace.

The only bathroom in the house had a cast-iron claw-foot tub, a sink and mirror, and the crapper, crammed into what appeared to be a former 5 by 12 foot closet. It was likely that the early residents were quite familiar with an outhouse, since the plumbing for this only bathroom was not enclosed in any wall. A shower wasn't installed until the 1970s, and it was simply a shower head and curtain for the existing tub.

The front door opened from the porch into a foyer with a stairwell to the second floor on the right and double door entry to the drawing room on the left.

Straight ahead was another door entering the middle room, later called the playroom. Over time, all the floors were covered with either linoleum rolls or vinyl tiles. The only room that was left bare was the living room, normally covered with a thrift shop rug which was changed out from time to time.

The dining room took up the space along the side yard, opening to the playroom on the right. There were three dining room windows enclosed in a bay. The dining room was connected to the living room by an open doorframe which may or may not have originally had double doors. Now, it was host to a long, solid dowel that went end to end in the opening and held a two-piece curtain that could opened to each side. Very Italian.

The kitchen ran the full width of the house on the north, back side. A small porch was situated off the northeast corner in the original house was later enclosed to enlarge the kitchen. A 4 by 6 foot pantry took up the northeast corner.

Stories over the years posited that the kitchen was actually an original, stand-alone building, with the rest of the residence added at a later date. As the story went, the kitchen was actually the original office and print shop for the Northfield Advertiser, the town weekly.

It was not out of the question architecturally, since the kitchen appeared to be of older beams, many of which appeared hand-hewn, and the kitchen was only one level. Add to that the fact that dozens of glass photo plates were uncovered in the back yard when the garden was first turned, and for several years after. Further evidence included the later appearance of a nearly identical, larger house next door built by the newspaper's owner.

In addition to the only bathroom, the second floor included three small bedrooms. The master was about 12 by 12 feet, while the kid's rooms were barely large enough for three kids beds. The boys room was slightly larger thanks to the bay window. Each bedroom had a small closet, and a single light bulb suspended from the center of the ceiling with a pull string. There were no wall switches or electrical wall outlets in the bedrooms. In fact, the only wall switch in the entire house was a double push-button in the entry hall that controlled the front porch light. All the wiring was original cloth wrapped copper with screw-in fuses and ceramic insulated stand-offs. The original 19th century electrical system was not very adaptable to modern appliances and posed more than a minor fire hazard.

A survey of the house from the street revealed the quaintly artistic flair of the late 19th century. A sitting porch stretched along the entire front of the house, with six very wide steps down to the concrete sidewalk. The porch railings were supported with turned stiles in the Victorian design, and the roof supports had decorative arches reaching to the ridge beams. They were probably more for design than support, as most mysteriously disappeared over time and the house didn't collapse. Two huge double-hung windows stood sentry over the porch, facing Hoyt Street .

There were two young trees marking the centerline of the lot as viewed from the street looking north; a Maple just off the street and a "twin" Pine, centered in the yard opposite the kitchen door. Small indigenous berry hedges hugged the west property line, interrupted only by a mature and somewhat rotten apple tree up past the twin pine. Near the back of the lot stood a bright red chicken coop, complete with a few layers. The last fifteen feet of the lot, at the top of the sloping property, was the smaller part of the garden. The rest of the garden occupied the northeast corner of the property, all the way down to the barn.

At harvest time, Mom could feed the whole family with very few store-bought items. The garden had a variety of fruits, vegetables and treats. Big Boy tomatoes were always a favorite, where one slice of tomato and some mayo made a complete sandwich. Green beans, peppers, carrots, radishes, raspberries, strawberries and, later in the season, melons were and annual treat. In those days, the garden served more as a food source than a hobby, as you would expect with eight kids. Italians didn't need the encouragement of the World War II "Victory Gardens" campaign.

Historically, they were farmers by necessity. Farm or starve.

The small barn held a tight position along the east property line diagonally adjacent to the pantry. There was just enough room between the house and barn for a concrete walkway. The barn was designed to resemble an English carriage house, complete with wide, double doors up front. Each door had three windows near the top, and wide, white 1 by 6 crossed beams creating a large X on the front of each door. The dirt and coal ash drive led from the red and white doors down the gentle slope to Hoyt St. Dad never used the garage to park the car. He needed the space for his gardening tools, fertilizer, wheel barrow and lawn mower.

Eventually, the house got so small that brother Rick decided to make himself a lair in the back of the garage. At first, it seemed like a crazy idea. The fact that the garage was nasty, dirty and smelled of fertilizer and lime, didn't at all deter Rick. Within a few weeks of starting. Rick had installed a new door in the back of the garage, cleared the entire back half, installed his own refrigerator, and of course, his stereo. He pulled a heavy duty extension cord through the kitchen window and into the garage window. He somehow managed to close both windows over the cord so that the weather would be kept at bay.

His next task was to install an antenna on the barn, which was easy for him as a radio hobbyist. Over the years, he had spent endless hours as a hobbyist DXer listening to radio signals from around the globe.

Soon, Rick had his own, private retreat with ready access to the house, sometimes through the door, other times through the second story window into the bedroom. That was his favorite way to escape the house late at night, before he finished his hideaway.

Some months after finishing his garage abode a strong thunderstorm came through the neighborhood. Lightning struck his new antenna and jumped to the power extension cord, zipped through the kitchen window, blew through the kitchen-dining room wall, continuing through the living room, through the TV and out through the living room wall. Amazingly, the only casualty was the old Black and White Zenith, which really wasn't a great loss. It did, however, scare the ever-loving crap out of everyone in the house.

Despite the fairly good quality of construction for the time, it's not a challenge to believe the house was always cold. Bare floors covered with thin linoleum, large, thin-paned windows in loose frames without proper drapes, no insulation anywhere, bedrooms without heat and a cold, wet basement.

The furnishings were no prize, either. The living room had a well-used second-hand couch and one upholstered easy chair. If more than four wanted to watch TV, they pulled in a dining room chair or sat on the floor.

The dining room was centered on the yellow porcelain table, with a second piece inserted to expand it for the larger groups. Up against the bay windows was a small piano, always cluttered with family photos and Catholic trinkets. There were never enough chairs for a large group, and the ones available were often a bit rickety, with a loose screw in the back or a missing foot. At the back of the dining room was a very old buffet, again cluttered with photos, trophies and sundry memorabilia.

The "playroom" as it was called for no relatable reason was stuffed with clothing and not much else. Some time in the '70s a store-bought washer and dryer were set up in the corner nearest the kitchen. Unfortunately, the dryer was never set up since the house wiring could not support it.

The kitchen was not the primary activity center for a family of ten. They spent far more time in the living room. Until the new washing machine was installed, an old electric washtub with attached ringer stood faithfully in front of the sink, almost blocking the door to the kitchen. All the cupboards had been replaced a few years after the property was purchased. The old wood and glass was replaced with modern olive-green aluminum cupboards and yellow countertops.

The kitchen always smelled like a wash room of detergent and wet diapers. Eventually, mold took over and was never remedied. Cooking was done on an early version of electric stove; four burners, an oven and a warmer underneath. It was amazing that a single appliance could perform such a huge task for so many years. Nobody in that house ever starved. When a kid was hungry in the evening, they would help themselves to some bread and butter or a bowl of cereal. Nothing much else was available. No pre-packaged energy packs and certainly no cupcakes or Ding Dongs.

The master bedroom on the second floor had a queen bed with a headboard and footboard from the Art Deco period, many years before. But it was sturdy furniture built to last a long time. There was a matching vanity with mirror opposite the footboard along the wall. And that was it. There was no room for loungers, dressing trees, or whatever else the furniture salesmen were pushing in the '50s. And certainly no money for anything new. Everything in the house was second-hand, a perk of living in a town of incredibly wealthy industrialists and financiers. Working on their estates for generations reaped occasional benefits beyond a handful of cash for services rendered.

The boy's room had a full size bed on the closet wall, and a second child's bed along the entry wall. Sometimes, there was a large crib on the third wall, for the youngest toddler. Even the sheets and blankets were second-hand, but good enough for the "hired help." Beggars can't be choosers, you know.

The bedrooms never had carpet, but always a roll of linoleum spread over the original wood floor. Cowboys on horseback was the theme on the boy's room for at least a decade. The only other piece of furniture that found its way into the boy's bedroom was the student desk Bob got for Christmas when he was ten.

There was no "girls" room until there were girls in need of something other than a basinet to sleep in. In a single day, the "spare" room, basically a junk room, was transformed into another bedroom with a couple of used beds and mattresses. There was never any other furniture in there.

It was a rundown ramshackle former blue collar class house, now with eight kids, a dog, one or more cats, and of course, the chickens! That simple, bare-bones hovel was the eventual growing field for eight Italian-American children. The house, the porch, the yard, the tree, but rarely the basement. The basement was always damp, cold and smelly. All the stories and experiences the kids would carry with them began at 41 Hoyt Street.

The house certainly wasn't middle class, but may have been when first built. But it could never be considered privileged class. Now, it was poor white working class. The poverty was easy to see. Threadbare blankets, hand-me-down furniture and junk cars in the drive were the obvious markers. There were times when school lunch was a tuna fish sandwich every day for a year. Strangely, there was always an abundance of sugar in Mom's cookies, Grandma's chocolate cakes and 7-Up or Coca-Cola. There was always sugar in a house that did not have a single toothbrush. Rotten teeth became par for the course for Bob. That made for many long, painful and sleepless nights. Mom would give Bob a baby aspirin to put on the tooth in hopes it would dull the pain. Since dentistry was so expensive, cavities were never repaired. Each offending tooth was eventually removed because that was the best you could get from Dr. Buccari for 20 bucks. Those repeated episodes revealed everything about the family finances.

But there was more to it than the physical senses could capture. Even on a hot August day, Bob could feel the odd coolness as his bare feet hit the cowboy-print linoleum first thing in the morning. As he sat in the living room on a fall evening, the slightest breeze could be felt on the back of his neck. Mom would say it was just drafty. But it wasn't just the house. There was something else, almost ephemeral. Something a young boy could not consciously perceive. But it was there, and it was a mystery that grew over time and would haunt him many times in years to come.

Chapter 3~Chuck and Angie

Dad (Chuck) was a talented, athletic and intelligent man. But, more importantly, he was a hard working and patriotic American, just like his father, Antonio. And just like his father, Chuck served his country in uniform. He signed up for the war in '43 and completed Diesel engine mechanic school before being deployed overseas. His assignment with the Army Air Corps was unique. He was sent to the ruthlessly frigid mountains of China to maintain all the diesel engines, including the diesel generators that supported the radio relay sites for the pilots flying "the hump." On the one and only occasion he spoke of it, he told of a time when he and his buddy were driving down the mountain to base camp to fetch some supplies and the mail. Without any warning, the Jeep they were driving slid off the icy road and skidded sideways down the mountain for what seemed an eternity. Luckily, the jeep got snagged on some trees and rocks, and ground to a halt. Chuck later joked about how war wouldn't be such hell if they didn't have to drive "those damn Jeeps!" Fortunately, only a couple of bumps and bruises provided any evidence of the accident. Except the Jeep, of course. It had to be towed back up the side of the mountain and sent in for some repairs. The most painful aspect of the whole mess was that nobody got their mail that day!

But, strangely, he never talked about the actual job of keeping the generators running or the hardship of living in the crazy cold at high altitude AND keeping the generators running! Perhaps he felt that his part in the war was far less important and didn't compare in risk to life and limb that others suffered "on the front." He just never talked about it.

After the war, Chuck did what was expected of all returning GIs; Take a bride, start a family, and chase the American Dream: A house with a white picket fence, 2.5 kids, a car in every garage, and a chicken in every pot. Of course, that would require finding a decent-paying job as a diesel mechanic in a quaint bedroom village where there wasn't much call for that discipline.

While looking for that opportunity, he went to work with Antonio, at the Failer estate as a caretaker. The money wasn't great, but after a long search, Chuck got a job as an auto mechanic at the Buick dealer in town. There, he worked his way up through the ranks to Parts Manager and Service Manager, only to be unceremoniously canned after 18 years, without explanation, without compensation. He continued to work as a caretaker throughout his life, and took other, lower-paying service station mechanic or parts jobs as they came up.

But Chuck was also a bit of a wheeler-dealer. He once uprooted the Japanese Maple from the front yard and sold it to a stock broker who was one of his landscape customers. Use the resources you have at hand. Survival.

Chuck and Angie (Mom) were married in 1946, when Chuck returned from the war. Unfortunately, Chuck never made enough money to support his family in any reasonable manner. Certainly not in the manner of "those damn rich people" as Mom would say. Despite the lack of well-paying jobs, Chuck managed to get a mortgage for the house in 1956 while working at the Buick dealership. It was later revealed that the Murphys "may have" helped with the downpayment. But that was the extent of his investments. Every other penny went to taking care of his eight children, with just a few bucks held back for his own menial entertainment purposes.

Amazingly, in addition to working two or three jobs at a time, Chuck always made time to coach Little League and lead the Boy Scout Troop, even two troops at the same time. There was never any obvious plan to use valuable time coaching, he just never let his lot in life keep him from doing for others in his own way. Such generosity would eventually get him in continuous hot water with Angie, who thought that his time was better spent with his own kids. That's not to say that he didn't spend time with the kids, but everything is relative and stories change over time. All of the boys had their turn on his Little League team. Four of the five boys were also in Dad's Boy Scout troop for however long they wanted. He also enjoyed playing board games with three or four kids at a time. His favorite was a penny game called "bank", which was really just a carnival game adapted for kids. Mom didn't like the penny betting for kids so young and always accused Dad of cheating. Monopoly was another favorite, but that usually ended with someone broke and upset.

He enjoyed teaching the kids about his Italian garden "just like" Grandpa Antonio's in the back yard. The only difference was the lack of grape vines. Every true Italian had grapes in the garden for wine making. Not at 41 Hoyt St. There was no alcohol of any kind in the house. Therefore, no grapes required.

And then there was always the wrestling. That was a right of passage for most boys in those days, to "toughen them up!" Of course, Mom had a real issue with it, especially wrestling in the house. But it went on for years, until Mom put an absolute halt to it with the younger kids. Alas, that didn't stop Dad from giving wheelbarrow rides to the sisters until Mom caught him and put a stop to that, as well.

Chuck didn't smoke or drink, and only occasionally did he bet on the horses or Jai alai. He was a good Christian man who did what he could to instill a lasting sense of right and wrong in his kids. The first four kids attended Catholic school and everyone went to Mass on Sunday. They were all properly Baptized, made

Communion and Confirmation. When they got married, most did it in a Catholic Church. Bob even attended Christ the King Prep Seminary for four years. He was going to be the "priest of the family." Every Italian-American family had the unspoken duty to produce a priest for the Church.

But Chuck wasn't a saint by any means. There was the occasional colorful language, especially when he was watching Friday night white on black boxing on the black and white TV. Like most guys, he also liked to escape from it all now and then. Sometimes he would head up to the country club to "sneak on" for nine holes with his brother and cousins. Other times he just went out to play some softball with his friends. That aspect of his life not only gave him some temporary relief from his responsibilities, but also seemed to make him a bit more human.

Angie was also extremely intelligent and talented. She was born to Michael and Anna Carchia (originally from Panni, Italy) and was one of three daughters. She was the middle daughter and would often tell about getting disciplined more often because Anne was the "oldest" and Carole was the "baby."

Judging by her early photos, Mom was a beautiful young lady, with strong yet gentle features, medium brown eyes and chestnut hair. When she was about 17, she was offered an opportunity to model for a ladies magazine. Her parents wouldn't hear of it, if only for the fact that she had to take the train to New York City. That was an opportunity lost that nobody was ever allowed to forget.

She prided herself on being self-sufficient and very creative. While she probably had dreams beyond being a mother, she never discussed them with the children. Angie was a great tutor and disciplinarian. She made no bones about the importance of not just an education, but of good grades. Studying was the primary after school task. There was no TV until homework was complete. She would help where needed and cook dinner at the same time. The result? All eight kids became excellent students.

Aside from her cooking, cleaning, ironing, sewing, shopping and raising kids, Mom actually found time to mentor a Cub Scout pack for many years. In her later years, she found time to join the Catholic Daughters of America. Angie loved to stay busy and help others.

When she got upset with Chuck, Angie would sometimes complain that theirs was an "arranged" marriage, a very common custom throughout history. That was more frustration than fact, but it made the kids a bit confused from just hearing it. Luckily, it didn't come up very often.

Chapter 4~Go Forth and Procreate

When Michael and Angelina Vitti purchased 41 Hoyt St. in 1956, they already had four children afoot and one in the oven. Michael, Jr. was the oldest, born 1947. He was followed by Anthony, 1948, Bobby, 1952, and Ricky, 1956. Johnny would arrive in 1958 in the new house. But there was more to come. After a brief hiatus, three daughters were born. Angela, Michele and Cheryl. The makings of the quintessential poor immigrant family with far too many mouths to feed.

But eight kids made for a solid Italian-Catholic family. To make it more interesting, Angie and Chuck tried to spell out the word M-A-R-R-I-A-G-E with the first letter of each of the kids names. It worked well for the first four: **Michael, Anthony, Robert, Richard.** But then came John. Since the Jewish name Isaac just wouldn't work in a Catholic family they used the next letter. Angela fit in fine, but all was forgotten after that. A nice try resulting in one of those interesting family stories no one remembers.

But what remained was the fact that there were ten mouths to feed, clothe, and shelter. All of this on a mechanic's paltry paycheck. Chuck supplemented his meager grease monkey income as a landscaper and estate maintenance man. He had been working at the Failer estate on Smith Ridge Rd since he returned from the war. He took care of everything from the grass to the rose garden to washing and changing out the storm windows each Fall.

On occasion, he'd take one of the boys out to help him with some chore or another. It was there that they saw their first cicada shell stuck to the trunk of the Chestnut tree and Mrs. Failer's dead butterfly collection hanging on the brown shingles in the never ending wrap-around porch. It was there that they learned to explore the woods and run in fear from the big, granite "devil's chair" and stay clear of the Gravely riding mower. It also was there that they learned, in short, simple lessons, the value of work. Some days they would help wash the storm windows before Chuck put them up, other days, they raked leaves. These essential work lessons would be learned and relearned throughout their lives.

In return for his landscape efforts, the family was allowed to live in the original servant's cottage at the back of the estate. But with a fourth child on the way, Angie and Chuck had to find a bigger place. 41 Hoyt St. was the solution. Feeding eight hungry children on a mechanic's slave wage was less than a fair challenge. There came a point when the family doctor recommended some new "vitamin milk shake" for Bob because he was "too skinny." It was no secret that he was underweight for his age. But, so was brother Tony. Grandma Vitti would often tell him "mangia, mangia, you too skeenee" in her best Italian-inflicted English. Too bad that "milk shake" tasted like warm moose shit! He managed to drink about a half of the first dose, and the rest went in the trash. "Do you have any idea how much money you just wasted?" And money was not overflowing the coffers in that house. If not for the skill of Mom in shopping and cooking for ten, they might have all ended up with a lifetime of eating disorders.

However, there would come a time when there were seven children sharing two bedrooms, plus the baby in the master bedroom. The overcrowding was only relieved when the oldest sons were drafted into the military.

Life on Hoyt St. was a grand mix of the good, bad and ugly. It's difficult to avoid fun when so many kids are involved. Although the boys invented Vittiville, an extensive dirt village in the back yard, the girls eventually caught on and put their own spin on the little unincorporated town. They would play grocery store by cutting coupons out of the newspaper and using them as shelf items in the imaginary store.

It was true mid-century playcraft for the poor. They made the best of what they had, under Mom's careful guidance and active imagination. Sometimes it was clothespins in a cigar box for the younger kids and home-made play dough for the older ones. Mom's knowledge and love of crafts was so extensive that she served several years as a Cub Scout Den Leader. All of the cubs thoroughly enjoyed her fun-based learning every Wednesday afternoon. And the learning part was never lost on her own kids. All the kids thought it was so cool to grow their own crystals in a jar!

Of course, one thing the boys enjoyed more than most was climbing trees and building forts. There was one time when Ricky was working on his own to build his "special" fort in the twin pine. Bobby and Johnny were playing in the yard nearby when they heard the strangest thwack, thwack, thwack, thump. As they turned to the sound, they saw Ricky making his final landing on the dirt under the tree. He looked up, looked at his brothers, laughed hysterically, and climbed back up the tree.

Between mudpie fights and burying treasure in the back yard, the Vitti kids rarely had a boring day. When winter froze the landscape, they would build snow forts and sled runs. Suicide hill was their favorite. It ran the length of the hill on the neighbor's property up past the garden and the chicken coop. It headed straight downhill for a while, then around a sharp corner and down along the briar patch. Unless you missed the turn. Then you ended up in the briar patch. A perfect run got you all the way down to the lot where the neighbors later transplanted an ante-bellum house. They trucked that massive house from the far side of town, all in one piece! As amazing as that was to witness, it ended up destroying the best sled run in town!

While they were rarely bored, and usually by choice, there were times that were better forgotten. Late one night when Bobby was around four, the two older brothers got to fighting in bed. While that was a normal activity for boys, they made the mistake of waking Bobby up from a dead sleep. Chuck got an earful from Angie and steamed up the stairs to the bedroom, his size 44 inch belt already doubled in his hand. His punishment was swift and accurate, and the two older boys exploded with tears of fear and pain. But it wasn't a true whooping. Just two quick lashes on each butt, and a stern scolding to stop fighting and stop waking up their little brother.

From there on, the threat of the belt was all that was required to quell any situation. Even though the kids would be in trouble from time to time, Dad never used it again. Ever.

Clothing was mostly hand-me-down, unless it was a Christmas or birthday gift. When a gift was clothing, it was common to hear a "Clothes, again?" complaint from one of the siblings. Many mornings, Mom would find a bag or a box of used kids clothing on the front porch, left by some generous townsfolk with knowledge of the need. The only other source of anything new was Uncle John and Aunt Anne Murphy, Angie's older sister. The Murphys never had any children. So, naturally, they enjoyed helping out the eight Vitti kids whenever they could. They were both employed in town. John was a Postman and eventual Postmaster, and Volunteer Firefighter, and a senior leader in the Knights of Columbus. Anne spent over thirty years as the Bookkeeper at Karl Chevrolet. The kids were all amazed that the Murphs could buy a new Chevy every two years, like clockwork. Working for the dealer had its benefits.

But they were also incredibly generous. Against all of Angie's protests, the Murphys would sometimes bring over goodies for the kids. It was never a flaunt of wealth, though. Most of the time it was some food treats or clothing. We often suspected that a little cash was passed "under the table," but it was never mentioned. Angie and Chuck were proud Italian-Americans, so taking money from an Irishman, even the kindest most soft-spoken Irishman on the planet, might bruise an ego. But sometimes, beggars can't be choosers. Uncle John never rubbed it in, never spoke of it, never held it as leverage. He was a true Christian man.

Television didn't exist in the Vitti house until the late sixties. That was one of the reasons the kids looked forward to going to Grandpa Vitti's house on Sundays. Not only was the authentic Italian food a real treat, they had a television that worked. The kids spent so many Sunday evenings filling their guts with real Italian food and watching Disney, Ed Sullivan and Bonanza. To add to the treat, Grandma Vitti always had Cott's soda and a chocolate cake with real shaved chocolate on top. It just didn't get any better than that!

Grandpa Vitti was born in Settefrati, Italy, in the mountainous region east of Rome some forty minutes. These were dirt-poor farmers, herders and masons grinding out a living in the unforgiving Apennine mountains of central Italy. While the actual reason for his emigration to America was never discussed, millions of immigrants had come to "the land of opportunity" to find a better life. While generational poverty or an oppressive government were contributing factors, it was really the draw of a better life for them and their families if they were willing to follow the rules and work hard. There were two major migrations from Italy at the end of the 19th century. One to the land of Vespucci, the other to the coffee plantations or Brazil. The Vitti clan spread themselves across the globe, from Italy to South America, to North America, to France, England and Spain, going where they could find work and a better life for their families.

Antonio came through New York's Ellis Island as a teenage boy just before the turn of the century. He came over with a dozen of his cousins and was sponsored by his Uncle Joseph, who had come to New York City some years earlier and settled in the Bronx, New York, the area that would later be referred to as "Little Italy."

As with most laborers, they went where the work was to be found. For Antonio and his uncle, it was Northfield, Connecticut, where manual labor jobs on the vast estates of the super-wealthy were plentiful.

For several years, Antonio learned the Mason's craft under the guidance and tutelage of Uncle Joe. When he was twenty, Antonio went back to Italy to take a bride and bring her back to America. He and his wife, Josephine, returned to Northfield where they eventually raised five children: Vincent, Michael, Carole, Emily and Alex. Five American children.

Grampa Michael Carchia, Angie's Dad, came through Ellis from Panni, Italy about the same time as Antonio. He met an Italian American girl from New York by the name of Anna DiMichael, and they were married. He, too, moved his new wife to Northfield where they raised three girls; Anne, Angelina and Carol.

Just like Antonio and so many Italian immigrants, Michael Carchia was also an estate servant. In his case, the Vandergarbs locked in his decades-long servitude by buying Mike a house for his family on Richmond Hill. The upside was that he never had a house payment. The downside is that he never had another realistic career choice. He was a 20th century indentured servant.

Both men understood the dedication, hard work and sacrifice that would be required to make it in the new world. They knew they would have to learn English, even if they could not adapt to the accent. They knew they would be treated as second rate, as the lower working class. What they didn't realize was just how severe the treatment would be at the hands of the unconstrained wealth of some. While so many of the townsfolk were outwardly kind, Christian folks, there was always some undercurrent of knowing your place in society. It was a daily struggle to break through and that struggle would be passed generation to generation. True acceptance would likely never happen for the immigrants. It represented too much risk to those in power. The kids would be told time and again that "those rich people are no better than you." Hardly a guarantee, but hope was always held out for future generations that the American Dream was real.

Chapter 5~Life on Hoyt Street

Feeding eight kids on a mechanic's pay took a great deal of imagination and effort. Of course, pasta was a staple and Mom often would spend the whole day making it from scratch. Her lasagna was so good that all her children learned to make it for their families when the time came. Much of the food was grown in the back yard which made the fall season much heartier and healthier than the rest of the year. And in the early years, there were chickens in the back yard, so eggs were always fresh when available.

While the kids never starved, the food was far from gourmet. Steak was far too expensive to feed a large family, as was fresh fruit with the exception of apples, oranges, bananas, and tangerines. The only fish served was tuna or "junkfish," what the kids called frozen the stuff normally fed to the seabirds. No salmon, crab or lobster. School lunches were typically bologna or tuna fish with a couple of Hydrox cookies, not the Oreos the rich kids had. The Vitti kids certainly were not the envy of the school lunchroom where potato chips and Twinkies ruled the day. Sometimes, Mom's Italian egg cookies made up for the absence of store-bought pastries.

A common misperception among Americans is that all Italians must be "mafia." Such a simple-minded labelling was pimped full-steam ahead by Hollywood.

But the Vitti family was far from mafia. There were no "made men" or Dons. If there had been any, the family wouldn't be eating tuna fish and bologna on a regular basis.

Bob didn't know anything about the mafia until he was on a first date with the blonde hair blue eyed lifeguard from the country club. Just getting that date was a Herculean feat, especially for a seminary student. They decided to go to the drive-in in Norwalk. Unfortunately, the only movie playing was the Godfather, Part II. It bored the crap out of both of them. At one point she asked Bob, "You're Italian, right?"

"Yep", Bob replied. But not that Italian!"

That appeared to just confuse her more.

"Not all Italians are mafia. And not all mafia are Italian."

She ended the conversation with a simple "Oh, OK."

They never had a second date. But that might have been because Bob was out of his social class, and two years younger than her. She was also the daughter of a local politician, if that mattered.

What Bob did notice about that date, but many, many years later, was that this tall, sturdy, good looking blonde was driving a Jeep and insisted she drive them to the movie. Interesting insight, but only understood in hindsight.

Mom was also unbelievably good with money. She would scour the newspaper ads to find the best deals at Grand Union and A&P, then make the trip to Norwalk or Broad River, if necessary for the better deals. She knew her way around the Bongo's discount store in Springdale and other bargain basements. Northfield stores were too expensive for almost anything other than the Sunday paper.

However, when the holidays came around, there was always a ton of food. On Thanksgiving, Mom would make a huge turkey with all the fixings, two or three pasta dishes, salads, rolls, olives, pickles, and, of course, cranberry. But the one item that every kid will remember long into old age is the fruit cocktail. It seems there was some long-standing European tradition where fruit was served before anything else to "cleanse the palate.." So, every Thanksgiving, the little pressed-glass cups with the long stems would come out of hiding filled with fruit cocktail. Everyone hoped for a cherry.

The festivities would repeat every Thanksgiving, Christmas and Easter, with some minor changes to the menu. Easter was always a ham dinner. Needless to say, all the kids looked forward to Mom's holiday feasts.

One of the most insightful observations Bob's wife Naomi later made regarding Bob's family was that it really was two families. The four older boys made up the first family. John and the younger sisters, the second. There was absolutely nothing deliberate about the way this turned out, but since the older boys were out of the house while the girls were still in diapers set the stage for endless drama on the topic.

The girls weren't bashful about telling Bob "You're the one who left home and never came back!" Well, dear sister, that's what life throws at you. Draft number 39 was not to be dismissed, and once Bob was out of Northfield, so many other opportunities presented themselves.

Bob made a valiant attempt to move back to Northfield after his first three-year Army hitch, but his attempt to get a teaching position at Northfield High School was unsuccessful. In hindsight of many years later, he theorized that despite his degree as a Secondary School English teacher, his Army background just wasn't a "fit" for Northfield. He had earlier believed that Army experience would be welcomed at any high school. He never got an answer and never expected one. He was trained to "kill commies" not teach wealthy teenagers.

The whole discussion of "leaving Northfield" was a sore point all around. While Bob never understood the girls' issue, especially since Mom always expressed pride in Bob's accomplishments, he figured a bit of life and career jealousy were the heart of the problem. He eventually took that to be the real issue, and avoided further discussions on the topic. Eventually, the sisters would understand that, despite the best-laid plans, life, and war, can get in the way.

Individually, Chuck and Angie were intelligent, energetic and generous. Together, however, they had their share of problems. Arguments between couples is almost expected, especially in Italian-American marriages. It's no surprise that most arguments began over money or Chuck's regular disappearing act. While the arguments often got loud, only once did one get physically violent. Fortunately, the only casualty was a dining room chair. Dad usually ran from an argument either into the basement or somewhere out of the house. He always yielded to the flight instinct.

These arguments, while not a daily occurrence, were not seldom, either. They were mostly devised of nasty remarks or cruel jokes. On the occasion of Dad's 40th birthday, Mom couldn't help herself and kept calling him "fat and forty." Sure, he was usually overweight, but that kind of name calling was something she constantly chastised the kids for doing! By the grace of God, they stayed together long after the children were out of the house. But they did, eventually, D-I-S-S-O-L-V-E the M-A-R-R-I-A-G-E.

Despite the continuing money problems, Christmas was almost always plentiful, thanks to Mom's financial ingenuity. Some years it was board games and dolls, other years it was bicycles and transistor radios. In the lean years, some good samaritan would leave lightly used toys on the front porch and they would find their way under the tree. One year someone left a whole box of Tonka trucks and bulldozers. Nobody cared that they were used. Vittiville was getting a new look once the snow was gone!

A long-kept secret, one that would make Santa Claus proud, was the "purchase" of toys from a catalogue points program from Dad's work, accumulated according to sales. One of the best gifts Bob ever got from Santa was a new student desk and chair made completely of cherry wood. He used that desk for years and retrieved it from his Hoyt St. bedroom after getting married. He re-finished it for his older daughter and still had it in the garage in his old age. Easy to say, he cherished that simple piece of furniture and it motivated him to become good student, and maybe even a writer some day. Over the years, many of those great Christmas gifts came from that catalogue.

As Bob got to be a little older, he became Santa's helper for the younger kids. He would stay up well past midnight, sneaking the gifts from their hiding places into the living room, quietly wrapping and labelling each one, and artistically placing them under the tree. And, there was always a stocking for each family member he laid out on the couch since there was no mantlepiece.

Traditions come from the most interesting places. The contents of the Vitti stockings became their own tradition. There was always a huge orange, a Chapstick and some chocolate Santas. These were supplemented with other items, such as a personalized bracelet, some Vitalis or a kid's nail grooming set, and always a candy cane or two. And don't forget the book of Lifesavers! They were always a crowd pleaser. Despite the poverty, the arguments, and the anxiety, Mom and Dad always pulled Christmas together, somehow. As a result, these Christmas traditions were handed down and merrily used for many years after. Chuck and Angie made sure there were plenty of happy times for the kids, despite the never-ending poverty.

Chapter 6~St. Alphonse~Patron Saint of Bullies

He never saw it coming.

"Hey, Vitti, you think you're better than us?"

"Whaa....?"

Then, a sudden, sharp pain between his shoulder blades. He lost his breath for a moment. The cowards laughed as they ran away across the parking lot.

He had attended St. Alphonse since first grade. Always an excellent student, taking top academic spot for boys for six straight years. But, for some reason, the seventh grade was different. He became a target of the over-hormonal "middle schoolers" who somehow made a full transition to evil over the summer break.

For two agonizing years, Bob put up with the bullying. Verbal name calling and taunting was a daily diet.

"Hey, look, Dumbo's here!"

"Yeah, do you think he could flap them and fly away?"

At first it just seemed like harmless joking. But as more and more chimed in, it became more than just schoolyard joking.

"Nice shirt, Dumbo. You get it from the thrift shop?"

Bob usually ran away from the harassment rather than fighting a mob, verbally or otherwise. But he had his own repertoire of insults and eventually hurled them without fear of consequences.

"Hey, O'Shea, is that your head or did your neck just puke?" The Irish punk would respond with his signature shit-eatin' grin.

"Is it time for your annual bath, Manfred?" That was another favorite. Manfred would just drool as his mongoloid brain took the time to process the remark.

This bullying became a pastime for these ignorant snotbags. While the smarter kids sometimes looked on, it was usually the really stupid ones that were prodded into doing the damage. On one crisp fall day, one of the idiots thought it would be funny to throw lit matches at Bob, without warning, of course. The first couple flew wide of the target, but the third hit his shirt just right of the pocket. The shirt smoldered with the help of the weeks of starching, resulting in a singed hole about the size of a pea before it whimpered out. Mom was not happy, yelling that someone needed to buy Bob a new shirt. But, like so many times before and after, the demand was never taken to the principal, or ignored when it was.

In those days, "Boys will be boys" was the standard response from the school leadership. Rough-housing was to be expected. It built character and taught boys to stand up for themselves. In reality, however, forcing the issue with the perpetrators would require the principal to go face to face with the wealthiest parents in southwestern Connecticut. These were the captains of industry, the kings of Wall Street. Their million-dollar mansion estates served as both a status symbol and a warning to the "townies." We are wealthy, you are not. Deal with it. And good luck with that shirt. Despite their pretense as "good Catholics", the reality was classic "we versus them" existence. Bob, the son of an Italian grease monkey, was not worth risking the wrath of the rich, which is why Chuck never took the issue head on. We'll pray for him.

The bullying reached a breaking point about two months before 8th grade graduation when one of the kids threw a pencil at Bob's head, striking him about an inch above his right eye. The pencil point make a permanent tattoo where it struck. These idiots lacked any sense of right and wrong. They were now getting way too dangerous in their stupidity.

Bob had had enough. He had traded barbs with them for months, but usually found himself avoiding them or even running away. But, not this time. Once he had realized what they had done, he took off full speed toward O'Toole, the clown that threw the pencil. O'Toole had at least 20 pounds on Bob, but blind rage yields to no logic. As soon as O'Toole saw Bob coming toward him at full speed, he tried to run to the hole in the back fence. He didn't make it. Bob was way too fast on his feet.

He tackled O'Toole football style from behind. They both slammed to the ground right where the asphalt met the grass, just a few feet from the fence. Dirt, leaves and small rocks flew everywhere as they both tussled to get the upper hand. Before either could throw a punch, Sister Mary Margaret witch-broomed her way across the parking lot. The little mob that had gathered quickly dispersed.

"YOU TWO, STOP WHAT YOU ARE DOING, IMMEDIATELY IF NOT SOONER!", she shouted. That was her favorite warning "immediately if not sooner." It was difficult not to laugh every time she shouted that. But, the boys looked both disappointed and relieved. "Get up off the ground, straighten yourselves out and get back to class."

But a message had been sent and received. Bob was willing and able to defend himself one on one. As they got back to their desks O'Toole said, "this isn't over." Bob didn't wince. He invited the end of this nonsense.

A short while later, a folded note landed on his desk. He opened it up to read "Be in the gym after school." "Finally," he thought, "this inane bullying is going to end."

At the final bell, he gathered up his books, pencils and paper in to his briefcase and headed down the hall to the gym. The others were already there. O'Toole,

Sweeney, McDonald and the new kid, O'Shea. He had just started at St. Alphonse at the start of the year. It didn't take him long to figure out what bunch of asses to hang with.

"OK, Vitti, this is what we're gonna do. You and O'Tool are going to finish the fight right now." Bob sized up his opponent. He was a chubby, sweaty shorty with a permanently stupid look on his face. His shirt sleeve was dirty and torn from the earlier encounter. His pants were stained with grass, but otherwise fine. He had already taken off his tie.

"You are going to have a slap fight. First one to quit loses." Sweeney stated.

"A slap fight?", Bob asked.

"Yep, no fists, no tackling, just open hand slaps."

Bob thought to himself, no fists, no wrestling, nothing but slapping? Isn't that girlie stuff?

"One more thing," Sweeney added, "O'Shea is stepping in for O'Toole."

"What? I wasn't fighting him! What the hell is this?"

"I'm fine," said O'Toole. I can take him."

"Well, O'Toole sprained his thumb when you tackled him, so he wants O'Shea to fight for him."

"That's bull!", Bob shouted as he took a step backward.

"Well, you can ask someone to stand in for you. You have somcone to do that?"

Bob looked around for an answer where he knew there was none. He knew that, once again, the odds were stacked against him. O'Shea was two inches taller than O'Toole, and much more athletic. His haircut was right out of West Side Story, as was his look of arrogance. He probably had a switchblade comb in his back pocket.

This was not going to be easy. He'd love to have Dominic or Rocco stand in for him, but they were both too big to ever be threatened by these idiots. Besides, they'd already gone home.

"We'll figure out who goes first with a coin toss. Vitti, call it in the air." A coin immediately went skyward and Bob shouted "heads." Tails came up. O'Shea got the first shot.

Bob braced himself for the first slap. Heck, he'd been slapped before by Mom or his brothers, but never in the face. Mom usually caught him on the way out of the room on the back of his shoulder. This would be nothing like that.

It wasn't two seconds before he felt the searing pain, the agonizing sting of O'Shea's hand as it ripped across Bob's left cheek, jaw and chin. He reeled back on his heels, but caught himself before losing his balance, lurching sideways with a slight stumble. He tried to shake off the pain as the whole side of his face was turning bright red.

"OK, your turn, Vitti', said Sweeney. Bob was a bit bleary-eyed in response the to pain, but that just added to the anger. Once again, they stood face to face, just a foot or so from nose to nose. Bob had never done this before, so he was in a quandary as to how to inflict the greatest pain. In the flash of brilliance, he recalled part of a golf instruction book he had read over the summer. He remembered that power doesn't come from the energy in a few small muscles, but from the combined power of the large muscles all working together. In order to generate real power, Bob had to coil his body in the wind up, turning his upper body against a stable lower body, and then uncoil in reverse order. The huge amount of energy from the large muscles would be instantly transferred to the upper body and then to the smaller muscles in the shoulder, arm and wrist.

"Let's go, Vitti. We aren't going to wait all afternoon!"

What the hell, he said to himself. It's worth a try. He spread his feet a bit wider and shifted a little more to his right side. He then turned his shoulders as far back as he could and stretched his right arm to its fullest extent. He immediately put all his weight back on his left foot which started an irresistible chain of events that he'd never experienced before. As his lower body went to the left, his upper body unwound in a flash, which resulted in his arm effortlessly flying through space. His wrist and hand became the end of the whip, smashing into O'Shea's face with uncanny force.

The impact was loud and ruthless, twisting O'Shea's head a full ninety degrees. His entire body followed suit, shoulders turning, arms flailing. In less than a second, that large bucket of turd fell in a twisted heap on the gym floor, sliding a few feet effortlessly as a puck on ice. His lip was bleeding and his face was beet red.

"Holy crap!" Screamed Sweeney, "I think you broke his jaw!" A screech came from the stage where two sixth grade girls had been looking on. One ran off down the hall to summon help.

Bob just stood there, his hand stinging almost as much as his face. It was a crazy good feeling. Of course he had tussled with his brothers before, smacking each other from time to time. But this was really, really……..fantastic! Without even knowing it, he had harnessed all the bullying and harassment of the past two years, and together with the pain of his stinging face and a bit of newly learned technique, he had smashed the living crap out of one of the biggest kids in the school! This is stuff movies are made of.

Bob turned to the idiot squad red-faced and shaking. "This is over, right? No more crap from you or any of your friends, you got it?" The shaking was gaining ground fast. They just stood there, frozen as the balls on an Alaskan brass monkey. Not a word. They were in awe of what they just witnessed

It was finally over. There was no Hollywood handshaking or new-found friendships. They would still throw an insult or sneer when they could. But it was over. No more schoolgirls giggling or shrieking with each encounter. No more need for anyone to talk to the principal. All these living, breathing lumps of infected flesh had learned and important lesson: don't poke the bear. Even the 5 foot nothing, 100 pound bear. When anger turns to rage, the bear strikes back.

It's called survival.

Chapter 7~The Altar Boy

Bob spent several years serving as an Altar Boy at St. Alphonse Church. He quickly learned that the 7am mass was not the preferred time for anyone, which is why the boys were not given a choice. It was a simple job, other than memorizing all the Latin prayers. Father Norton and Father Hussey were both mellow and very instructive. Monsignor Fox, however, needed a little extra help to get through the service. At his advanced age, the boys never knew if he was going to be able to get up once he knelt down! That kept them on the alert throughout the mass.

A fun part of the service was the "smells and bells." Although only used as part of the High Mass, the chore of loading and lighting the incense burner was a challenge in itself, but well worth the effort once the smoke hit the nostrils. It was a smell only experienced in the church. It was the signature smell that made an indelible memory.

On occasion, Bob would be called to serve a wedding. It was pretty much the same effort, but always rewarded with an envelope from the bride. Not enough to buy an island, but it would cover a few of Nicoletti's "sangawishes."

In all his years as an Altar Boy, Bob never, once, was a "victim" of a predatory priest. In later generations, it somehow became a "widespread problem," for which the Church paid dearly in both money and reputation. Through more than 16 years of Catholic schooling, Bob had never even heard of such a thing. He could never reconcile his personal experience to that of so many others, labelled "victims" of allegedly wayward clergy.

He eventually figured out that some of his teachers in high school were "batting for the other team," but he was never approached and never observed such warped activity in or around the school. Not even during the two week adventure to Canada was there any indication of such nonsense. And there are few better target-rich environments for predators than a campout with young boys. But, that deviousness just never happened. Was he really that naïve, or just very lucky?

The only kind of church-related incident Bob witnessed was far less noteworthy. Two of the eighth grade boys disappeared during recess one day. They were located when school let out for the day, rolling down the hill between the church and the school, both completely shit-faced on altar wine. Nothing was ever publicized about that incident inside or outside the school, and the mutts were back in class the following Monday, no worse for wear.

In later years Bob's wife joked about why Bob cursed so much, especially on the golf course. Well, he was an altar boy, a caddy, a press room worker and spent 13 years in the Army. It doesn't take any more than that.

In Nomine Patris, et Filii, et Spiritus Sancti, Amen. I'm sorry, you were expecting a different answer?

Chapter 8~The Best Friend

Bob met his best friend and eventual wife at the Ft. Leonard Wood Officers Club where she worked as a bartender. She accused him quite often of sitting at the bar sipping his ginger ale and eating the cherries right off the waitress station. It was a challenge to see how many he could eat before she removed them from his reach.

Her name was Naomi. Bob had never known a Naomi, outside of the Bible. She was a medium height brunette with a warm smile and a kick-ass sense of humor. She also knew how to work the bar, and the drunks that come with it. She could hold her own in any conversation and Bob was soon convinced she could handle herself in a bar brawl, if need be. But, that would never happen in an Officers Club. Just unheard of. NCO club? Sure. But never in an O Club.

Bob continued to "politely" harass her while she worked, eating the cherries and making bad jokes, puns especially. That had been his humor specialty from grade school. All spontaneous retorts, usually at the most inappropriate times.

There was one noteworthy exception to his pun king antics. While a Sophomore in high school, Bob came up with the brilliant idea using his little sister's Fischer-Price windup music box. It played just one song: Frere Jaques. Perfect for Mr. St. Laurent's French class. Bob got to class a bit earlier than normal so he had time to wind the music box and slide it under Laurent's desk. He kept his foot on the box to keep it from starting before the teacher was settled in. He just sat there innocently until the class started. Then, BOOM! He took his foot off and let it play. Mr. St. Laurent broke stride in speaking English. He turned to the sound, eyes popping out of head, "What ees dees? What ees dees I am hearing? The students inadvertently aided the escape by cracking up loudly enough to distract St. Laurent from the sound, giving Bob just enough time to retrieve the box from under the desk with his foot and stuff it back in his briefcase. Not a pun, but damn funny and a great start to a usually boring class.

After about a month of harassing Naomi at the bar, Bob found the guts to ask her out. Of course, he couldn't do that with all the other patrons around, especially the Field Grade Officers, who firmly believed the club belonged only to them, including the staff. LTC Bailey was a prime example. He hung around the bar like some bat in a nasty cave, constantly begging Naomi to go out with him. He was beyond obsessive, obvious and always drunk. If you didn't know his rank you might think him a high school freshman who just saw a cheerleader's panties for the first time. A pathetic sod who needed to learn some decorum and act like an officer and a gentleman.

When Bob finally got up the courage to ask Nye out, he figured he'd catch her by surprise outside the O Club. So, one warm summer evening, he left the bar a bit earlier than quitting time and got into his 914. His plan was to drive up on Nye as she went to her car after her shift. When he saw her leave the building, he slowly drove around the parked cars and approached her without startling her. The good news is that it got her attention. The bad news is that it got her attention. There he was, of all things impossible, at a loss for words. Nothing. After she greeted him with a simple "Hello, what are you up to?" He blurted out, almost mumbling "Play your cards right and I might give you a ride sometime." At that very moment, he wished he had just kept his mouth shut! Where in the hell did that quirky line come from? An old Bogart movie?

Nye just looked at him and chuckled, "We'll see about that."

Bob couldn't get out of there fast enough. Of all the gin joints in all the towns in all the world, he thought to himself. "What an absolutely dumbass move!" Then again, what would you expect from a guy who just graduated from seminary school?

They quickly parted ways with a mutual chuckle that he took for a hopeful sign, to meet again on another evening.

Their first "date" was some tennis and a feeble attempt at chess on a Saturday afternoon. Bob learned a lot in those couple of hours, like he had no clue how to play tennis and neither Fischer nor Kasparov had anything to worry about.

It turned out that Nye (her preferred nickname) had three young kids from a previous marriage. It was not a kind marriage for her. Her husband was a violent drunk and she had to depart Maine "under cover of darkness," so to speak. She was fortunate to have the full support of her parents, who put her and the kids up in their Army-provided housing until Naomi could find her own place. It had been barely two months since she left the marriage and Maine with the kids. But Bob, always the never-say-die hero, was undaunted.

Strangely, once Bob started dating Nye, he received orders for "funeral duty" at a rate inconsistent with an honest duty roster. It was easily twice a month that LT Bob was leading a team to one or another cemetery to dutifully bury a veteran, which normally took the entire day. That was in addition to the other more "regular" duty roster assignments, such as Staff Duty Officer (SDO) which put the young officer on duty the entire night for the safety of the troops. In one instance, LT Bob got back from a funeral and went straight into the SDO mode. Something seemed rotten in Denmark!

Nye had found a cheap trailer to rent in a park just outside the front gate. That's where Bob met the kids for the first time. He was greeted at the door by Sandra and Sharon, ages 5 and two, respectively. The older child, Carl, was in the back bedroom playing. Bob no sooner got through the door and both the guitar and the small black and white TV he was carrying disappeared into the trailer, courtesy of the two girls. Outside the trailer sat a '67 Comet convertible, which barely got Nye to work and back, but ran. Bob soon got a real-world grasp of the gravity of the situation. Here were three fatherless kids stuck in a trailer park. Nye was working as a bartender and looking for a second job. The furnishings looked like they came with the rent, broken down, sad-looking pieces from the '60s.

Bob and Nye spent the summer enjoying each others' company, often at the place she worked her second job. The Running Chef was the Army's take on a fast-food hamburger joint. When it came to being a trainee at Ft. Leonard Wood, MO, beggars couldn't be choosers. The burgers were acceptable, if for no other reason than the Army's meticulous and frequent inspection of these facilities. They might no be the greatest of burgers and fries, but they wouldn't kill you!

Their discussions covered every aspect of their lives, and eventually approached the subject of their future. After just a few short months, Bob and Nye had become fast friends, despite the fact that their lives had taken very divergent paths to this point.

By about mid-Fall, Bob brought up the subject of better housing for the kids. His only option was base Officer housing, but that meant they all would have to be immediate family to qualify. The only way that could happen was if they got married!

These two good friends decided to look into getting hitched. There was no Hollywood down-on-one-knee proposal. Just a conversation over a cup of tea leading to a mutually beneficial decision.

They visited every priest, minister and preacher on post, including the local rabbi, but were turned down each and every time for one or another religious dictate. In once case, it was the difference in religions, Catholic vs Episcopal. They just couldn't allow that! In another case, they would have to endure months of "marriage classes" before getting hitched. They dropped that one at the curb! It appeared that none of them appreciated the value of getting the children in a better place, even if it meant bending their arbitrary and capricious rules just a bit. Well, to be fair, converting to Judaism was a bit unrealistic.

Bob and Nye decided to put everything in a holding pattern and see if anything worked out down the road. Turns out, it eventually did. While Nye's parents watched the kids, Bob and Nye drove to CT for the Thanksgiving break to "meet the parents," so to speak. It would obviously be far more involved that that, with Bob's siblings, their spouses, their kids, Uncle John and Aunt Anne, the grandparents, and certain friends who might be in town for the holiday.

While the initial meet and greet went well enough, the later "behind the scenes" discussions were not so wonderful. Mom was adamant that Bob "couldn't marry a divorced woman with three kids." It would ruin his life being saddled with such huge responsibly while trying to build his career. Dad, on the other hand, was more supportive, saying "You're a smart, educated young man. I'm sure you'll do what's best." Not exactly warm congratulations or wise words of encouragement, but the message was clearly received.

It ended up being a civil ceremony at home, back at 48 Hoyt St. Bob's buddy Jim had convinced them that "Since we're all in town, why not?" Bob scheduled the local Justice of the Peace and Mom, of course, laid out a ton of food. Bob and Nye had gone to a local big box store to find something worthy to wear for the occasion. Nye ended up in a white jumpsuit with turquoise accents, while Bob sported a nearly psychedelic printed shirt and leisure suit— all cheap crap that was never worn again and eventually ended up at the thrift store.

When money is always tight, it was a challenge to get what you need in the most creative ways. When Bob and Nye decided to get married, they ended up buying the rings at a Spencer Gift store. They were minimally designed plastic bands painted silver. They couldn't afford any real precious metal rings, so the good fakes would have to do. They didn't go out of their way to show them off to anyone, especially Mom, who likely caught on anyway. If she did, she didn't say anything at the time.

Several years later, when Bob and Nye had put a few bucks in the bank, they went to the PX and bought a couple of real gold rings with a nice oval-cut design around the circumference. Mom definitely noticed the new rings and commented, "You got new rings?"

"Yeah, Mom, the other ones were just temporary."

The topic never came up again.

As always, Mom put all her opinions aside and prepared a full feast for the ceremony. She made several salads, fresh bread, a full condiment tray, and, of course, enough lasagne to feed an Army. And, totally out of character, Mom purchased a few bottles of A&P champaign. As it was later recalled, "Bob and Nye tied the knot somewhere between the lasagne and the I do."

But the marriage ceremony was never about the food or the clothing. Rather, it was all about getting a piece of paper which would get them into post housing back in Missouri. And in that endeavor, they succeeded. There would be no "honeymoon" if for no other reason that they spent their wedding evening searching for, Bob's oldest brother, Mike.

Mike had just gotten divorced from the mother of his kids, and was devastated. Rumor was, he was wandering around town looking for some place to release his anger. Another brother mentioned he always wanted to "get back" at the rich snobs and that managed to unnerve the younger siblings, who begged for someone to "go look for him." So, on their wedding night, Bob and Nye jumped in the 914 and drove around town for an hour or two. Nothing. Mike was not wandering around town with an axe to grind. All nonsense. While Mike had been the king of pranks since he was a kid, he wasn't up to anything that night. Turned out, Mike just wanted to commiserate with someone, but they were all busy with a wedding. No harm, no foul as usual.

The 10 hour drive back to Ft. Leonard Wood was uneventful, except for the exploding champaign bottle in the boot! Mom had passed two unopened bottles of the grocery store champaign to Rick before everyone left. After the "search" for Mike, Bob and Nye ended up at Rick's house, where they managed to work through the first bottle. The second bottle somehow ended up in the trunk of the 914 (in the front of the car for a mid-engine sports car.). At some point in the trip, it got just a little too shook up and blew its top. Turns out that grocery store champaign was not very well sealed. It was everywhere. Bags, shoes, clothes, whatever. No real damage done, and a good laugh in the end.

Upon returning to Leonard Wood, Bob put in his request for base housing and was told it could be up to two months on the waiting list. It turned out to be five weeks before they were able to move the kids into their new digs on Humphrey St. It was a classic split level, indicative of the times. Enough bedrooms for all the kids, living room, kitchen, two bathrooms, but no air conditioning. Oh well, they thought, no big deal. They grew up without, they'll deal with it. The attic fan would do the trick just fine.

The kids were soon settled in their new school and all was right in the kingdom!

There wasn't any hubbubandarub when folks found out that Lt. Bob got married while on leave. A question here and there, and, of course, the mostly insincere "can't wait to meet her" comment from a few. There was no secret that Bob had been dating the O Club bartender since June. Connecting the two ideas should was not rocket science.

With the mission complete, Nye and Bob went on with their newfound military lives with three kids and a place to live. Nothing much mattered beyond that. Life went on. Never stop drumming.

Chapter 9~Find a Need and Fill it

One of Chuck's favorite sayings. "If you want to be successful, find a need and fill it." Bob had taken that to heart as a young teen, and it served him well throughout his life.

When immigrants came to America, the smart ones brought with them some sellable talent, even if was a menial skill. Grandma Vitti had two sisters who lived with her eldest daughter, Bob's aunt Carol. They lived and worked in her basement. Bob never knew the details and it wasn't ever discussed.

The two sisters were old maids, never married, and only wore black. An old country tradition brought to the new world and never explained. The two sisters made their income for decades doing just one activity: peeling garlic. They were so efficient that almost every restaurant in the county, and several from the NYC, brought their garlic for peeling.

The one and only time Bob got anywhere near that basement, the thick wall of garlic stink almost made him puke. Once was enough. Further admonishments from Mom to stay away from that house were not required.

Bob had arrived at the University of Dayton in August 1970 with about a hundred bucks to his name.

All the money he saved as a newspaper boy, yard ape and caddy, all $1,222 of it, had already gone to pay tuition, room and board, and fees. He still had to buy books, though. There was no room for little luxuries at that point, although he always came up the the twenty-five cents for a pack of smokes. Luckily, he was not a heavy smoker, so two packs would last him more than a week. He recalled smoking his first cig, a non-filtered Camel, around age 15. He was standing on the concrete porch of the new Pro shop and found he was a bit too close to the edge when he took his first drag. Had he not been able to grab the roof support post, he may had ended up on the wet grass three feet below. But, that was more enticement than deterrent. He ended up smoking for another 15 years until he quit cold turkey.

He managed to make it through several weeks of college on his hundred bucks and a few more that Mom and Grandma sent him on occasion. He really didn't expect much, since Mom was still feeding five kids at home and Grandma was on social security. Since financial budgeting had been his hobby for years, he had some idea about when he would be totally broke. Luckily he had the dorm to sleep in and a food ticket for the semester.

In mid-October, Bob was assigned to cover the ROTC Annual Fall Ball for the school paper. He was fortunate to run into a local photographer, Wayne, who was hired to shoot the formals for the couples. In between shots, Bob and Wayne got to talking about photography and earning money from it. By the end of the evening, Wayne, a full-time employee of the Power Company, a part time Baptist preacher and part-time photographer, made an offer that Bob just couldn't refuse. Once Wayne approved of Bob's work, Bob would start shooting his own assignments for profit. Bob shadowed Wayne at his next wedding to prove himself. Over the course of the next three years, Bob would complete 125 weddings and a handful of schools and bar mitzvahs. At first, he was working Wayne's "overflow", shoots. The ones that Wayne couldn't handle on his schedule. After about six months, Bob had built his own reputation and was getting continuous referrals from his work. He didn't have a free weekend for many, many months. But the money didn't start to flow until the middle of the second semester. Fortunately, he had already applied for college loans and grants, so almost all his expenses were covered. Almost. But, he never went broke.

He also figured that if he were ever to get out of the noisy, smelly cinder block dorm, he'd have to pack some money away for rent, utilities, etc. That's where the weddings really paid off. Eventually, business was so good, that Bob was able to finance a new car. That would be a first for the Vitti family; buying a new car!

But wedding photograph wasn't all about cute but nervous brides, bouquets, and cake. The stress of documenting "the bride's most important day" wasn't lost on Bob, who was known as a perfectionist in all his endeavors. While he had only a couple of equipment failures, he managed to correct each situation without losing the business or his mind.

During his very first wedding which he undertook at his friend Greg's request for his sister's wedding, the brand new flash Bob had just purchased slipped off the mount and crashed to the ground. Luckily, it happened in between the ceremony and reception, allowing him a little bit of time to find a remedy. His only thought was to drive the five miles into town and visit the camera store. Perhaps they could loan or rent him a unit for the afternoon. He jumped into his '65 Corvair and raced through the countryside on the nasty, bumpy New England roads, sometimes completely losing contact with the road! The owner of the camera shop was unwilling to rent or loan a unit, but did suggest Bob contact Syd, the head photographer for the Advertiser. He had run into Syd once or twice as a newspaper boy, but really didn't know him. Nonetheless, he had bride, groom and wedding party waiting on him, so he decided to call Syd at home and beg for a flash unit. Syd was gracious and dredged up an old Honeywell he kept charged up in his basement. Bob accepted the generosity and sped back to the wedding as fast as he driven to town.   The rest of the wedding went on without a hitch and the photographs turned out quite well, especially for his very first effort.

Later that evening, as Bob drove home, he noticed the engine was running excessively hot. He went on to discover that he had blown the belt off the air-cooled engine, which eventually resulted in seized engine just a few days later. Sadly, his very first paid wedding, turned out to be a very, very expensive endeavor. For a less confident fellow, that might have been the death knell for his paying photography jobs. He considered it a trial by fire and carried that caution into every other wedding he shot.

He experienced other, less dramatic problems. In one memorable incident, he loaded the film incorrectly despite having done it perfectly a hundred times before. After fixing the problem and reloading a fresh roll, Bob had a chat with the bride and groom, who were already enjoying the reception. They agreed, almost cheerily, to invite all the guests and the priest back into the church to "recreate" the ceremony! It all turned out better than expected, even though it was a bit "posed." The wedding party got a good chuckle out of it while Bob ate a little professional crow served up by the bride's parents. Another valuable lesson: check, check and re-check.

Bob went on to build the business by going in with Wayne to construct a color photo processing lab in Wayne's basement, from scratch. It took just a few weeks to build and furnish the lab which meant they could maintain complete control over every aspect of the business, from shutter click to finished album. In the process, they also increased their profit margins significantly!

Bob went on to take other bookings. He spent a whole summer shooting picture frames for a catalogue. He found that to be monotonous and boring work, but it paid $5 and hour, which in 1972 equated to 20 packs of cigs, or about five lunches at Bob's Big Boy. He had not attained the financial "yacht class" yet, but for the first time in his life he was financially independent! As a college kid.

He was still shooting for the college newspaper and yearbook, but wasn't getting many assignments. He figured that was their loss, since that left him more time to make money with his camera!

Chapter 10~The Work Ethic

Some folks predisposed to ignorance would gladly blame the failure of the poor on their own cultural laziness and apathy. Of course, there was always plenty of that in the peasant workforce. After all, animals, by their nature are lazy. Lions don't kill prey unless the are hungry. However, apathy is strictly a human attribute.

Apathy has become a Badge of Honor for many. Bob had come across at least one fellow who believed that "If it doesn't affect me right here and now, I just don't give a shit." That attitude bugged Bob his whole life, rather believing that everyone must care for something or someone or society falls apart. He also learned that he could not force people to care. Just like he couldn't force people to accept others with different pigmentation.

Unfortunately, over the generations, the government has taken that to extremes (historically, extremes are the norm for government). Tens of billions of taxpayer dollars were spent on social welfare programs which only served to enable more laziness and apathy. As long as the government check was there on "Mothers' Day," as every other Tuesday became to be known in the welfare culture, there was no reason to do anything for themselves. Government (taxpayer) dependency had become a grand sport of benevolent politicians in their constant drive to buy votes. But Bob noticed, as many others also did, that the overall state of the poor was not improving over decades of free money! "Projects" (tenements) built in the '50s were being torn down by the '90s. In most cases the endemic apathy of the welfare recipients had led to the nearly total destruction of the very welfare housing they occupied. "Why would I take care of a place that ain't mine?" was a common retort to the question of maintaining good order. In one way or another, laziness and apathy was always turned back into an excuse to blame others.

What kept that welfare farce going as "hope for the future" was the constant and clever marketing of any kid that made good. While almost every tenement kid had dreams of playing pro ball, nobody ever had the guts to tell them that achieving that success was more difficult than getting a seat on the Space Shuttle or wining the lottery. You just can't kill dreams, even years after the opportunity is gone. But, as long as the media pimped the "success" stories, the rest of the peasants would continue to hold out hope for their house in suburbia, a new Cadillac, and fame and fortune at every turn.

❈❈❈❈❈

Since Chuck was almost always working, it was left to Angie to make sure the kids were fed, dressed, educated and kept busy. She knew what kind of trouble kids could get into without any effort, so she made sure their minds did not become the devil's workshop.

Each of the sons became newspaper boys for the Northfield Advertiser by their eighth birthday. Bobby was playing in the brook at Cosgrave's house a few doors down Hoyt on his eighth birthday, which just happened to be a Thursday, newspaper day. As always, he could hear Mom yelling from the front porch, "Bobby, it's Thursday. Time to go see Mr. Harris!" There was no hesitation as he ran up the steep drive to Hoyt, past two more houses and bounded up the stairs. Mom was waiting there with a sweater and a handful of change.

"Go see Mr. Harris at the Advertiser. You know where that is, right? Right next to the movie theater."

"Yeah, Mom, I know where it is."

"Be careful crossing the streets. Look both ways. Drivers aren't always paying attention," she added. "Go directly there! Mr. Harris is expecting you."

Bobby grabbed the sweater and the loose change, bent over and re-tied his well-worn canvas sneakers. "OK, I'll be safe," he replied as he bolted up the street. It was barely thirty running paces to Maple St. which led around the corner to Main St. He passed the Ferrity's, the Lutringer's, Domino Bruno's house, and Barlow's big, green house on the corner. He reached the next corner at the new real estate office quickly, but was getting a little out of breath. He slowed down to a quick walk as he passed the public library, crossed the street, and cut through the public parking lot behind the Mobil station. It only took two more minutes until he was pushing open the large wood and glass door to the front office of the newspaper. Emblazoned on the door in gold lettering read "Northfield Advertiser." Below that in only slightly smaller lettering, "The Next Station to Heaven."

He introduced himself to the lady behind the counter, and she summoned Mr. Harris, who showed up in mere seconds.

"Hello, Mr. Harris, I'm Bobby Vitti. My Mother said you were expecting me."

"Nice to meet you, young man. Let's chat a bit about being a newspaper boy," the boss replied.

Mr. Harris, a tall, sturdy man, went on in clear and concise words about the job responsibilities, how to treat customers, where he was allowed to sell and not sell, and how to manage the money he collected. He then reached over the counter and pulled out a canvas newspaper bag. It was almost larger than the boy, with a wide shoulder strap and a flap that folded over the bag to keep the rain out. Again, the words Northfield ADVERTISER were printed on the bag, in bright red block letters.

Bobby hardly noticed that the bag was slightly used. After all, he hadn't ever seen a new one. The ones his brothers had were also used. Mr. Harris handed him ten crisp newspapers fresh off the press. He could smell the barely dry ink blended with the scent of rag paper. Through the next door he could glimpse the chattering, thumping machinery that turned out paper after paper. He was invigorated by the excitement of the activity, the scent of the newspapers and, of course, the opportunity to earn his own money for the very first time!

"When you sell these, you can come back for more," finished Mr. Harris as Bobby hit the street.

For the next several years, Bobby spent every Thursday afternoon and evening selling and delivering newspapers, sometimes well past dark. While he started with no regular customers, he made a few deals and took over a few routes from "retiring" paperboys. By time he was twelve, he had a route of over a hundred and twenty homes and businesses. He also sold on the street, at the Grand Union supermarket, and the train station. He sold so many newspapers that, after just a year of working at the Advertiser, Mr. Harris presented Bob with a brand new canvas bag! That was a great reward for young boy just starting out on his first real job.

The train station presented his first opportunity to show some creative initiative. The New Haven Railroad had a spur that ended in the middle of town from NYC. In earlier years, it served as a route to the city from the horse farms and shoe factories in town. Once the Industrial Revolution ran its course in Northfield, the railroad saw even more potential in shuttling New York City commuters to the wide open pastures of the quaint bedroom community.

Paperboys hustled for the best positions on the train platform. Some took the front or the back to try and jump on the train and sell as the passengers exited. That never worked. Others simply stood their ground on the platform and sold as many as possible as the commuters hustled to the parking lot.

After about three months of this fracas, Bobby decided to try something different. He wrangled one of the other, younger paperboys he semi-trusted to work with him. The plan was to buy two round trip tickets to the first station on the line headed back to NYC, Talmadge Hill. They would take the current train there on its return, and ride back to Northfield on the next train from New York. They managed to sell out the train in the eight minutes it took to get back to the station.

The ingenious plan worked perfectly for all of three weeks. Then all the other boys caught on. Each week, another two or three world jump the train to Talmadge Hill, making it all but impossible to execute the sweep. The jig was up. It was no longer profitable.

Bobby went about his business week after week, regardless of rain, snow, sleet, heat, cold, homework, or other distraction. Over the course of seven years, he never missed a Thursday. He had no problem riding his hand-me-down bicycle in the snow to get to all his route customers. After about three years, the price of the paper went from ten cents to fifteen, and his cut went from two cents to five. Selling 125 papers every week, the money was good!

Once Bob turned ten, he was allowed to work in the printing press room flying the press and jogging in the sections. This was a whole different environment from selling papers on the street, carrying golf bags at the club, raking leaves or shoveling snow. This was a greasy, noisy, smelly, hot press room where every other word was banned by the FCC. Bob was a quick study when it came to all things mechanical. After just a few minutes of instruction, he was flying the papers off the press and onto the jogging line. He wasn't allowed to work the jogging line until he had worked flying the press without letting any fall on the floor. The speed of the press, while incredibly quick, was not impossible to keep up with. It was critical that all sections of the paper made it into the proper order and all the commercial ad inserts made it to the final paper. That was the purpose of the jogging bench. Pull together all the sections into a single, complete issue.

Bob was soon enthralled by all the smells and sounds of the press room. A massive roll of printing paper, probably five feet in diameter and ten long, was loaded into the Webb press by the senior pressman. Once the press was started, the paper ran quickly through a series of rollers and inked plates which impressed the image on the paper as it made its journey from the Paul Bunyan sized roll to the final end-point rollers, printed, dried, cut, folded and ready for jogging. Bob could smell the wet ink and the fresh paper, along with huge aluminum/lead ingots slowly melting in the electric pot mixed with the smell of Davie's Pall Mall cigarettes. Off to one side and closer to the front office stood two huge typesetting machines with their incredibly experienced and competent operators, who set up the text for every column inch of the weekly paper. One of them was nice enough to type out and mold Bob's full name for his personal use.

On the other side of the room was Dave, the lead picker. He set all the headers and anything the typesetters couldn't handle. He sat in front a rack of molded lead letters of different typefaces and sizes, he never took his eyes off his copy sheet as he picked letter after letter and slipped them confidently into a print tray, despite the fact that everything was backwards!

This was real work. The work ethic drilled into his head by Mom and Dad was on full display in the print room. These were the kind of skills that required specialty training and years of practice to attain the level of expertise and productivity this crew produced. It was amazing to watch and a thrill to be just a small part of. Bob found himself growing up right in front of his own eyes. No other kid in St. Alphonse would ever have this experience to learn and enjoy. It was all his own.

At the age of ten, another Vitti tradition was thrust upon each son: caddying. The golf season in CT normally began some time in April, so, once again, Bob was given the opportunity to make some good money right around his birthday. Mom drove him to the Country Club of Northfield to meet the Head Pro, Mike Bickle and the Caddymaster, Pete Socci.. Pete gave him the lowdown on caddying and sent him out with a senior caddy for nine holes to learn the ropes on the course. He caught on quickly and had his first loop the next weekend. He was tired after carrying a heavy golf bag for eighteen holes up and down the Connecticut hills. After all, he weighed barely a hundred pounds, dressed. Each bag weighed upwards of twenty pounds, and those were the light ones. He'd soon learn how heavy a golf bag could get when the member tossed in a couple of extra clubs, a rain suit and an extra pair of leather Foot Joy shoes.

But, hell, two dollars is two dollars.....per bag! The was the same as 40 newspapers! Now he was making real money. Before the end of his first month, he had looped four times and even carried four bags at once when he was the only caddy left in the shack. That was a disaster that almost got him permanently tossed by

Socci. Turns out it was more an initiation than a real loop. It could have turned out much worse for all concerned had the four old women actually been serious golfers!

The stories he lived in the next seven years as a new caddy (called leaches) and eventually promoted to Caddymaster would have made for a great Hollywood comedy. It was almost a daily contest to see who could carry the day with jokes, harassment, or comments about the "over-dressed, ever-boastful, old fart members" who mostly "sucked at golf." The challenge, other than getting the better players to caddy for, was to have fun while staying off Socci's radar. But, there were also the women who frequented the golf course. For young, horny caddies, it became a contest in its own right to see who would caddy for the hottest women at the club. They were always perfectly dressed in the appropriate golf attire and smelled like Saks Fifth Avenue. Oddly enough, a couple were actually decent golfers, another plus to a caddy.

But some of these caddies were always looking for trouble, teasing or otherwise exerting their dominance. One such "dustup" actually involved dust. It was called the "Russian Stomp" for reasons unknown. The willing participants would form a circle around the subject in the dusty caddy yard. On command, they would all kick dirt in the offender's face while spraying coke on him. The end result was almost always someone in or near tears, coated with dirt and sticky coke. Never did a victim stick around for the rest of the day, since he had to retreat home to get cleaned up. While most of the caddies could find their own way home, either walking or hitch-hiking, some of the "leeches" had to call their Mommies for a ride. But the message always got through: "toe the line or suffer the consequences."

In another similar caddy incident, Bob's little brother, John, got into a tussle with another Italian kid. John ended up chasing the kid back into the caddy shack where the kid slammed the door in John's face. John was unable to stop his momentum, and careened right through the half-glass door. He immediately started to bleed from his right bicep, repeating "holy crap, holy crap!" A fairly large chunk of flesh was hanging, blood red, from John's arm. Bob came to his assistance with all his Boy Scout First Aid training, and found enough clean towels to dress the wound well enough to get John to the Emergency Room in Norwalk. While John showed no panic throughout the incident, the wound was severe enough to require twenty stitches and a rather large compression dressing. The remaining challenge was trying to explain to Mom and Socci just what the hell happened. Fortunately, to borrow a popular phrase, "All is well that ends well." That included John's return to caddying after just a week, while the other kid was never seen at the country club again.

But Bob also found himself along the periphery of a world he could never enter. Members of the club were super rich. All of them. Otherwise, they couldn't get membership. They were also mostly white Brits, Irish, Scotts and other European Anglo Saxons. Membership in most country clubs around the world was restricted back then. No Jews, no Blacks, and certainly no Italians, even if they had the money. The only Italian in the clubhouse was the locker room attendant, who spent hours each day just making sure all the member's golf shoes were cleaned and polished. Nobody made any fuss about it. It was just the way it was. It was clear that no one from "downtown" would ever be on the invite list for membership. The Vitti name would never be seen on the New Year's Eve party list at the country club.

That wasn't the world that intrigued Bob, however. He knew there was an abundance of both old money and new money. Blue blood inheritance and new 20th century geniuses were both represented. What he didn't know was how much he could have learned had he been encouraged to just listen. For a caddy, a poor kid from downtown, absolute privacy for members was an unspoken rule. What the members were talking about for three hours on the course was none of his business. Years later, he wished he had broken that rule and eavesdropped on all those Wall Street wizards. Who knows how differently things might have turned out? He might have picked up some wisdom on IBM or Xerox, not that he would know what to do with that information for years to come. He certainly had no way of taking advantage of any Wall Street intel at that age.

One lesson came through loud and clear, however. You don't get wealthy, or stay wealthy, by giving your money away. That principle was proven day after day, loop after loop, when only a few members would give the caddy a tip. There was one exception. Dr. Kirkland and his wife always added a quarter or fifty cents to the standard fee. The guests also tipped fairly well during the member-guest tournaments. But that was it. If you were lucky, you got a soda at the turn after nine holes. Beyond that, the members pretty much kept their hands in their pockets. But, again, that's just the way things were.

As the kids grew older, they all got "regular" part time jobs after school and weekends. Bob worked at Barlow's news and variety store perfectly situated in the middle of town on Elm St, adjacent to the public parking lot. It had one entrance on Elm and another on the lot. They served as a news stand, gift shop, record store, toy store. They had two floors of pretty much anything you could conjure.

Old man Barlow worked his two grown kids hard but still needed part time help for things like stocking, sweeping and trash. Bob started working at age 15 1/2, the earliest any kid could work in CT. He made a dollar an hour after school doing whatever the old man needed.

This was an introduction to yet, another culture he didn't find at the country club. The Barlows were Jewish shopkeepers. They were not only demanding when it came to getting the job done, but they were absolute penny-pinchers.

"Anything you find on the floor when you sweep you give to me", the old man would say. "Even if it's just a penny, you give it to me." That's the kind of survival attitude earned through hard, hard experience.

So, being the good Catholic school boy, Bob did just that. Every penny, every dime, every torn greetings card, every half-eaten candy bar and piece of chewed Bazooka bubble gum he gave to the boss. Everything that looked like it still had value he gave it to the boss. Plus the gum, just for kicks. It was one of those cultural lessons learned early in life and lasting into eternity.

Well, almost everything. He once found a ring watch that he though was lost by a young girl being led out of the store by her Dad, all the while insisting that she "lost something." He held on to it hoping the little girl would eventually return to the store so he could return it. He never saw her again.

So on it went from there. Newspapers, caddying, store clerk, leaf and snow removal added to homework, music practice, after school helper, altar boy, boy scouts, little league and, eventually, television. There was never a spare moment except at bedtime. Then, he was usually too tired to do much of anything, anyhow. All according to Mom's plan.

But, his favorite activity for most of his teen years was Boy Scouts, especially the camping. It was certainly a great learning experience to go from one rank to the next. Tenderfoot, Second Class, First Class and so forth. The activities and badges became both a duty and a challenge to conquer. Over the course of the years, he earned over forty badges in everything from archery to zoology. He gained rank all the way to Life Scout, just one short of the top rank: Eagle Scout.

And then it came to a screeching halt. Bob lacked just two merit badges: swimming and lifesaving. And although he tried his best at every summer camp, year after year, to become a decent swimmer, it never happened. It had everything to do with the summer of 1959 at the Kiwanis pond. Mom had taken the three oldest boys to swim lessons. This was Bobby's first year. Mom told the instructor that Bobby was a new swimmer and needed to start from scratch, but Bobby took exception to that. He saw that all the beginner kids were just babies, and he wasn't a baby! After throwing a mini-fit, Bobby convinced Mom to put him in the next higher class.

That almost turned out to be the mistake of a very short lifetime. The instructor gave each child a small, red foam kick board and told the kids to kick their way across the pond. The board was no bigger than a minute and didn't even have handles to grab. Just a small, slippery slab of foam. Bobby never had a chance.

Less than halfway across the small pond, he lost the tiny board and immediately started taking on water. Angie, the ever-vigilant mother, screamed a bone-chilling "Help him! He's drowning!", as she rushed toward the pond.

And he was. By the time the lifeguard jumped off his perch and into the rowboat, Bobby was on his second trip toward the bottom. Luckily, the lifeguard needed just two good heaves on the oars and he was there. He reached over the bow, grabbed the panicked boy by the pits, and dragged him onboard.

Fortunately, although Bobby had taken in a good bit of water, there was no need for any smacks on the back or CPR. Just a towel and some TLC wrapped in proper "I told you so!" scolding from mom. But it was a lesson for a lifetime about egos and limits. It was also the catalyst for him to never like the water. He refused to take any more lessons at Kiwanis and it wasn't until he was in the Army that he managed to cover the required distance in the survival pool to pass that test. Barely. But he would never become a swimmer, nor a friend of open water.

Unfortunately, it also kept him from becoming an Eagle Scout, despite the fact that he met all the other criteria and challenges. But it was one of those times when working hard just didn't have its expected reward. As a sort of consolation prize, Dad, who was the Scoutmaster, made him Jr. Assistant Scout Master, a real leadership position, but not what he truly wanted: Eagle Scout. Eventually, his age pushed him into the Explorer troop, who were, of all things, Sea Scouts! Go figure.

Chapter 11~Spreading Wings

Despite his failure to reach Eagle Scout, Bob had the opportunity to learn about every aspect of survival in the wilderness. From basic fire starting to first aid to knots and proper use of the axe, knife, and firearm, what he took away from those great years was invaluable. But, what he enjoyed most was the freedom of camping. The troop would schedule a weekend every month and two weeks every summer to Camp Mawehu at Candlewood Lake. Some sites were close by, like Luckhurst and Brown, others were a bit of a drive, like Housatonic State Park.

He looked forward to each opportunity to get out the house, and explore the outdoors. So obsessed with the outdoors was he, that he managed to camp at least one weekend a month for fifty straight months! While the only recognition he received for that accomplishment was a series of small "year" pins presented at a Troop meeting, it was a big deal to Bob. Fifty monthly campouts straight, regardless of weather, location, or company. Every chance, he would pack up his gear, put together some grub with Mom's help and head for the hills. It was his first real taste of freedom and individuality. Something most kids his age never experienced.

There was one campout, in particular, that he would never forget. On this occasion, the troop had to hike into the campgrounds from the parking lot for about a mile. It was cold winter weekend in January of '66. They had never camped at this site, so that presented an extra challenge.

Camp setup and wood gathering went as well as could be expected for January. "Get all the wood you think you need for the night, then go double it! Keep moving to stay warm." Words of wisdom from the Scoutmaster.

This was one of the few times they used a large, eight-man tent. It was far more difficult to pitch than the small 2 or 4 man tents, with a heavy ridge pole and a ton of tie-downs. But they managed, with the Scout Master's assistance, to get it high and tight up against a few logs to block the wind at the back.

The snow started around the time they were finishing dinner and cleaning up. The snow came quickly, with little warning, in fat, wet chunks. Before an hour was up, there were two inches on the ground. Because of the snow and wind, it became a chore to keep the fire burning out in front of the tent. Before long, they had to close the tent flaps or be covered in snow as it drifted. Whatever heat they had in the tent at that moment would be the most heat they would have for the rest of the night.

When young boys get scared or nervous, they tend to get chatty. The wind was ripping at the tent and sailing the flaps. As the snow piled up on the roof, the boys would beat on it to get it to slide off. The last thing they wanted was for the tent to come down under the weight of the wet snow. Nerves were starting to fray. Not much sleep ensued.

Before long, some not-so-nice jokes were being tossed across the tent. Each joke, funny or not, got louder and louder, with more and more cuss words. So loud, that the Scoutmaster finally came around to check on all the noise. He stood there in the piling snow and listened just long enough. Then, in his booming voice, through the snow, the wind and the canvas he bellowed, "Would your mothers approve of that language, boys?."

Instant silence.

They all survived the night, but found it impossible to start a fire at dawn. They opted for cold snacks and water while breaking camp in two feet of fresh snow! Packing back out to the cars could have easily turned into a scene from <u>Call of the Wild</u>. Fortunately, the Scoutmaster and senior scouts had the wisdom and experience to get them safely out of the woods. It took a while to clear the cars and beat a path to the road, another 50 yards or so. The boys worked in shifts, a few moving snow while the others warmed up in the cars. Needless to say, most of them slept all the way back to the Congregational Church in Northfield, home for Troop 31.

On the slow, trudging walk home from the church, Dad had just one thing to say. In a calm voice he said to Bob, "There's no call for that kind of language. You are better than that. I expect you to set the example." And that was that.

Other camp stories could fill a book. But one that always stood out was a summer camp at Candlewood Lake. One humid, stuffy evening, thunderstorms fired up coming across the lake, and they were violent. Bob was sitting on one cot and his best friend Jim was laying in the other when a powerful bolt landed just few dozen feet away. In that microsecond, Bob was involuntarily blown out flat on his cot, and Jim was bolted upright up on his! Fear turned to nervous laughter and eventually, a bellicose roar of "Holy crap! Holeee crap!" when they realized they were still alive!

On another occasion, Bob had lost his brand-new Timex Boy Scout watch. It took him quite a while to save up for the watch and meant a great deal to him. Despite an extended search for it, the watch never turned up. The following year the boys were walking down from the campsite to the mess hall when they spotted barely a glint of light from the road. Upon closer inspection, and a little prodding with his knife, Bob recognized his "new" watch. It was covered in that gooey tar oil used on the old dirt roads back then. He spent an hour carefully cleaning it, trying not to scratch it. And then the time came to wind it. Amazingly, it worked!

"It takes a licking and keeps on ticking," as the commercials promised.

One of the greatest challenges and honors Bob had as a scout was the ritual of becoming a member of the Order of the Arrow. This was a special honor bestowed upon only the most worthy scouts, those that had distinguished themselves as exceptional "braves" among the rest. It was a two day ritual, culminating in a moving ceremony that included senior scouts in full tribal regalia and dance.

However, to get to that ceremony required discipline, bravery and service. The service came in the form of making repairs and improvements to the camp. They spent two days rebuilding and reinforcing the trails up and down the hillsides. The bravery came that night, when each scout was led out to a site with just his sleeping bag, his knife, and a canteen of water. He would spend the night, all night, alone in the woods.

However, the discipline came as the greatest challenge to Bob. They were not allowed to speak for the entire weekend. They basically got two strikes, because if you opened your mouth a third time, you were out. And his chance of ever being nominated again were pretty much nil. To encourage silence, each candidate carved a small arrow about the size of a pencil from a branch and attached a string to each end.

The arrow hung around his neck when he wasn't holding it in his teeth. It served as a reminder to shut up.

But Bob spoke twice. Both wise cracks. He came that close to getting tossed! He spent the rest of the weekend chewing on the arrow until he almost chewed through it.

The ceremony was probably the first time Bob had been moved emotionally by anything. It was chilling to watch the braves in their full regalia, summoning the great spirit to the beat of the Northern drum to accept the young braves. It was warming to then have the elder brave call him to the fire and drape the simple red arrow sash over his shoulder. "Well done, young scout. Well done."

Chapter 12~Where The Girls Are

One of the book's early draft reviewers asked the question "Where are the girls?" Since Bob was never real popular with the opposite sex and eventually a seminary student, the question made its point. He had to include girls in the book. What's a story without girls (or sex)? So he reached back into that part of his memory that had the most faded images and began to add girls to the story.

Bob learned in his English class about Keats' <u>Ode On a Grecian Urn</u> about the never ending search for Truth and Beauty. What he remembered the most was the description of the endless pursuit of the girls by the boys, around an around the urn. That's exactly the passage a young, hormonal teen would remember:

What pipes and timbrels?

What wild ecstasy?

What mad pursuit?

What struggle to escape?

That Ode pretty much summed up Bob's love life, as it was called back then, as an endless pursuit. He met many girls, but failed to get past a first date with most. There were a lot of "pretty girls" in grade school, considering the standards of Catholic grammar school kids.

One of Bob's early crushes was Dorothy. She was the tallest girl in his class with a bob haircut that curled up at the bottom. Of course, like all the girls in grade school, she never gave him a glance. All of his grade school crushes were absolutely one-sided. Several other girls got Bob's attention, especially after they started to look like young ladies. The two Barbaras distracted him from his work from time to time. There was also a Jane, the first short-haired blonde Bob knew. She was the second shortest in the class, but always smiling.

About the time that Barbara Ann started playing on the radio, Bob was attracted to a new transfer student named, yep, Barbara Ann. She was a very thin, strawberry blonde with hazel eyes. Her shyness seemed to attract Bob even more than other characteristics. Once again, song or no song, Bob got no notice.

The most memorable girl Bob met was a year older and quite well developed. She was the daughter of a local store owner, so she could be found downtown almost any day after school. Unfortunately, she attracted several older, wise guys who enjoyed cracking dirty jokes in her presence. And while Brenda was sharp and in tune enough to keep up with these jokes, on one occasion, one of these older guys decided to make Bob the butt of one of these less than clean jokes forcing Bob on a quick retreat up the street and into the alley to get out of range of their cruelty.

Needless to say, Bob never had the chance to get to know Brenda any better.

So, there was Jane, DeDe, Barbara and Brenda, Kathy, Patricia, and a couple others whose names have faded with time. But, alas, none of them ever gave Bob a glance, a chance, a simple smile.

But Bob's attractions weren't limited to real life. He had a crush on several TV characters in his adolescent years. At the top of the list was Emma Peele, played by British actress Diana Rigg. He watched many an episode just to see her in her skin-tight body suit, deliriously fantasizing while crazy jealous of John Steed.

Rigg wasn't alone at the top of the list, though. A show called <u>Lost in Space</u> aired about the same time, with a cast of hotties suited to the 1960s "sexual revolution." Both Angela Cartwright and her TV mom, June Lockhart were excellent eye candy. Bob sometimes wondered why he had such an attraction to full body suits, but it eventually came to him. He also didn't learn until decades later that he and she were the same age! Unfortunately, seeing the evil Dr. Zachary Smith in a full body suit kinda broke the "hottie" scenario. Fortunately, the sexy, older June Lockhart balanced out those scenes. But, alas, all mere fantasy to sell commercial products and having no impact on real life.

Things didn't get any better once Bob entered high school. He became a student at Christ the Prep Seminary in Southport, CT. It was an all boys school, so getting a girl at a school was a non-starter. Bob would have to fish in another pond. On the other hand, he was on his way to becoming a priest; a celibate priest. So what was there to fish for? If it happened, it happened. It was all a matter of fate at that point.

He managed one movie date with the blonde life guard. One bowling date with the redhead from the library. One tennis date with the Irish girl. One non-date with the skinny girl. Never more than one date. So much for fishing. His only girl to get past one date was Cheryl, the incentive for the start of this novel 50 years ago.

Once that relationship ended, the opportunities dried up. Bob had zero dates in college until his senior year. He met a sturdy Polish blonde at a wedding he was shooting. After the reception, a few of the taffeta-dressed girls, mostly drunk off their asses, were dancing the Polka. Bob didn't dance at all, but that didn't belay the blonde, who strolled over to Bob, grabbed his arm and said "Let's dance."

Bob protested vehemently. "I don't dance and I certainly don't know whatever it is you're doing out there."

She ignored him, introduced herself as Laura, friend of the bride, and all her friends, whose names Bob immediately forgot.

The two of them flailed about for a couple of tunes before she realized she was way too drunk and Bob was a horrible dancer. They went back to where Bob had started packing up his gear. They sat there and chatted for a bit as Bob finished his Coke and Laura capped off her Vodka Collins. He got her phone number and address, not expecting to ever need or use either.

Bob and Laura spent the remainder of his senior year in a very Platonic relationship, becoming pretty good friends in the process. When Bob graduated UD, she was there to congratulate him with a couple of nice gifts. They lost track of each other after college. The one time Bob tried to look her up, her mother quite brusquely told him that she moved to Florida. It was clear she didn't want Bob to contact her. So be it.

If Bob was writing about his love life, it would have been a very, very boring short story. Unless it was a book about Naomi, his best friend and wife. Then it would be a volume large and exciting enough to make Steven King and James A. Michener proud.

All in all, Bob's love life before Naomi was as close to nil as is possible in the real world. Certainly not one to be the basis of a Hollywood movie.

Chapter 13~Listen to the Music

There was always music in the house. Mom had taught herself to play piano and accordion. She played a lot when the older kids were at school and she was nearly alone. But, it took a great deal of prodding to get her to play for a group. The accordion never came out of the case without great fanfare and convincing, usually at a birthday party or Christmas gathering.

But the piano, her piano, the only item of any significance she ever bought for herself, stood proudly under the bay windows in the dining room. It was the one item in her life she absolutely cherished and protected. As a child of the depression and war, she felt very fortunate to have her own piano in her own house. Bob could listen for hours to Mom and her piano. He'd sometimes sit on the front porch by the open window and marvel at her talent, though she never had a music lesson. He really didn't care what she played or sung, it was all wonderful.

Her repertoire was replete with big band tunes and movie tracks. She adored Glenn Miller, Tommy Dorsey, Duke Ellington and pretty much anything played on WNLK radio. WNLK broadcast out of Norwalk, came on in the morning on the portable radio, and didn't go off until bed time.

More incredible than her playing was her voice! She could be heard singing to pretty much any tune that came on regardless of who was around. Every day, the radio served as both entertainment and learning new tunes as Mom worked around the house or cooked dinner. She truly had the voice of an angel.

In her later years, Mom would play and sing for the Catholic Daughters of America, the local nursing homes and other select venues. She was a hit wherever she played and rarely, if ever, was paid to do it. It was her passion. So much so, that at age ninety, even after her stroke and three brain surgeries, she still managed to sing a simple tune with the help of her daughters. Passion so powerful it never faded.

WNLK was a far cry from WABC in New York, a top 40 station with the likes of none other than the teen favorite DJ, Cousin Brucie. Mom never compromised her music with the likes of Elvis, the Beatles or the Beach Boys. For her, great music was hard come by after 1960. But she made sure that her kids were music literate, regardless of the genre. In those days, schools were instrumental in getting kids into music.

The training started in first or second grade at St. Alphonse Catholic school, where the children were taught to read music. Each classroom had one of those five-chalk tools that the nuns used to draw the music staff across the blackboard. While this training was primarily intended to develop good church singers, it carried over easily to learning an instrument.

Michael started with the trumpet in grade school, and moved over to the F-horn in high school. But, even later in life, well after high school band, Mike taught himself the piano and organ. While he enjoyed playing while serving in the Air Force, opportunity was slim at most the places he was stationed. After retirement, he improved his talent and played as both a restaurant entertainer and a choir director. And he, too, had an excellent singing voice.

Bob was always drumming on something. It just came naturally. But Tony got the drum. A single snare drum. He played on and off for a few years, but lacked the time and energy once jobs, marriage and kids played in. However, after his children were grown, Tony purchased a complete drum set and got back into beating the skins just for fun.

Bob was set up to be the next Benny Goodman with his clarinet. How he came to own a clarinet is a story in itself. On Memorial Day, 1962, he was returning home from the parade and festivities in town. As he came flying down East Maple Street on his hand-me down bike, flags mounted on the handlebar and baseball cards flippity flapping in the spokes, an older couple in their Chrysler New Yorker backed out of their drive and all the way across the street. That left nowhere for Bob to go. He smashed into the rear fender of the green beast, and was launched several feet into the grass, brush and rocks that lined the Barlow's yard.

He came to a skidding halt on top of a flat piece of granite, quite awake but a bit dazed. Although he felt no pain, the "holy crap" fear effect was in play. The driver and his wife immediately came to see how Bob was. They carried him into the back seat of their car and headed off to Dr. Cody, just a few blocks away. It's amazing how fast old farts can move when they need to, but Bob was still feeling no pain. Shock can do that.

Upon closer inspection, Dr. Cody found that a few layers of skin had been peeled off Bob's right thigh. Beyond that, he was in perfect working order. After a bit of cutting, cleaning, disinfection and bandage, all was fixed. Well, he did have to have a tetanus shot, standard fare whenever an injury was suspected of having "dirt germs" in the wound.

A week or so later, a nickel-plated clarinet showed up in a case in the living room. Turns out that the old folks who tried to kill him not only paid for the doctor, but added enough cash to the mix to buy a clarinet. About thirty-five dollars worth of used clarinet. Why enough money to buy a clarinet and not a new bike? That's because Mom told them the bike could be fixed, but he needed a clarinet! Fifty years later that nickel clarinet was sitting in the back of the closet, still in its original, now broken down and taped up case. Bob had contemplated turning it into a lamp, but never saw that through.

Brother Rick and the younger siblings all had their shot at a musical instrument. Rick tried Tony's drums. John was into guitar and eventually mastered the mandolin. Angela took up the French horn, Michele dabbled with guitar, flute and singing. But, it was Cheryl that inherited Mom's phenomenal voice. Since Bob had gone off to college and the Army at 18, he didn't hear Cheryl's voice until Michele's wedding, many years later. He was amazed that such vocal quality and range could be passed on through the genes. That was also the one and only time he heard her sing. Such talent. Such shyness.

Bob stayed close to music in his own way. While there was no band at the small high school he attended, he did get his hands on a guitar and taught himself some contemporary songs. He also found time in college to serve as president of WESB, the campus AM radio station. While he enjoyed all genres of music, thanks to Mom and his high school Humanities teacher, he had a tough time keeping track of group names, song names and performers. So, he left that to his programming staff, which turned out to be every DJ in the place. He managed, quite by accident, to put together the first, truly free-form radio station. Too bad no one was listening. WVUD, the campus FM station had been around longer than WESB and already had all the listeners. It was an FM station in the nascent years of FM broadcasting. The station was also firmly hooked into the university's communications curriculum, so they got both the money and most of the talent. There's nothing like broadcasting the <u>King Biscuit Flower Hour</u> every Saturday night to cement a solid and loyal listening audience.

At his first active duty assignment at Ft. Leonard Wood, Bob took a part time DJ position on Sunday mornings at a country-western station. Of all the genres he'd heard, played or studied, country-western was not one of them. He didn't know Jonny Cash from Merle Haggard. But, music is music, so he hung in there. To shake things up a bit and see if anyone was actually listening on Sunday mornings in St. Roberts, Missouri, he would play Doobie Brothers' <u>Listen to the Music</u> as his lead-in cut. Funny how that job didn't last very long.

Another wonderful task Bob had to do was read the obituaries on Sunday morning. One chilly October morning, Bob read the obits with a bit of a head cold. He had no idea how his delivery sounded until he got home and Nye told him his sniffing from the cold made if sound like he was truly mourning each and every deceased. He didn't let that happen a second time. Fortunately, no one complained or even commented. Maybe there wasn't anyone listening, after all.

Bob never stopped drumming on anything within reach. He was one of the few kids that could drum Wipeout correctly. Indeed, he banged on the glovebox of the old Buick wagon so much that he broke the latch! Mom wasn't very happy that the glovebox was permanently open. She should have gotten him the drum instead of Tony.

Chapter 14~COL Spoonbender and other Miscreants

The invitees were always expected as Commissioned Officers, to make the drive from Augsburg to Munich HQ for the annual Christmas party. This was planned as a formal dinner, dress blues required. Wives were dressed to the nines in their favorite holiday gowns with hair done up and makeup perfect

The usual hors d'oeuvres were plentiful, accompanied by small talk of no consequence. Butter bars (newly commissioned Second Lieutenants) trying to impress the Field Officers, usually to no avail. Mind numbing discussions about Christmas plans and new assignments in the new year. Everyone just waiting, drinking, filling their guts with shrimp, waiting for the dinner bell.

The bell soon rang and the partiers filed into the ballroom. Lines of long tables were set up facing the main table and placards were posted with the name of each attendant. Very formal, indeed.

Dinner was served after the invocation, and folks ate in quiet conversation interrupted only by the sounds of clanging silverware and glasses. As the desert was being served, the Group Commander rose to give his Christmas message. The audience expected the run-of-the-mill Christmas blessing, "duty, honor, country and importance of family" speech. Instead, the Colonel began speaking, in full gory detail, of his experience in the Vietnam war. There have been thousands of stories relayed by actual combat veterans. Gruesome, terrible stories of death and unbearable pain. The Colonel, however was an Intelligence Officer, most of whom sat comfortably in a quonset hut or underground bunker out of harm's way. Regardless, his story was wholly inappropriate, gross and damned disgusting. But, with his reputation as a self-anointed "spoonbender."the Amazing Kreskin of the 55th MI Group, most of the officers were not at all surprised at his choice of topic for the Christmas Formal. Here, we had a "full bird" colonel with nearly thirty years in service, the commander of an Intelligence Group, making regular claims of being able to bend a spoon with his mind! This brought up the concept of his fitness for duty, especially in his current condition. But no action was ever taken to have him complete a psych eval, or any other review of his behavior. He just plodded on, making command decisions for over two thousand troops located all over Europe. All the officers knew he wasn't fit for duty, judging only by his capricious and arbitrary decisions he made on a daily basis.

Col Spoonbender once chewed out the Battalion Commander because he hadn't sent a team to the

Group softball tournament. Instead, the battalion had arranged for winter training for about 100 soldiers in the Bavarian Alps. It was a simple scheduling conflict that the Colonel had blown out of proportion to suit his ego. On a separate occasion, the Battalion Commander asked the Soldier of the Year to formally greet the Group Commander on his visit to the Battalion. The Spoonbender saw it to be a deliberate insult to his ego and his position, and lectured the Battalion Commander on the need for his personal attention when he arrived to visit. He also later relieved the Battalion Commander, but no one really knew why.

Putting this all together, it was very easy to judge this fellow as a genuine nut bar. Yet, there he was "relating" all the ugliness of war at the Christmas Formal. One of the "great leaders" of the late 21st century with the power to make or break careers, was a certifiable mental case! And the Army just looked the other way.

While the Spoonbender never made General, he retired with a full pension and immediately picked up a 6-figure position with a beltway bandit consulting firm near Washington, DC. He was never criticized, reprimanded or punished for his wanton, unprofessional behavior as the Group Commander. Whatever standards his superiors were using, he must have met them, despite what the troops witnessed. Alas, this was the Army of the '80s. Nothing but ass-kissing and politicking to get ahead. Real leaders need not apply.

The ongoing saga of the Command Sargent Major also illustrated the lack of leadership and importance of networking in the Army. The Battalion CSM was the most important and powerful person in any Battalion. He didn't just support the Battalion Commander, but actually ran the unit. He was also the brother of the CSM from another Battalion in Europe. They have been scamming the assignments officers back in DC for years, many times just swapping assignments rather than accepting a less-than-glamorous duty assignment somewhere else. To add insult to injury, the CSM was a functioning alcoholic. Barely functioning!

Bob, now a Captain, had been commander of the Headquarters company for about 6 months when he became fully aware of the CSM's drinking problem. He saw it as his duty to place the CSM in a recovery program. He filled out all the necessary forms, consulted with the Battalion Commander, discussed the program with the CSM's wife to make sure a support environment was available, and counseled the CSM. That was the most difficult session he had experienced, including all his work in the Drug and Alcohol Counseling office during an earlier assignment. The CSM was livid and screaming at the CPT along the lines of "You can't do this to me!"

When all was said and done, the CSM knew what he had to do, and reported to the hospital for his recovery. He was returned to duty two months later, when he, once again, plotted to trade assignments with his brother.

As it turned out, the group commander wasn't the only "slipped stitch" in that unit. There were constant rumors about drugs and racial conflict. Regular unannounced drug tests always came out clean. Surprise walk-through inspections turned up nothing. It wasn't until a trusted Platoon Sargent blew the whistle on the offenders that the CPT was able to start an official investigation. He determined that his Supply Offer, also a CPT, was selling marijuana to the troops at their regular weekend basketball games. The dope was stored in the suspect's freezer in the Bachelor Officer's Quarters. It wasn't difficult to get to the truth once Bob interviewed the strangely cooperative Supply Officer peddler. It came out that there was an unofficial Black Officer's group that played basketball every weekend. While there's nothing wrong with that, once they started distributing dope to each other and the troops, it was a massive criminal issue. The leader of the gang was Maj. Carter, the Executive Officer. While he apparently kept his hands clean of any drug involvement, he had to be aware of what was happening right underneath his nose.

Bob filed charges against the Supply Officer under the Uniform Code of Military Justice (UCMJ) and sent it to his commander for approval, deliberately avoiding the Executive Officer. Within two weeks, the Supply Officer was reassigned to Chaplain School stateside. No court martial, no UCMJ punishment, no reprimand, no reduction in pay or rank. Just sent him off to become a Chaplain. Seems the Army was very short on Black Chaplains. Seemed fair. From that incident, which also implicated the Battalion Executive, Major Carter through the black basketball games, the Group Commander (COL Spoonbender) ordered an official AR15-6 investigation into racism in the organization. Soon after, an overweight, slovenly Major Feinberg showed up from The Intelligence and Security Command in Maryland to conduct the investigation. Every soldier and civilian in the Battalion was interviewed by Major Feinberg over a two week period. It took another month for the official report to be returned to the Battalion Commander. "No signs of endemic racism in the 502nd." Of course, everyone knew that, despite what the Spoonbender was led to believe. It was a well-hidden drug problem disguised as innocent basketball games.

Shortly after the he began his investigation into a supply officer for selling pot to the soldiers, Bob came up positive on a field drug test ordered by the Battalion Commander. Popping positive as a Private is bad enough and punishable by UCMJ Article 15, but as an officer and Company Commander, it was a career death sentence. Bob knew this was all a bit coincidental, but it still scared him until the formal lab result returned as negative. The Battalion Commander followed command policy and issued a written warning to the Captain, basically threatening to remove him from command if the lab test also popped positive. UCMJ action would likely follow, with a general discharge, at best.

Once the official lab test proved that Bob never, ever did drugs, the field test was never spoken of again. But the snide remarks and raised eyebrows of the truly guilty parties continued to be a nasty undercurrent for weeks. Bob was convinced that one of Carter's "gang" had contaminated his sample, reminiscent of a prison gang coordinating the demise of an enemy. It didn't work. This would be Bob's "reward" for rooting out bad actors in the command and forcing the CSM into alcohol rehab. No good deed goes unpunished. It was eighth grade all over again.

❋❋❋

Among the not-so-great leaders are the ones who have no one to go home to at night. LTC Green was on of those. He was a mild-mannered enough to lead the Battalion of prima donnas, but found ways of irritating his subordinates by way of "leadership example."

Bob woke up from a deep sleep with an angry grump when the Motorola walkie talkie screeched its alert tone at 2am. He answered with some groggy mumbling.

"Captain, this is the colonel", Green announced.

"Yes, sir. What's the problem?" Bob asked.

"I count at least two pintle hooks that are not secured in you motor pool. They need to be corrected, immediately."

"At 2am Sunday morning, Sir?"

"Do you know when the Ruskies will attack, Captain?" Green asked.

"No, sir, I don't. I'll get it fixed immediately." Bob responded.

"Roger, out." Closed the Colonel.

Pintle hooks are used to connect the trailers to the vehicles. They are secured with a large cotter pin. Although there were no trailers hitched up on any vehicle in the motor pool, two of the cotter pins had be left dangling by the drivers. If they weren't secured immediately, we wouldn't be able to defeat the Russian offensive through the Fulda Gap!

And so goes great troop leadership. And defense readiness.

Priorities.

❊❊❊❊❊

Among the many failures and cover-ups Bob witnessed in his government years, the testing of a tactical Air Defense weapon was one he never understood or forgot.

The field testing at Ft. Hunter Liggett went as well as any, but the final report included a "failed" test score for the remote control component. What it meant for the system operator was that, regardless of weather, the operator would not be able to remote the system to a "stand off" position. The operator's cupola was known to reach 130 degrees in desert conditions. More expendables.

The response at the final test report meeting was a blatant failure to follow the multi-volume Acquisition regulations, in that the Program Test Officer does not have the power to overturn the results of the test organization. Yet, that's exactly what he attempted, demanding that the entire section be removed from the report.

That blatant attempt at a cover-up was only partially successful. Someone higher in the testing chain read the original report. The outcome was an order from the Congressman who was selling the system to the DoD to deliver all data tapes, all data reduction software and the actual computers used to process the data! Bob's staff ended up packing and shipping hundreds of 9 track data tapes, the original executable software and removing the fairly large VAX 780 mid-frame computer system from the computer floor and shipping it all to Ft. Lee, Va. so the

Congressman's hand-picked (gold team) staff could re-run the entire data reduction and analysis process on their own terms.

Word came back months later that the test results did not change. The remote component of the system was deemed a failure and removed from the integrated system design after the fact, but before production. Bottom line, a great deal of time and money was wasted trying to disprove what the test data confirmed. What the greatest minds in operational test had already reported was confirmed by the Congressman's Golden Boys, certainly against his desires.

✣✣✣✣

So few things bothered Bob more than phonies. His first memorable example was the new St. Alphonse church bell. The parish and diocese determined that the old church was getting "too small" and started a campaign to collect money for a new church. It was a grand design (what Catholic Church isn't?) With the Alpha and Omega as architectural inspiration. The building footprint was the Omega and the bell tower was the Alpha. The design was met with rave reviews as "avant garde" and "a modern, fresh, forward-thinking design." As a wannabe architect, Bob liked the concept and design. Until he learned that the bell would be "electronic." That just tanked the whole idea in his mind. All the bell sounds would be imitation. Computerized audio files. After all, it was the 1960s and things had to move into the new age of electronics. But, Bob knew it just wouldn't sound the same and the congregation would have to re-tune their ears to the new, electronic noise lacking any fidelity to the original.

But, alas, it was a new, much larger building and the priests wouldn't have to schedule so many Masses on Sunday. They spent several million dollars on the new church, the vast majority from the parishioners. Uncle Murphy told Bob that they had received a "bill" from the church for $25,000! That was their "fair share," according to the Monsignor. Bob never did find out what the Vitti's "fair share" was. He didn't really want to know, especially since his future was in the Army because they had no money!

✳✳✳✳✳

While Bob was working as the Assistant Program Manager for a Defense contractor outside Washington, D.C., he had been through countless contract discussions with his subcontractors. Usually, they were just a matter of confirming a rate, or a staffing level. Since Everyone knew the terms and conditions of the contract, these discussions were normally civil. Except this one time. A subcontractor's money man called to dispute charges and payments on a recent invoice. Bob pulled the invoice and found everything to be in order. Unfortunately, the subcontractor was having a bad day, month, year, whatever, and needed to "take someone on."

Of course, that wouldn't fly with Bob. He knew every T&C forward and backward, and knew the rate structure for every position. That didn't deter the sub from threatening Bob to "take you out back."

Bob tried real hard not to laugh into the phone, but offered just one question: "What is this, eight grade? You want to go out to the parking lot and resolve this?"

Bob quickly recalled is middle-school horror show and quietly said. "Feel free to call back when you cool off." And quietly hung up the phone.

He briefed his boss on the conversation and nothing ever came of it. The parking lot? Really?

✵✵✵✵

Bob's knowledge of automotives served him well when dealing with most car salesmen. However, that was not always the case.

On one especially complex transaction, the salesman agreed, as part of the new car purchase contract, to replace the oil-burning valve guides on his old Acclaim, rather than trading it in. After several weeks of hearing absolutely nothing, Bob pressed the salesman for the status of the old car. All he got was the two-step shuffle of deceit. After a lengthy "discussion" and a chat with the sales manager, Bob found out that his car was sent to the wholesaler, "by mistake," of course! Livid was an understatement.

Bob eventually convinced the General Manager to pull his car back from the wholesaler and make the promised repairs. In the meantime, the salesman was still trying to get Bob to sign the contract and "close the deal."

"Not until you show me you have my Acclaim back in the shop. How long do you need?" Insisted Bob.

The salesmen stuttered, stammered, cussed and tossed the contract through Bob's window, just missing his nose as is flew between the steering wheel and Bob's face. When the salesman walked off, mumbling about being a "millionaire and not needing any of this crap,"and "I know where you live" threats, Bob noticed that the clown prince had tossed his personalized pen with the contract. Bob bent over to pick it up and noticed the gold engraving of the salesman's name. The pen was probably an award for meeting some sales goal. An award that nasty idiot would never see again!

❋❋❋

There he lay out in the middle of a farmer's field happy that he put his poncho on the ground before getting comfortable. Not only was it getting a bit chilly, but the dew was forming, creating a sci-fi mist as far as he could see in the dim moonlight.

The radio crackled just a bit. "Simba Two this is Simba One, radio check, over." It came across muted but understandable.

"Simba One this is Simba Two, reading loud and clear, over." Bob Replied in a tactical whisper.

"Simba Two this is Simba One, Roger, out."

That was the sum total of all the comms that night. The radio never crackled again. As Bob started to doze off, pulling the drawstring on his OD green jacket tight, he could hear nothing but the singing tires from a road that was easily a half-mile north of him. He imagined it was Bubba and Mary Sue returning from another fun Saturday night of drinking and dancing at the local saloon. The sound of the tires seemed to go on for ten minutes, changing tunes with the distance and eventually fading into the next county.

As he drifted off, Bob tried to figure out what he had gotten himself into. There he was, alone, in the middle of a farmer's field, slightly damp and cold, babysitting a stolen tactical radio.

His instructions were clear, but not very informative. A senior member of the cadre had pulled him aside just before the Escape and Evasion exercise began and told him he had a "special mission" for Bob. It was simple, but critical to assess tactical reaction to adverse events. Since Bob had been assigned to that platoon, he hesitated right up to the point of questioning the cadre. "Steal the radio?" He asked the Captain.

"We want them to believe that the enemy has infiltrated their camp and made off with their PRC-25." He replied. You just need to take whatever opportunity to obtain the radio, then find an out of the way place to hide until dawn."

That was it. The entire mission statement. No contingencies. No clarifications. No rendezvous coordinates. No comms unless contacted by them. Just go. Bob easily absconded with the platoon radio at the first smoke break and quietly snuck off through the sparse cedars and maples until he came to a spot where he could pull out his map and compass. He spotted a clearing on the map about a quarter a mile north of his position, just across a fordable stream. Off he went, arriving at his "hiding spot" just as the sun was setting. He nestled up against a large boulder after checking for critters, so the boulder would block some of the eventual northern wind.

He gobbled what was left of his lunch C-Rats and drowned it with a half-canteen of water. He pulled out his poncho and spread it out next to the boulder. The air began to chill right after sunset, so he put on his jacket and snugged the collar.

As he lay there, eyes half closed, wondered if he had become that traitorous, weasel doctor on the <u>Lost in Space</u> TV drama, who would do anything to anyone to save his own ass, regardless the consequences to the rest of the crew. He immediately shook off that thought. After all, he was following the orders of the senior Cadre, the folks who were running the exercise. Still, the words "naive" and "gullible" haunted him all night.

The birds were his first notice that the sun was up. He gradually raised himself up to sit against the boulder, rubbing his eyes of the farmer's dust. Soon enough, he had to relieve himself. Since he was the only human for miles, he simple moved around to the sunny side of the rock and did his business. He suspected he would be moving on soon, so no harm done.

He had written down the exercise end-game rendezvous point, so he knew that if he didn't hear from anyone soon, he'd just make his way to that spot, about a mile east, just on the other side of the stream.

Bob sucked down a couple of dry crackers from the last C-Rat can and wished he had a lot more water. He thought about heading back to the stream to dip his canteen, but even though he had that little brown bottle of Halazone tabs, he decided against that play. They may purify the water, but they tasted nasty and the shelf life of an opened bottle was about three days. He wouldn't dehydrate anytime soon, and would just have to suffer the dryness left from chewing on the crackers. He could always get some dew off the leaves, if necessary.

He figured it would take the platoon about 90 minutes from dawn to the final coordinates, even though he had to guess at their last location. It would only take him 10 or 15 to the same spot. He figured he should arrive there before the platoon and seek out the cadre to close out the story of the missing radio.

He made his way across the recently harvested fields toward the rendezvous point only to find the stream had gotten somewhat wider than his earlier crossing. He managed to find a downed tree that crossed near the widest point. It would be a bit risky, "but what the hell?" he mumbled to himself. He thought back to the first obstacle course he ran as a boy scout. He learned to keep moving once you start across the log. Pick a focus point across the stream just as an artist draws to a finish point when making a line across the canvas. The constant forward movement kept the momentum moving to the finish, which means it's less likely to be going sideways.

He only had one minor slip as he stepped on the stub of a broken branch protruding from the top of the log. He recovered quickly and luckily, his momentum direction didn't change. In about six grand steps, he was on dry land, no worse for wear and all his gear intact. The radio was cinched so tight on his back, it didn't budge.

It was just another 500 yards or so to the finish. He hoped the cadre was already there, waiting to welcome their "special mission" back. Bob stepped out from the woods down a couple of sandy steps to the dirt road. About 50 yards up the road he could see the glint of unsubdued weapons and the muffled sounds of the cadre as they smoked their Marlboros.

One of the senior cadre shuffled down the hill to greet Bob.

"What are you doing here?" He asked.

Bob replied: "I haven't heard from you since commo check last night. I just figure I'd make my way to the rendezvous point to find you."

"Well, your orders were to hold tight until you heard from us. I guess following orders is not your strong suit, Cadet. Grab your stuff and head down to the clearing. Your compatriots will be along soon."`

"What about the radio?" Bob asked.

" Not my problem, said the Captain. You'll figure something out.". Bob gave the arrogant bastard a sideways glance, the evil eye, and headed down the road to the clearing. He'd figure something out.

✦✦✦✦✦

After Bob left the Army he went on a job search in California. He came across a local ad for a startup company inviting "interested" individuals to attend a briefing at a nearby hotel.

When Bob arrived, he first noticed a wrinkled bedsheet hung from the ceiling, not making the best impression on a job candidate. The fellow in charge, who turned out to be Don, the "President and CEO" of the company, was immediately eager for Bob's help in straightening things out to make them more presentable for his slide presentation.

Don was less than presentable himself, wearing a far-too-large suit jacket and a wrinkled white shirt. His shoes look like they never saw a brush or shoe polish. His leprechaun stature just made him appear that much more pathetic.

Despite appearances, Bob reminded himself that some of the best minds in history were always disheveled and decided to hang around for the presentation. After about 30 minutes, he was glad he did. There were only three prospectives there, so the discussion was direct and lively.

While the illustrious leader was less than properly dressed for the executive office, his technical and marketing ideas were cutting edge and filled a real need in the publishing world. This fascinated Bob, especially after 13 years of tired military ideas.

The leprechaun posited the idea that he could design and implement an integrated system for producing text, line art and graphics for the highest quality printing, including those slick magazines used in the fashion industry. Up until that point, everything in the printing world was still cut and paste, old style, with X-acto knives and rubber cement. It would require the best minds in the graphics and software industry, as well as some brilliant folks in the printing and publishing realm to move the industry out of the 19th century.

The hardware systems needed to host the integrated publishing system were already commercially available, although there would be some negotiation with producers to reconfigure their systems for the final design. Creating software to work across multiple, diverse operating systems would be the real challenge.

All in all, Bob saw this as the challenge he always cherished. Systems Engineering in the Silicon Valley was a real career-maker, if successful.

Unfortunately, all the great ideas and talent were no match for the leprechaun's incompetence and lies.

Turns out, while he had convinced everyone he had a promise of big funding from a large corporation once they saw proof of concept and a sourcing plan, the boss had no money to get the project to proof of concept. The only money he had came from his mother, who was not an endless deep pocket. Within a couple of weeks of hiring on, at a very good salary and promises of equity ownership, Bob noticed that bill collectors were at the office almost every day. One morning a fellow came in to repossess the fax machine!

In an effort to get his back pay from the boss, a fellow employee, who was hired long before Bob, brought two "tough guy" actors to accompany him to the boss' office. The two behemoths, wearing pinstripe suits, just stood at either side of Don's office door while the "negotiation ensued." After a few short minutes, the boss left with the employee and his "enforcers" in tow to the bank to make a withdrawal. It worked. Bob thought maybe he should try the same tactic, but as the saying goes: "Fool me once….." Don finally cut Bob a check for half a month's salary, but it bounced. Twice. Bob's final severance check from the Army was now decimated because he had no pay coming in for nearly three months.

Bob finally threw in the towel and went on a job search that maximized his military experience and technical computer training. Don's check never cashed.

Chapter 15~The Novelist Goes Back in Time

It was the year 2020. There he sat, in front of the TV watching Hulu and Prime videos. He hadn't written a single word in over a week. Every day was a challenge to corral his anxiety over the fake world pandemic that had shut down almost every civilized country. He knew he had to dig deep to get back on the keyboard and create. Things had gotten so Orwellian that old folks were out walking their dogs in the Texas sunshine wearing a mask! Young folks had been so brainwashed by the education system that they accepted the risk of taking a vaccine that was rushed through development and testing. Even the mighty CDC, kowtowing to the WHO, had fewer and fewer answers as time went by. Their website was nothing more than a propaganda ploy, without any two-way communication. All they chose to do was tell folks to "wash your hands", keep away from other humans, and wear a mask. Eventually, they were told to take the experimental vaccine, and volunteer to be the guinea pig for Big Pharma. Anyone who died from the vaccine were reported to have "obviously died from something else." And the sheep fell for it. All of it. The old folks were bitching about not getting the vaccines first. Some signed up for the shot on several lists, desperate to get poked and "save Granny." He was totally baffled by this penchant to just "Do what you are told and don't ask questions." Even his grandson who was studying medicine in college believed that "fixing" this virus was important to the old folks so they could "get out of the house." Really? We were being ordered to take an experimental vaccine that might be 95% effective to protect the world from a virus that was less than 1% fatal across all age groups. Hell, maybe his grandson's rationale was closer to the truth.

He spent endless hours mulling over the idiocy of it all. Wasted cycles. Added frustration. Elevated blood pressure. No writing. Frustrated as hell! His unique and potentially fatal ability to internalize everything in the world took him beyond the point of frustration day after day. He knew that it would be a mental challenge to punch through the pandemic-induced brain fog to get "words on paper." He had to learn to not give a shit about things he had no control over. He had to unlearn a whole lifetime of care and concern. He had to come to grips with the fact that he would never be one of the the heroes he admired since his childhood. Not Superman, not Ben Cartwright, not Batman, not John Wayne. No hero here.

But, as always, he chose to trudge on, albeit very, very slowly. Not that it was drudgery, but it took a great deal of directed energy. He tried to activate the dictation function on the Mac, but found that Apple required all voice translation be done in the "cloud" and they insisted that all personal contacts and other sensitive, personal data had to be copied to them, as well. His only option? Don't use it. The option he chose, of course. Let them eat cake.

So, he set off, once again, to put together the novel he'd begun fifty years earlier. He worked his way past his less than secretarial ability to type. He felt he spent more time deleting and re-typing, resulting in an effective rate about 30 percent short of acceptable. More wasted time.

Soon, another whole week had passed and he hadn't written one damn word. This time he rationalized he had a great excuse: Texas FROZE OVER! Temperatures were below freezing for a week with ice and snow not seen in Texas in a century! The cooperative that ran the Texas Grid instituted rolling blackouts across Texas, leaving residents in the dark and cold every day sometimes twice a day for hours on end. And it was never announced when the blackout would occur.

Bob's engineering experience told him that this massive system failure was most likely a combination of institutional apathy and engineering incompetence. Even without any failure data, he could determine that those in charge of designing and testing the grid for extreme conditions failed miserably. Gas lines and generators froze on the first day of the storm, cutting off 40 percent of the grid's generating capacity! Unacceptable incompetence was the way he saw it.

Surely, there would be investigations and lessons learned, but there was little public confidence any improvement would be made ahead of the next weather disaster. They had one job and they failed miserably.

He put that all aside and decided to search for his original manuscript from 1970. It was an easy find, stuck in a large manila envelope with all the other college and high school writings he saved. He had placed the envelope in the bottom drawer of the filing cabinet, where it sat for 50 years.

He was amused to find not just the original story, but several papers from English, History and Philosophy classes. They included a report on the Communist Manifesto, a review and commentary on current American politics and a Modern Contextual Criticism of Walt Whitman. The diversity of thought was a real eye opener 50 years later.

He spent many hours over the next couple of weeks deciding whether to include the original text in the finished book. He read the manuscript several times and was concerned that the writing style, word usage, and character descriptions were amateurish, almost childish.

That put the brakes on inclusion of the original text. Then it hit him, even a bad example can be a good example. So, taking this tack, he mulled over how the text could illustrate the five decades of maturity in his writing ability. Besides that, it was almost Quixotic to publish his first draft for all to see. All the ugly there for the world to see. But, if the book was to be educational AND entertaining, why not include it? And so he did. The original, untitled, hand-typed manuscript he scanned from the recycled paper (it was already printed on one side with a play script of unknown origin) read like this (unedited for authenticity):

Preface

Well, it's a new year and I'me damn glad of it, being that I just spent the most boring New Year's Eve in all of my eighteen years. I felt the inspiration to write...well...this. I've got the radio on any my mother is having a fit. She has herc usual right to be mad. It's the middle of the night and my little sisters are asleep.

To resume, I feel the reader should be warned. Read with an open mind and with caution. Do not take everything as fact or fiction. It is, on the contrary a suspended mix of the two. Imagination is the spice of life. Warning you may not be the best way to start off, but it shouldn't bother you at all if you are reading with an open mind.

Chapter One

"You're going to a party."
"What?"

"I said you are going to a party. Are you hard of hearing?"

"No, but I just got home from work and I'm dead tired. And besides, you know I'm no good at going to parties."

"Well, you'll get some practice tonight. Grab some dinner. I'll be over in fifteen minutes."

I didn't bother to get all dressed up. Just put on a sports jacket and something to get rid of the airs of the day. I had an excellent dinner of cookies and a glass of milk. I was still munching on the cookies when Jim arrived.

"You got here fast enough."

"Yeh, the car's running well. It takes the curves real nice with the new tires."

"Well, take it easy. I wouldn't want to get killed by my best friend who drags me to crazy parties."

"You'll have fun. Just keep a beer in your hand and a pretzel in your mouth. Besides, there's going to be girls there."

"Girls? What are you driving so slow for?"

"Anyone ever tell you that you're crazy?"

"Yeh, but I don't believe them. Whose party is it?"

"Everyone is home for Thanksgiving and they're getting together. You know Greg, don't you?

"The one with the Camaro?"

"Yeh. Well his girlfriend and her sisters were invited, so naturally Greg was invited. It just so happened that they needed som guys to balance if off so Greg invited us."

"You mean we actually qualified?"

As we entered the driveway, we could see figures moving back and forth in the dimly lit house. I knew we were in rich country by the size of the house. Too bad it wasn't very good looking. But then again, the party was inside.

Something hit me in the nose when I walked through the door. What a stench! I had no idea what it was, but the beautiful sight that hit my eyes compensated for the smell. She was good looking, both facially and bodily. She kept my interest...and every other guy's. I found out later that she was holding the party and only to spite her boyfriend who she was giving her a "lot of shit."

After a while, I got the impression that this was a "walk-in" party. Everybody and their brothers were gaining entrance. It was almost dull. Everyone seemed to be playing pool in the next room. I had no idea so many people could share a table that small. I walked in the room, took a look around, and retreated to the kitchen to gather my thoughts. I took a seat and lit up my pipe. When I came around to looking up, Jim was standing there with a couple of girls. He didn't say anything. He just looked at me, then at one of the girls, and then back at me in a somewhat persuasive manner. I looked him in the eye and he knew where I was telling him to go. The girl he was pointing out to me was fairly fat, had fairly brown hair had a fairly pudgy nose, and was fairly bombed. She was also a fairly rotten conversationalist.

"Hello, Bob"

"Greetings."

"Jim told me your name. He mentioned that "Bob is the one that's
always dressed up."
"You got one?"
"Oh, I'm Barbara. Pat's sister."
"'Who's Pat?"
"Greg's girlfriend. Your invitation."
"You're her sister? You don't look a bit like her."
Do you live around here?"
"All my life."
"Well how old are you?"
"That's for me to know and for you to find out."

She left and I was relieved. She soon had all her girlfriends over to take to me just to find out how old I was. I decided to play a little game with them by not telling them for a while. I don't really know why. I guess I just felt a little embarrassed that I was only seventeen. They complimented me by telling me that I looked like a junior in college. Well, being the honest guy I was, I just had to tell them the truth. It didn't matter any. The party went on as usual.

I soon found myself in the room with the pool table and the fireplace...and a beer. Where I got it from I'll never know. I couldn't stand the taste but I drank it just to make it look like I was having good time. I wasn't. Then it started, Candies and marshmallows were flying through the air. The laughter rose above the music, which was damn loud in itself. Just to get in to the act, I chugged the last ounce of beer, shouted "hit the deck" and and dove under the pool table. I looked up from the floor and there she was. She was a very cute chick. But something besides looks made and impression on me. She was just standing there smiling at all the action, occasionally ducking an M&M. Something made me call up to her.

"Hello there.

"Hi. What are you doing down there?"

"Playing it smart. Come on down,"

"No thanks.

Just then, something hit her in the eye. I jumped gallantly to her assistance if only to get a closer look."

"Are You ok?"

"Yes. Only a marshmallow. It didn't hurt."

The bombardments retreated to another room and she and I were left standing there. The doors to opportunity were open and staring me in the face. I liked her already. We exchanged names and talked about the party. She told me she didn't drink. I liked her even more. She was pretty, quiet, and a good conversationalist..

"I'm glad someone around here doesn't drink besides me."

"If you don't drink, then what were you doing under the table?"

"I only had one beer and that was due only to the pressures of society. I dove under the table so I could meet you."

She just smiled and started to walk away. I wanted to talk some more. I stepped in front of her and started asking her some more idiotic questions. I found out that the was also Pat's sister and they lived up the street. I somehow guessed which house it was. She kept on asking me how I knew. I kept asking myself the same question.

Someone suddenly shouted out the good news that the parents were home. The doors flew open and everyone, including myself, was outside running for cover. It was a false alarm. I was glad about that. For a while I was afraid that I wouldn't get to say good-night to my new acquaintance. I found my way back into the house only to find her cleaning up the house that was by now a total wreck.

"Why are you cleaning up?"

"Someone has to do it."

"Why should it be you?"

"Oh, I don't mind."

Every little thing that she said or did made me want to know her even more. She told me that Shelly was already in enough trouble with her parents for even holding the party. If they came home and found it in that condition she would have probably been shot. I helped to clean up while she took Shelly up to bed to sleep it off.

"Let's go Bob. It's time to hit the road."

"Not yet, Jim. Wait a while."

"Wait for what? The party is over."

"This place is a mess."

"Well , that's not your worry."

"At least let me say Good-Night."

"To whom?"

"Never mind. I'll be out in five minutes."

She came back down and I told her that I had to

leave. She thanked me for helping out. I asked her for her telephone number and I had a hard time getting it. I did finally get it and bade her adieu, promising her that I'd call.

I went out the the car only to be affronted by. Jim's command, "let's get the hell out of here." Then he started in.

"Who is she?"

"A very nice girl."

"That's good. Who is she?"

"Pat's sister."

"Barbara? She's pretty good looking."

"No, not Barbara. Cheryl."

CHAPTER II

I slept most of Sunday. It wasn't until Jim called that I decided to get up. He invited me over for a while to "mess around," as he always put it. So we messed around at nothing all day, We did our usual bullshitting about girls, but for once we actually had some girls to bullshit about. Since he was already going steady, he was more interested in "Pat's sister." He kept trying to convince me to get to know her better, a thought that had been a dream to me all the previous night. I assured him that I would at least call her. I never even dreamt what was to come in the next few days. It just happened.

Monday was one of those crisp days that frequent early winter. I decided that it was a day for a ride after school. Driving up in the area of the week-end's party was the first idea that came to mind. I wasn't quite sure of my goal. Perhaps to find that road, that house that I believed she lived in, and possibly her. For some strange reason, I felt like a real ass. I didn't know whether I was chicken, or just mad at myself for wasting gas on such a wild goose chase.

Upon finding the road, I began a quick search of the area in which I had guessed the house to be. There it was, as broad as day. Too bad the mailbox had the wrong name on it.

I must have gone up and down that road at least six times. No luck at all. I decided to give up the search and enjoy the scenery. A street full of newly built housed caught my eye as I headed back down the road for the last time.

Upon turning in to investigate, I noticed that most of the houses were not even complete. The road led straight up a hill to a view that encompassed all of long Island Sound. But the view only help my attention for a matter of seconds as I turned to look at one of the more finished houses there appeared a familiar face. Greg. My first thought was that he had obtained a new job for he was carrying a large box into the newly finished abode. But then my mind really started into circles. There appeared another familiar face which struck me as quite a coincidence. Pat. They recognized my car as it had previously been described to them and started to wave. By this time I had the window rolled down in eager curiosity.

"Hey Greg! What the hell are you doing here?"

"This is the place!" came the reply.

Everything hit me at once. I couldn't decide whether or not to go in, or to just take off as if in some kind of hurry. I just couldn't pass up this chance. I was there, She was probably there. And I had nothing better to do. I shut down the car and proceeded down the incline to the big gray house of hazards unknown to the commoner. I had many thoughts as to how I should present myself. The problem was that I was not quite sure how to act or what to say. I knew I had to give her at least a reason for being in the area.

After all, it wasn't quite my daily route home from school.

As I entered the house I had the feeling that I was being watched. I passed it off without a second thought. The first room I encountered was quite messed up and it smelled of children. I just stood there for a few minutes waiting for Greg to come back from whatever part of the mansion he was in. In those few minutes there passed through my mind at least a million and a half thoughts as to what her father's occupation was. He certainly wasn't the grease monkey that I was so used to at home. The room that I was standing ing was large enough to be the complete first floor of my family's humble shack in town. My eyes lightly touched one a fireplace, a color television, a bookcase, some furniture scattered here and there, and a double door leading to the back porch which rose twenty feet abovo the ground. Then Greg popped in.

"She's in there." He pointed to the kitchen.

"Thanks, but where's there?"

"The library. Go into the kitchen and take a quick right."

I proceeded into the designated are only to be met half way by Cheryl, herself. She looked as stunned and dumb for words as I felt. Our conversation started out with a bang."

"Hi."

"Hello, Bob. What brings you out here?"

"I just felt like taking a ride in the country. I also wanted to find a certain road with a certain house of a certain girl that I met at a certain party over the weekend."

"You found what you were looking for."

"Yeh, But I had given up the search and decided to take a look at the new houses. It just so luckily happened that Greg and Pat were outside and they invited me in."

There was a pause as she lead me back in to the library where she was cleaning up. I glanced around the room in a somewhat perplexed state. Books lined one wall while on the opposite side of the room there hung several plaques of merit and pictures of moments in the history of her father. This few seconds of investigation was soon interrupted.

"So how have you been these last couple of days?"

"Oh, just fine, considering school." I couldn't resist throwing that in for the kids.

"How's Christ the King? That is the name of the place, isn't it?"

"Yes, that's the name of the institution of higher learning which I attend. Funny name, isn't it? It's actually coming along pretty well. I had a short yearbook meeting after school today."

"Are you on the yearbook staff:"

"I'm the photographer."

"Are you really a photographer? I've been wanting to get a camera for so long. I'd like to photograph flowers and insects and things like that. You know, with the special lens and equipment."

"You mean a close-up lens, right?"

"Yeh, I guess so."

"I'd like to get some equipment myself. I've been working with nothing for a long time."

There was another momentous pause while we both tried to think of something to talk about. I wasn't thinking too hard, though. I was busy trying to figure out just exactly where I was. The house was more like a castle. I wanted to cure my curiosity by asking her a few questions but I didn't have to. When I turned to look at her as she hung something up in the closet, I accidentally leaned up against the wood panelling and it swung open in front of me. There, staring me in the face, was the most fantastic conglomeration of stereo equipment I ever laid my eyes upon. There certainly wasn't any need for a question. It was written all over my face. I just stared at it with stern interest and amazement.

I was soon to realize that this house had almost every living comfort conceivable. Besides this, it was, for once a good looking large house. The only reason it was good looking though, was because it had the markings of children. I almost felt at home as I finally spotted one of the little devils peeking around a corner from the hallway. She quickly slipped back around the corner as soon as she realized that I had spotted her. Then, around yet another corner popped a second, and a third, and a fourth. By this time I knew that I had to start asking some questions. I just didn't know where to start. Cheryl was looking at me with a smile. She could see that I was more than just curious. I was plainly perplexed!

"Where are they all coming from?"

"Oh, they're all over the place. Come on out kids, he doesn't bite."

I had the distinct impression that they a didn't believe her. All they did was stick their heads around the corner again, give a little giggle, and duck back around the corner. Cheryl motioned to me to follow her. We went through a door behind us around a couple of corners, and up behind the little rascals. That a was all they needed. They took one look, and off they went scattering in all directions. We just stood there and laughed.

" I take it that that is the rest of the clan?"

" That's part of it. The others are around somewhere. Probably messing something else up.

"And we didn't when we were their age?"

She just smiled and started back into the library.

"How many of them are there? I counted five,

"There's nine of us altogether. Barb went back to school. Tom is upstairs studying. Pat is with Greg. Little Greg is outside playing with Rick, and the rest are running around here somewhere."

"You beat us by one. There's eight in my family." We kept on the subject for a while, but my mind was somewhere else. The answers were coming out of my subconscious, by instinct probably. I was concentrating on the probability of the whole experience. There I was, in a strange house, laughing at strange kids and conversing with a not so strange and very nice girl. It just wasn't me. I couldn't convince myself that I was really there. I had to get out. I wasn't nervous or scared or anything of that sort. I just had had enough unbelievability for one day. The funniest thing about it was that I had only been there for 10 minutes. But then I had the thought that maybe she was thinking the same thing I was. She seemed none too sure about the situation either. She kept herself busy with the housework. I decided to stay as long as was politely practical.

"You're always cleaning up. It must be habit by now.

"I don't know if I'd want a habit like this. My parents expect if from Pat and I. We're the oldest that are still home."

"And it looks like you're the most experienced. What do you do for fun?"

"Go to parties, but I don't really like to. I only go because both my sisters go.

I'm sort of the chaperone for the neighborhood parties. You know what I mean. And whenever any of the kids in the neighborhood have a problem, they know they can come to me. Sort of neighborhood psychologist"

"I liked the way you acted at the party. You were a lot more mature than everyone else. Why don't you like parties?"

"It's a long story. I just remember one party that I went to that really shook me up. Everyone was drunk out of their minds to the point of disgust. Now and then I have a bad dream about that night. I just stand there, scared, while everyone else is drinking and making noise. That dream always scares me."

"That's kind of interesting. I haven't been to very many parties myself. It is just not me. For one, I can't really drink, and for two, I never really want to. I've got to be in a fantastically crazy mood in order to go to a party."

"Were you in a crazy mood last night?"

"Not really. Jim dragged me to it. I didn't get into a crazy mood until I got there. That was only because I didn't know anybody and nobody knew me, so I really didn't care what I did. I just let my instincts take over as usual.

We just kept on talking about the party for a while and exchanged an occasional smile. There was something there. We just seemed to get along. After about an hour of just talking about things, mainly points of introduction, we were both relaxed.

I didn't feel so awkward any more. I felt like staying for another hour or two. But it was nearing five o'clock and I hadn't been home yet. So just to avoid interrogation when I got home, I decided it was time to leave. We were now in the kitchen where she was getting dinner ready. Something was there, and we both knew it. "I probably got in the way more than I helped." She just smiled as we walked to the door.

"Take it easy, now."

"'Ok you too. And don't be afraid to drop in if your ever in the area. The door is always open."

"Thanks I just might do that."

I walked up the hill to the road where my car was parked and got in. I just sat there for a second, and the whole afternoon flashed by in one big scene. I felt good about something. I just couldn't figure out what it was. I waved to her through the window and buzzed off down the road. The car was driving itself, I was riding the clouds. What she said about ever being in the area struck me as funny. I guess she didn't realize that my house was only about a mile away. I know I told her where I lived. She just didn't know where the street was. I knew I was going back, and soon.

"And where have you been until six o'clock?

"It's just after five, Ma." Mom had a habit of stretching the time. But she was only half serious.

"Are you going to tell me that your yearbook meeting lasted until now?" She was more curious than anything else. It was a habit with her.

"No, I've just been around."

That was a usual answer, Either that or bumming.

I went upstairs o get rid of my books. The room was its usual mess, so I just dropped my books on the bed and went down to dinner. But I was still thinking about that something. Mom knew I had something on my mind. I always thought that parents had some way of seeing into your mind. I had all sorts of wild theories about it. For some reason Mom didn't bother to ask any more questions, although I was sure she would. I guess she was waiting until she had a question that I couldn't get around.

CHAPTER III

It was another chilly morning, but the antique wheels started as usual. The ride to school was not the usual, though. Everything that always bored me on this small trip seemed not to do so today, Some things even looked worthwhile, when actually they were the same trees, houses and people that I saw every school day. Colors were more vivid, smells more sweet. For once, I actually felt as if I were going somewhere. I even wanted to go to school. I couldn't translate my thoughts into any shape or form. My emotions were reaching out for their fill that they had long awaited. I felt a type of excitement in just knowing that I soon would be talking to the guys at school about someone that really meant something to me. My new acquaintance had stirred up something in me that I had no control over. My dreams from the previous night were playing games with my conscious. I started to have some trouble separating the two. It was going to be one hell of a day.

I sputtered into the parking lot only to be met by Mr. Cool, himself What an honor to be greeted by such a one as he so early in the morning. I almost had my breakfast again. But, people will be people, Perhaps someday someone will tell him what he is. "Good morning, Bob. What's up. I hear you got a new girlfriend."

"Is that right? Where did you hear that?"

"It's all over time school. Really moving out, huh?"

"Yeh, Terry, really moving out."

I just took my time and let him go on ahead. He bugged a lot of people. So it's all over the school? Considering that the school was a whole hundred and forty-two people large, one could assume that there was a little exaggeration put forth in the minds of the mass. Now I knew I was in for something. But the guys were quite humorous. There wasn't any malice to be afraid of. Just quite a bit of teasing. I claimed no prize yet, and they all knew it.

I closed the car door and walked almost briskly up to the back door. I never could figure out why we had to enter by the back. It's amazing. Some of the things that you don't learn in school that is. The guys saw me approaching and decided to start the day off right. I was used to most of it by now.

"Hey, guys. Here comes lover-nose. Hey Vit, you better not try to kiss her. You might knock her out! I just looked up at him and them gave him a profile of "the nose"

"There he is, Romeo of Southwestern Connecticut," shouted the Lumberjack.

"I learned everything I know from you, Playboy." I had to come back with something or they might have thought that I was sick.

As I entered the door and started up the stairs, there came a voice from behind.

Went to a party over the weekend, hey, Bob?" It was another wise guy.

"Yeh Thom, but it wasn't all that fruitful. Just another party."

"You lying sack of shit. We all heard about it."

I jumped down the stairs and he took off. Typical of any underclassman,

Afraid of their own shadows, But around there everyone knew that the other guy was only kidding, even if he was an upperclassman. I started back up the stairs to my locker to get rid of the books and coat.

"Hello, Bob. How's it goin'

"Pretty good, Jim!" Amazing! A quiet one. Either that, or he was still asleep. I followed him into the classroom where everyone was waiting with their own two-bit words of wisdom. But I was, as they often put it, saved by the bell.

The comments about Cheryl weren't as bad as I thought they were going to be. Most of them said their say before the first class. It wasn't until I told

Phil and Jim about going over to Cheryl's house that the comments started to fly.

What bugged me most though was the typical asinine questions about such things as her body that the more moronic guys got their kicks out of. Those I just brushed off with a "real fine!" Or an "I have no idea" answer. It wasn't so bad when the idiots asked those type questions, but when Ralph, or "God's gift to the female sex ", started in, then

I really got a laugh. "Is she nice?" he asked.

"Definitely, Frank. She's a real nice girl." I just had to tease him in return.

"No, I mean is she nice nice? You know," He motioned with his hands

the symbol for a well built broad. I started to laugh. He had those kind of facial expressions that could make anyone laugh.

"For the sake of your stupid curiosity, Frank, yes, she is nice." He looked sort of disgusted as he walked out of the room. I was glad as all hell that he didn't start giving me some of his tips on How to Love! The day went on as usual, except for the way I felt about everything. I didn't really have any idea how I felt, I just took all the sarcastic remarks with a smile, for I felt sure that it wouldn't last very long. After all, these were a swell bunch of guys. Most of them knew when to stop. If for some reason, one of them didn't know when the joke was up, they'd find out soon enough. Someone would either tell them, or they'd figure it out when they found themselves to be the only ones trying to be funny about a worn out subject. It was soon last class and I had the feeling that someone was going to ask for a ride home. There wasn't any way I could avoid it. I certainly wasn't about to say no. Especially in the mood I was in. I managed to stay in this peculiar mood all day, despite all the wise cracks. I still couldn't figure out what it was though. I knew it had something to do with Cheryl, but I just couldn't pinpoint it. Maybe I didn't want to. At any rate, just before class was dismissed, Jim and Phil came up to me asking for a ride.

"Well, OK, guys. But don't expect this service too many times" I must have given them that line a hundred times before. But it wasn't all that bad. Things sort of evened out when one of the other guys drove and I took the bus. But after taking that bus for three years, I tried to drive to school as much as possible.

We all went out to the car, after a stop at the john, and were soon on our way home and soon on our way to a conversation that took a more serious tone than I had encountered during he day.

"So you went over to her house yesterday, huh Bob?"

"Yeh, Jim. You wouldn't believe that place. It's a mansion. It's almost the size of the school."

"That's impossible. I realize our school is small, but there's no house around here that big."

"Well that's with a minimum of exaggeration, believe me, that house is big."

"This I've got to see. What does her father do? sell slaves?"

"Knock it off, clown. Don't you worry none Phil. If I know you, you'll get around to seeing it, sooner or later."

"If it's up to him, It'll probably be sooner.", replied Jim.

"Where is this place, Bob."

"You'll never find out. You'll probably go up there and paint red hearts all over her front door.

"That wouldn't be such a bad idea, "would it, Jim?"

Come off it, Phil. What would you want to pimp him for?"

"I'll give you a hint. Do you remember where we were filming our movie last year? Let me put it this way. You've stood where her front yard now lies."

"What do you mean by that? Is it a new house?", asked Jim.

"Certainly is. You were there when it was nothing but a pile of dirt and cow shit."

"How far is it from your house, Bob.

I tell ya, Phil, it's about a mile... and almost straight up."

"OH, so she lives in a tree?" That was Jim again.

"Not quite, funny man. Try on top of a hill." They were quiet for a few seconds, just mumbling things to themselves. I couldn't believe how curious they were about where she lived. It was typical, though. Then Phil came out with a close proximity.

"Do you mean that new road off of that old road?"

"Very good, Phil. But I think there's a couple of those around."

"I got it, Phil, "blurted Jim, "Remember that hill where we filmed out over the Sound? That's got to be the place."

They just both looked at me, eagerly awaiting an answer. I knew that they'd kill me if I didn't tell them soon. He had the right place. No use trying to keep it from them any longer.

"That's the place. If that house was there when we filmed, we would have gotten a fantastic tour of her living room."

They looked a little astonished. I didn't expect any less. I felt the same way when I first saw all those new houses up there.

"You got to be kidding, said Phil." They don't build houses that quick.

"That's where your'e wrong.

There's about eight new houses in there. They all had a great view of the Sound from on top of that hill. I wouldn't mind living up there.

"Yeh," replied Jim. "Especially now that you know she lives up there.

"Hey, Jim. Don't you think we ought to make him take us on a tour of lover's lane?"

"I think so, Phil. How about it Bob? "

"Are you crazy? You don't really think I'd take a couple of clowns like you two up into a sophisticated area like Sturbridge Hill, do you?

I'm afraid you might start yelling some obscenities out the window at all those nice people."

They knew I was trying to be funny. They just looked at each other and laughed. But I could always count on Phil to come up with some brilliant idea.

"We'll come up and visit you two sometime in the hear future, When are you going to see her next?"

"I have no idea when I'll see her again but even if I do, you sure as hell better not pop in on us until introduce you to her, in due time.

Give me a chance to get to know her first. O.K.?"

"I'll have to think about it," was the reply. He was always good with replies, too, He seldom missed a trick. It's a good thing he was a friend.

We approached Phil's house where I let the two of them off. Phil had offered to Take Jim home, in yet another town. Our school had guys from all over the county.

As I went to bed that night, the feeling that I had awaken up with fifteen hours earlier was now stronger than ever. The beautiful dreams came again that night. (I still couldn't figure out what was going on in my mind.)

CHAPTER IV.

Wednesday afternoon found me wandering in Cheryl's neck of the woods again. I was contemplating whether I should drop in on her again. I had the invitation to do so. I also knew where the house was this time. There I heard the the baby of the family. She was a very cute child, now that I finally got a close look at her. I was no longer a stranger to them, either.

As soon as I stepped inside, they all came charging at me to grab a hello. They all wanted to lead me into the dining room where Cheryl was, once again, cleaning up. There was no doubt in my mind as to the success of my finding her. Not with the multitude of little scouts I had leading to the way.

"Hi! So I see you took your chances on coming back here."

"Don't be ridiculous, I'm getting use to leaving one house full of children and stepping into another house just as full. So how have you been since Monday?"

"Oh, pretty good. I had a German test today. I think I did pretty good on it."

"That's good. I see you're still cleaning up. You're going to make some guy a good housewife,"

"I wouldn't be too sure about that, Too much more of this and I'll get sick of it. I wouldn't want to keep a clean house."

There was a pause while she finished dusting. I found myself looking for something interesting to talk about, again. She put the cleaning cloths away and invited me into the library where we had a seat. She went over to the tape deck and turned it on. The music was familiar, but I couldn't place it. I think it was the sound track from a Broadway show.

Cheryl hastened into the other room to yell at the kids, who were making the boisterous noises of play that children usually make. It became quiet.

When she came back into the room she pointed out a picture of her father at his graduation ceremonies at Culver Military Academy. Flanking that were two plaques commemorating Mr. Steel's 100,000th mile in the air with TWA airlines. It had something to do with the Ambassador Club. My first impressions were that her father was some kind of V.I.P. My curiosity started to take over.

"This is all your fathers stuff?"

"Yes. That's his graduation picture in the middle, The other is of a company picnic or something. It's just a whole lot of junk that he always puts up on the wall as soon as we move into another house.

"This says he graduated from the Massachusetts Institute of Technology. He must be a fairly smart man."

"What does he do for a living?"

"He's a management consultant,"

"What's that?

"Just what it says. He consults managers of different companies around the country on how they should run their business.

"I take it that he travels a lot. I wouldn't want to do that unless I was independent. That way I could go wherever and whenever I wanted.

"Well, he hasn't been the only member of the family that's traveled

The whole family had lived in over twenty five different houses across the country. I've lived in about twenty two different houses myself."

"You must be kidding! How could you grow up like that? I've lived in one town all my life and I'm glad of it. I've gotten to know this town real well and It's gotten to know me."

It didn't really bother me all that much. It's only that just as we were getting use to a place and getting to know some people well, we found ourselves moving to another state. I figure we've lived in about eight different states. The good thing about it is that you get a well rounded view of the country and you get to meet a large variety of people, It's a good experience. The only real problem is leaving behind any friends that you've managed to make."

So far there was only one difference between us. It was the fact that I was brought up in one place, while she'd lived all over he place. This didn't bother me all that much, though.

We went on talking about ourselves, our families, our backgrounds. There were many similarities between us. Both our families were large. We were both third children. We tended more toward the conservative side of life as well as the optimistic side.

She was from a dutch or German background. I was strictly Italian. She even looked the part. She had sort of a pudgy, but cute, nose , rounded cheeks, long brown hair, and beautiful brown eyes. I don't think I took my eyes off her once the whole time we were talking. I was making a sort of long term survey, but it was quite involuntary. She was something to look at. Her body was as nice to look at as her face. I could help but noticing how well built she was. She had it, and I could see it. But for once, it wasn't the body that I was concentrating on. She was a very interesting girl. I knew that I could sit and talk with her for hours on any subject.

We talked on for about an hour and a half, just about us and our families. We asked each other questions on anything from how we liked our coffee to what church we worshiped at. We were both Catholic. For some reason, that was good. It was probably the way I was brought up by those dear nuns. But I realized that being Catholic wasn't "it."

Although we did managed to talk for some time, we barely scratched the surface of each other's background. But I had to get going, and before I left I had something to ask her.

"Are you doing anything Friday night?"

Tomorrow night? No. Why?"

How would you like to go out, Perhaps to a movie or something."

"I'll have to see what mom and dad say, but I'm sure there won't be any problem,"

"OK, then. I'll see you around seven tomorrow evening."

"That's fine with me, Good night now."

"Yeh, see you then. Take it easy."

I left through the same door that I came in. It was a side door in the front of the house, To me it was another front door and I couldn't figure out why someone would build a house with two front doors. But then I remembered her saying something about that door being for the children so they don't bring dirt in through the parlor. Whatever it was that was trying to break through the seal of my conscious was still working hard at it. It was getting stronger as the time passed. The unfortunate thing about it was that it showed and my mother saw it at dinner, She finally came up with that one question that I couldn't get around without lying.

"Bob, have you got a new girlfriend?" To her, all girl friends were girlfriends. And the "new" had to be put in there for clarification, even though I never had had a girlfriend.

"Not yet Mom, but I did meet a real nice girl at the party I went to last weekend. That got her. She wasn't a girlfriend yet.

I went to bed that night with Cheryl on my mind again and believe me, I didn't mind at all. I kept on thinking of what mom had said about a new girlfriend. She didn't mean much by it but for some reason it stuck in my mind. Things were still very foggy in my mind, though. I couldn't put anything together except that which actually happened in the last few days. Being that I had never experienced something such as this before, everything was really mixed up, Chance and logic seemed to fighting each other within my mind. I just prayed that everything would clear up soon. Before I knew it, Friday morning had arrived. The sun reflected the brightness of my eyes as I looked out the window as I got up. I was ready to get up because I wanted to get the day over with. I was super anxious for seven o'clock to come around. But, as usual, when you want time to fly, it seems to go backwards. The day dragged on but it didn't bother me too much. About ten of the guys asked me if I was going out with Cheryl that night. I felt proud to be able to tell them that I was. The feeling inside me was larger by the minute. I couldn't yet figure it out, but I knew I soon would.   The afternoon took longer to pass than the morning simply because all I had to think about was seven o'clock. I went up town just to pass the time, but that didn't help much. It seemed as if seven would never show up.

CHAPTER V

It was finally nearing zero hour and I getting more anxious by the minute. I was all out for a good night and nothing was going to get in our way. It wasn't the first date that I ever had, but there seemed to be something different about it. Maybe it was that for once, I knew who I was going to be taking out. I never had a blind date that went over very well. As a matter of record, I never had any date that went over very well. Tonight was going to be a first. I finished dinner in a hurry and just as I was about to get up, Mom came out with another of her logical questions.

"What's your hurry?"

"Nothing much, Ma. Just got to be going."

" Uhuh! And just where are you going tonight, Young Man?"

"Out." We were starting that usual cat and mouse game that we always used to answer our questions.

And just what do you mean by that? Are you taking your new girlfriend out tonight?"

"You got it! It shouldn't have taken you that long to figure it out. You're kind of slow today."

"Never you mind." She often ended her conversations with a line similar to that. She reminded me that I was still her son when she threw a line like that at me. I went up to my room and proceeded to get ready for my date. I wanted to take a shower but I couldn't. It wasn't that I was all that tight for time, it was our only bathroom didn't have a shower. Our house was quite old and all we had was an antique bathtub, I didn't want to chance taking a bath. I knew that I'd probably jump in and lose all tract of time. That I definitely wanted to avoid. I wasn't sweaty at all. It was winter and I never got that way at that time of year. I had my Right Guard to depend upon at any rate. I also had some lime cologne that I received that previous Christmas. It did a good job.

I was the type of guy that got dressed up for just about anything. So I put on my best pants, a white turtleneck sweater, and my fishbone sports jacket. I was hoping that I looked as good as I felt, but I couldn't tell. When I went downstairs to take off, I met my mother at the door with her parting line. I almost expected it. She was just curious about Cheryl as anyone else around.

"Well how do you do, handsome!", she exclaimed.

"Wow! Bobby's all dressed up," came my little sister, Angela.

"Your big brother is going out tonight, girls," replied Mom.

I didn't say much. I just smiled at them all and gave them a couple other funny looks. I went into the next room to get my overcoat, only to run into my other two little sisters.

"Ohh! Bobby stinks!" shouted little Cheryl.

"I stink?"

"Oh, you mean his cologne, He stinks nice." said Mom.

I laughed and walked over to Cheryl. I wanted to tease her so I bent over and planted a little kiss on her nose.

"You stink." she repeated as she ran into the other room as if trying to hide. All the others, including myself, brought down the ceiling with laughter. We all know that she was running away from the kiss more than the odor of lime. The children were always embarrassed when someone tried to kiss them. I didn't know why.

Well, I was all set to go. I felt really fantastic. The little episode I had just encountered had a lot to do with it. Children are fantastic, especially when they're happy. And when they said something like little Cheryl had just said, I knew they are too young and innocent to mean anything by it. I said good-bye to everyone and went out to my car.

That little automobile was my pride and glory. Never gave me any trouble and always there when I needed her. She started up in her usual brave manner and I was soon on my way to Sturbridge Hill. I didn't actually know where I was going to take Cheryl that night. I remember her saying something about some movie that was playing in the area. A thought occurred to me that was in something that I had read a while back. It had to do with dating and how the boy should decide where he was going to take the girl. I never did believe everything I read.

❋❋❋

He read it over several times. After scanning it into the Mac, he spent several hours correcting the text and filling in what the scanner missed. By time Bob was done, he had a greater appreciation for the effort he put in on New Year Eve, 1970. It was quite a serious start on a novel that kept growing in his head for decades. Adding story after story, but never committing it to paper.

He decided that including it in this chapter would give it a proper place in the book, and impress upon the reader just what it takes to write what now felt like the never-ending-story.

Chapter 16~The Renegades

By the summer of 1969, all three of the guys had purchased a motorcycle. At 17 years old, they had grand plans to travel around the country. Greg bought a Norton 750 and immediately put his art skills to the task. He re-painted the entire bike and sculpted a devil's face into the top of the gas tank. Greg had natural art talent. He could take a spray gun and freehand comic book artwork on a t-shirt with incredible results. Unfortunately, he never used his talent to make a buck. He didn't have to. His parents (which were revealed decades later to be his adoptive parents) had plenty of money, so Greg just had to argue it out of their wallets. He had bought and sold several cars before his 18th birthday, painting each of them to his whim with gnarly results. He even turned an old 13 window VW bus into a work of art before selling it. What an ability!

Jim purchased a Triumph 650 with a raked and extended front end with ape bars. He eventually convinced the others to design and order a club patch. They decided to represent "Fate" MC from Connecticut. The three naïve kids had no idea what life was like as authentic "bikers." Luckily the patches never saw the light of day, but were safely put away awaiting stories like this decades later.

Finally, Bob found an old Honda Cb160, barely an engine compared to the other two monsters. They all followed the law and got their motorcycle licenses and insurance. They mostly just bummed around town or biked between their houses.

Bob spent a lot of time "fixing" his used bike. The foot gear shift ended up being a small vice grip, since the original shift lever was broken. The headlight was loose and threw light into the woods with every bump and eventually failed completely on his way home from Jim's house one night. He quickly learned to follow the moonlit tree line as a guide to where the road went. Other than that, everything worked most the time.

Both he and his Honda were put to the test on one sunny Sunday morning when the guys decided to take a ride. They were barely out of town, going south on South Avenue when they heard a siren behind them. Greg was quick to shout, "We gotta go! NOW!" None of them had violated any traffic laws and certainly had no warrants out against them. But before Jim could ask Greg what the problem was, all three of them were accelerating down the avenue toward the Merritt Parkway. Greg, in the lead, veered off into the highway maintenance yard at the intersection of South Avenue and the Parkway. The huge piles of sand and salt were surrounded only by a guardrail of sorts, constructed with recycled telephone poles that were cut to about 5 feet, each half-buried in the ground. They were connected to each other by twisted steel cable, designed not to keep people out, but most likely to keep vehicles from rolling into the highway.

Greg accelerated up the side of the sand dune headed for the Parkway. It wasn't until then that Bob noticed that Greg was not riding his 750, but some rice burner trail bike. He made it look easy as he launched off the sand pile, over the guardrail and down the embankment onto the parkway. It was fortunate that it was a Sunday morning, so there was no commuter traffic headed into NYC. He was headed south on the Parkway before Jim made it to the pile. He struggle to get some height without fishtailing in the sand with his 650. Rather than trying Greg's "Great Escape" jump, he goosed the bike throttle until the front wheel of the bike was almost hovering over the steel cable. Then, in one, sweet, powerful motion, he drove the bike over, using the back wheel to propel the bike off the cable. Bob got a sand shower in the process.

By the time Bob had reached sand pile, he had decided to take a third approach. He rolled the bike carefully down back side of the dune, got off the bike, lifted the front wheel over the lowest point of the cable, then throttled the bike, basically "walking it over" the obstacle. But, it wasn't over yet. It wasn't until he got over the guardrail that he found himself at the top of a small embankment, maybe 20 feet from the Parkway. The tracks the other two left behind revealed that they both fishtailed a bit down the embankment, finding upright only when they hit the asphalt road. And then, nothing but the sound of their powerful engines in the distance. He eased the bike down the grassy bank in neutral, and made it safely to the highway. In one quick motion, he was back on the bike and going through the gears, trying to catch up.

It would be hard to tell if he was shaking more than cussing! The cheap sunglasses he wore were no contender for the wind that was slashing at his eyes. Tears started rolling down his face, which could be the result of the chilly wind or his fear and anger. He got the little bike up to 80 when he noticed the guys pulling off the exit almost a mile away! He throttled back since he knew where they were headed, and really didn't want to become a 120 pound bloody blot on the Parkway. And then he noticed that there was no one following him. No cops anywhere!

When he finally arrived at the Sunoco station just off the exit, he saw Jim and Greg having at it over on the side of the building. They weren't fighting, but very close to it, involving lots of shouting, poking and intimidation.

Bob could hear part of the "discussion" as he pulled up beside them, despite his helmet being half full of sand.

"Where did you get that bike?" Asked Jim.

"I found it on the side of the road near my house and hot-wired it", Greg responded, a bit red-faced.

'So this bike is stolen?" Jim shouted.

"Well, not really. It was just sitting there, abandoned. So I though I't take it for a spin."

"Are you out of your fuckin' mind? That's why we just ditched the cops and nearly killed ourselves?" Jim shouted at the top of his lungs. Bob never saw Jim so red-faced and trembling.

Bob was just listening and trying to stop shaking, himself. His heart rate had to be higher than anytime in his short life. The adrenalin was still circulating in his young system.

"You've got to be shitting me," Bob blurted out, half choking on the thought of being dead for such a stupid reason. His composure had not yet made a return visit.

As was his style, Greg started up his bike, shouting "I'll catch you guys later. I've got to put this thing back where I found it," he shouted, half chuckling.

That was Greg's common reaction to any conflict: run away. Perhaps for the best, most times. He'd run away now, twice in 15 minutes.

Bob and Jim looked at each other, started their bikes and left. No more drama, no more adrenalin. Just a "holy crap" moment to learn from, hopefully.

None of these three amigos were criminals in any way, shape or form. While Jim and Greg were known to have a beer while looking at a Playboy, they were what was referred to a "a couple of good kids, not "troublemakers." They both had jobs after school, respected their parents and went to church on occasion. They each had an indelible influence on the others through the years they hung out.

The only thing that may have outpaced the stupidity of that Sunday morning was their "party" on New Years Eve, 1970. It ended up that it was just the three of them in Greg's dingy basement. The girls Greg "promised" never showed up, and it's entirely possible that Greg had nobody else to invite. A month prior, Bob's girlfriend had ditched him for a drug addict who was headed to the same college. Jim was always "in-between" girlfriends, but he had enough to form a harem. Greg had been going steady for a couple years with the much younger sister of Bob's former. Nonetheless, none showed up on New Years Eve!

Jim started the festivities by popping open a Bud and handing it to Bob. But Bob was not an experienced drinker, so he was very hesitant. Turned out that he hated the taste, but thought the buzz was OK.

Unfortunately, Greg's basement was not a bright, welcoming space. His parents had chosen puke yellow wallpaper and a Spanish-style drop lamp that looked like a flying saucer made of starched fabric. It barely gave off any light, creating the feel of a denizen of ill repute. On one wall was a large poster depicting a grand bullfight, with the pics sticking out of the bull's back. After two beers, Bob was having a very loud conversation with Ralph while riding the porcelain bus, the tortured bull charging right at him from the adjoining room, which didn't help matters. Jim just kept his pace with no problem. Greg was in another room, lighting up a pipe. Jim had to explain to Bob what Greg was up to. "Smoking hash", said Jim. Bob had no idea what that was, but Jim was happy to explain.

"You guys want some of this?", asked Greg, not yet stoned.

"Oh hell no!" shouted Bob.

"Not my thing," replied Jim. "I'll stick to my Bud."

The horribly boring "party" went on for a while, until Greg, now fully stoned, suggested that we go "cruisin' for chicks." After a ten minute argument, Greg grabbed his coat and headed to the carport in a huff. Jim and Bob followed suit, not knowing what was going to happen. Do they go along with a stoned out Greg or jump in their own car half plowed from Bud? They decided to go with Greg, just to keep an eye out for him.

While the snow from the prior night had been plowed and sanded, the secondary roads were still a bit sketchy. All three of them were stuffed into Greg's BMW 2000i headed up 123 to town. All the while, Greg was insisting that, although he was still a bit stoned, his senses were sharper than usual and his reflexes lightning quick. He claimed that was the big difference between pot and hash. Hash doesn't dull your senses like pot.

They managed the trip to town without incident, drove the main streets, knowing that prospects were less than thin on a freezing New Year's Eve, then eventually headed back to the house for, as Greg put it, "another hit." Bob noticed right off that Greg was being unusually cautious in his driving, but he was still very concerned that Greg was somewhat high behind the wheel, even with the windows wide open in the cold, winter air!

That was the first and last time Bob witnessed Greg "doing shit." It was also the first and last time Bob drank more than one beer! Lessons learned and nobody got dead.

And so went the story of three guys at the very bottom of the teenage serious offenders list. A bit of mischief, a little common sense, and a lot of luck! But, alas, no chicks! Par for the course.

Chapter 17~Never Poor Again

He first entered active duty in August of 1974, after being commissioned at Ft. Riley, KS at the end of a grueling summer training program in the unbearable Kansas heat. A photo and press release were sent to the Northfield Advertiser, exclaiming the latest local boy who was ready to "Kill a Commie for Christ" in Vietnam (reading between the lines).

When Congress initiated the birthday draft lottery in the mid-sixties, Bob came up as number 39, out of 365. He was on his way to war if he didn't find way out. A college exemption and ROTC was the obvious answer. This way, he met his patriotic obligation serving as a Commissioned Officer rather than an enlisted man, and he didn't have to "escape" to Canada, as so many "Conscientious Objectors" had done.

He had all the brains and education to get into most colleges, but no money. His Northfield Savings bank account had $1,222.00 when he left for the University of Dayton. That's all he had to show for all the newspapers, golf bags, birthday gifts for the previous 8 years! But, alas, that could have easily been a big, fat zero if it weren't for Mom's insistence that he save money. And he did.

Chuck once told Bob that he had a simple choice: college or the Army. Since there was no family money to be had, Bob was on his own, either way. Chuck and Angie had nothing to offer of substance, although they did send frequent mail to Bob at college with a couple of bucks. The original "care package" was a real morale booster for a fellow on his own (truly) for the first time. The only other funds came from the local Board of Realtors, who offered a $500 scholarship to a high school senior with financial need and with scholarly potential. Bob was the lucky awardee that year. In 1970, $500 was a real pot of gold! But everything together still failed to cover more than the first semester's tuition, room and board, books and pocket money. He quickly learned how to apply for loans and grants. The fact that his family was dirt poor had its advantages in that regard. But this financial assistance still fell short of the real costs of being on his own in college. He knew he would eventually have to find a source of income which didn't detract too much from his studies. He refused to take a menial job bussing tables in the dining hall for $1.45 an hour!

Once Bob built a relationship with Wayne, the wedding photographer, Bob covered 125 weddings over the next three years! All while going to school. Granted, he had no other "interests." The only time he went to a UD football game was on assignment from the Flyer News. Since he didn't drink or smoke dope, his party schedule was mostly empty. In fact, the only time he was "invited" to a party was as a photographer for the event! Alas, he never saw a dime from those stoners, but really didn't expect to.

Bob charged forward on making money. While shooting weddings in college, Bob and Wayne decided to build and operate their own color processing darkroom, which was pretty much unheard of in those early days of color photography. They built the darkroom in Wayne's basement and Bob was processing film and prints in less that two weeks. They no longer needed to send their film by mail to Florida for processing. They could now ensure a more consistent quality of their work, while dropping their costs by 75%! They were soon taking in processing jobs from other local photographers and rolling profits back into the business.

Bob had come a long way from contact-printing pictures from negatives in his tiny bedroom closet. When he was 12 or so, he got a printing "kit" for Christmas. It contained a 6x6 inch metal box with a built-in light bulb, a push-button manual exposure switch, a few wallet-sized processing trays and a chemical starter kit. He set himself to learning how silver halide processing worked and printed dozens of pics from the old Kodak Brownie, until he ran out of photo paper. The photo bug had bitten him! Even the smell of the chemicals left him wanting more. About a year later, he built his first makeshift enlarger. He found a book in the library which detailed the pieces and process needed to make an enlarger. So, he "borrowed" his mom's Brownie box camera for the lens, cut the leg off an old pair of corduroy pants for the focussing bellows, built a rudimentary light box with a toggle switch, et voila! An enlarger. Too bad he damn near electrocuted himself and burned down the house because he had absolutely no knowledge of how electricity worked! When he went to plug in his makeshift device, sparks and smoke poured from the ancient wall outlet and he got a good shock. Once again, but by the grace of God, he survived.

There was no going back from there. The next Christmas, he received a brand-new "Swinger" Instant camera. What a hell of a treat that was! No need for processing, just shoot and wait 60 seconds for the photo. The only downside was the insane cost of the film cartridges. That constrained his eagerness and creativity in an instant.

In the summer between junior and senior year, Wayne decided the partnership had too many "conflicts" and offered to buy out Bob's share. Wayne never explained his imagined "conflicts." As it turns out, Wayne, a fully employed, salaried power company worker, treated the business as a hobby. Bob, on the other hand, considered it his financial life-blood and had no patience for "trying this" or "trying that."

Bob never received a dime for this share. Wayne considered it fair compensation for not charging Bob any rent while he lived there, in the chilly, wet basement next to the lab, his entire Junior year. No lawsuits, no lawyers, no fights. Just adios, Amigo, and good luck with school.

Wayne basically kicked him out with no compensation, but Bob had followed his financial plan and had enough savings to take him through senior year. He did, however, find himself seething and having nightmares of those events for years afterward. He was asking himself how people could be so cold and callous. How a "partner" could just "change the locks" and end it all was beyond his young years. Especially a Baptist preacher. Bob would never trust a Baptist, again. Ever.

Bob managed to finish out the small remainder of weddings on his schedule before putting Wayne in his year view mirror for good. Off to bigger and better things, he figured. Senior year was going to be ball-buster anyhow, and it would require all his energy and attention. The money was in the bank and he knew how to stretch it for another few months.

❖❖❖

Despite being careful with money and fastidious with budgeting, Bob faced poverty once again in 1979 after he had left the Army to work with Jim in the camera store in Hillsdale, NJ after Jim's relentless prodding.   After just a few short months, the store partnership did not work out. The second time that a partnership failed miserably. Bob moved his family from New Jersey to Connecticut to pursue his Master degree on the GI Bill. Since the GI benefit did not sufficiently pay the bills, Naomi took a job at the local convenience store and was soon promoted to manager. That helped greatly in feeding the three kids, but provided no benefits, whatsoever. Of course, this was the '70s and no one was whining about "entitlements" and "everything they deserve."

Naomi came home from work one cold, windy and snowy night with a blazing fever and chills. Since they were both raised in New England, they figured it was just another winter virus floating around and she could gut it out. It has been snowing for two days, so the roads were in terrible shape. Even if they could go somewhere, they had no money for doctors and drugs, so they hunkered down with Tylenol, soup and a warm bed. As the night wore on, she kept getting worse. They didn't even have even a simple thermometer in the house to check her temp. For the first time in his life, Bob was absolutely helpless. He had absolutely no control over the situation and could offer nothing to help Naomi. He got obsessed with not knowing her actual temperature, and decided to brave the weather and head out to find an open pharmacy. His many years winter driving experience were put to the test immediately, as he slowly made his way up the steep drive in the 914. All Porsches were great road cars, made for ugly weather in Germany, but Germany rarely gets more snow than Connecticut's average. He managed his way into the small town, searching for a place to get more Tylenol and and a damn thermometer, but nothing was open, anywhere. His desperation maxed out as he almost did a 360 taking a corner a bit fast, but recovered nicely. He couldn't stand the taste of failure, especially when it came to his best friend. He headed back to the house, almost in tears of frustration and fear.

He pulled into the drive and parked at the top of the hill. He turned off the engine and began yelling "What the hell do I do now?," as he beat repeatedly on the steering wheel. But, there came no answer. Only the light in the bedroom that beckoned him back to her bedside. He just sat for a moment, shivering. From cold or fear, he wasn't sure, and it didn't really matter. He knew he had to go back in with no help from anyone, anywhere. The snow was still falling, lightly now, as he quietly let himself in the front door.

Naomi was still asleep and the shivering had almost stopped. He checked her forehead with his hand and it seemed she had stabilized out of the danger zone. She slept until noon the following day and by that evening, the fever was gone. This was the first time he realized just how strong she was. Most folks born in Maine are very strong physically, it turns out. Nature or nurture? Who knows? Who cares?

But that also comes with a large dose of stubborn. For example, because of the illness, Naomi hadn't smoked a cigarette in three days. Bob pushed her to quit, altogether, but she was having none of that. She was convinced that there were always frustrating days ahead so quitting her one and only vice was out of the question. She finally managed to quit about ten years later when she started her government job in the newly established "smoke free" environment.

Sometimes, it seems the bigger decisions are the easiest to make. They were nearly broke at this point, with just enough in the bank to cover a few month's living expenses with no frivolities. A decision needed to be made regarding their future and this gut-wrenching episode was just the catalyst they needed to effect great change. Bob offered the idea of going back in the Army, where the pay was not generous but consistent, and health care was there for the whole family. They would never suffer another such episode as they had just been through. It seemed, at least in hindsight, the best option. Bob's advance degree in computers would have to be delayed, again. Certainly not the end of life on earth, since the military would give him all the training it deemed necessary.

After weeks of phone calls and letters, Bob received orders to report to Fort Gordon, GA in April to attend the Signal Corps Officer Advanced School. They were back, though the residual fear and agonizing frustration of not having any health care would take a while to wear off. And the horrifying feeling of being helpless was never forgotten. Bob made a promise to himself: never again. NEVER AGAIN!

Over the next 40 years or so, the family finances, while sometimes a challenge, were never a risk factor. So what if the kids didn't get the latest and greatest toy for Christmas? They still made out like bandits, just bandits on a strict budget. And life went on, at least for a while, back in uniform.

Bob and Naomi managed to raise kids, grandkids and a foster son, and still put together money for retirement. It was no small feat, taking excellent planning, superior cost control and the endless determination of a solid life partnership. They were never poor, again! But, after 13 years in uniform, they would suddenly lose the security blanket of the Army and would, once again, be on their own.

Officer promotions in the Army were never guaranteed, unless you were some politician's kid. They had to earn the promotion through years of service and top notch Efficiency Reports.

Bob's career came to a screeching halt when he was passed over for promotion to Major on the first review. He proceeded to do everything he could to improve his record (or at least the way the promotion board saw it) before the next review cycle. He completed a thorough audit of his official record and had his official photo retaken, completed Command and General Staff School on independent study, which required an "on-site" segment at Leavenworth, KS, at his own expense. He had already completed every lower level officer course offered, with honors. But, he had three career "flaws," so to speak. One was the fact that he was a Reserve Officer, not a Regular Army Officer. Second flaw was a short stint of about three months in a Reserve Unit in Rhode Island. His efficiency report from that short assignment should have never been entered into the official record since it did not meet the minimum number of days for a report. Despite his formal efforts to get the report tossed, it remained in his record for the Board to see. While it was not a terrible report, it was also not a "top block" rating necessary to get promoted to Major. The most significant shortcoming was the absence of a "combat arms" assignment. Despite his critical support assignments for 12 years, he was never assigned to a combat unit. Turned out that was an indelible black mark on his record and the most likely cause of his promotion denial. Ironically, he often joked his mustache was keeping him from promotion. He'd heard more ridiculous things in his career, but tossed that one to the curb in the end. He was basically a geek with no combat arms experience. Despite what he'd been told as a young Signal Corps Officer, there was little room at the top for Officer geeks.

Ironically, the whole mess could have been avoided had Bob lowered his integrity standards when he was ordered back to active duty. Once he got to school, he was informed that his personnel record had been destroyed in a warehouse fire. The LTC in charge gave Bob the opportunity to "re-create" his own record! Bob might have given himself better efficiency scores, or more years in service, or any number of other "self-promotions." But he stuck to his guns and did the right thing, as usual. He decided that if he couldn't offer positive, written proof of something (an award?) then it didn't go into the re-created personnel file. Almost as if the Sisters of Notre Dame were looking over his shoulder!

Little did he know what the eventual impact on his life would be.

Chapter 18~And Thank You for the ....

What many folks fail to realize, even after decades on this planet, is that there are great and not-so-great in every discipline. Good teachers, bad teachers, good parents, bad parents, good doctors, bad doctors, good leaders and bad leaders. Usually very bad. While Bob worked for some great officers, there was one that should have been shown the door before making it to Field Grade. Maj. Carter, assigned as Battalion Executive while Bob was serving in Augsburg was one of those. He was a light skinned African who constantly chomped on a pipe and kept his Afro skin-tight. He was a seemingly intelligent man, at least not giving any indication to the contrary.

When the Battalion Commander, LTC Beaty, Bob's boss, was relieved from Command by COL Spoonbender, Bob decided to play hero and talk personally with the Group commander just to impress upon him how great LTC Beaty was. Bob drove the hour to Munich after making a proper appointment with the Commander's secretary. The meeting was very short, and not very sweet. You see, John Wayne always rode in at the 11th hour. Bob showed up well after crisis midnight. The deed was done, as the COL didn't hesitate to impress. He also advised that Bob return to Augsburg immediately to tend to his own issues.

Those issues came very clear once Bob was back in Augsburg. In the parking lot, waiting for him, was the CSM, the very same CSM Bob had forced into alcohol rehab.

"The Commander needs to see you." "The Commander was just relieved," he thought to himself. Then it hit him like a brick shithouse. Carter, as XO, was now the Interim Bn Commander. He steadied himself for a verbal beating as the two of them climbed the marble stairs to the Commander's office.

The CSM turned into his office across the wide hall, leaving Bob to request Carters' permission to enter. Carter was solemn and polite, directing Bob to take a seat in front of the huge mahogany desk, once the formal salute was rendered. Carter's desk wasn't unlike any other senior officer's mahogany battleship, complete with the carved wood nameplate from Korea and the large tempered glass writing surface centered on the top. Carter's pipe was stuck firmly in the corner of his mouth, a wisp of smoke escaping with each breath.

Carter began the conversation, "Captain, going to see the Group Commander was a foolish move." He paused long enough to puff. "You were questioning the judgment of an Officer well above your station. While that does not rise to the level of insubordination, you did go around me as your Commander, which can be considered insubordination."

Bob was not surprised, but really had not prepared a response for this. He managed to stumble out a few words, "I thought it appropriate to stand up for our Commander. He's a good leader and this unit has never seen these efficiency and performance marks before…"

Carter cut him off immediately, slamming his pipe on the glass in rage. As hot embers flew everywhere, he continued his rant, his already large nostrils flared. "You had no right to go down there. I am relieving you of your command," he stammered as he plopped back into his chair.

"You can't do that! Bob shouted. "You are only an Interim Commander. You do not have the authority!"

As soon as the words left his lips, Bob knew he was wrong. Once the orders are cut, the power moves to the the XO and he BECOMES the Commander.

At that point, Bob knew he had to change lanes and try to salvage his career.

Carter looked down at his calendar and said, "You are done, Captain. There's no more to be said. You'll get career credit for 12 months command time. But no more. You are done. I'm putting Lemon in your place as Company Commander, immediately. You are to report to the Operations Chief in the morning. He'll find work for you for the rest of your tour."

"Major, for the sake of the troops, and my self-respect I'd like a formal Change of Command. I deserve that much."

Carter picked up his pipe, shoved it in his mouth, and after a very long draw on it, calmed a bit, spit out, "OK, OK, 7am tomorrow morning out in front of Company Headquarters."

That's the best Bob could ask for. His breach was certainly not on the level of LT. Calley's murderous offenses in Vietnam, but in the officer ranks of this Intelligence Group, Egos were more important than beans and bullets and were to be protected at all cost. Period. Years of real, measurable accomplishments meant nothing at that point. He'd pissed on the King's shoe. "You are done," as Carter so eloquently stated. "You are done."

As Bob left Carter's office, he noticed a couple of embers still smoldering on the Carpet. He gave a little chuckle to himself and moved on. This was not the way he wanted to leave his command. The troops were special to him, and mostly vice-versa. So much so, that his NCO cadre presented him with a framed Signal Corps scarf after the ceremony. The troops stayed in formation and gave a group salute as Bob left the trite ceremony. A real bittersweet moment that nobody would lose sleep over, other than Bob.

He had never been so pissed off. Not when his classmates abandoned him at the Worlds Fair, not when he cracked his Deep Purple album over Rick's head, not when Cheryl left him for the drug addict. Nothing had ever hurt this bad.

Nothing added up to this anger, a product of years of disciplined and loyal duty, horrible assignments, and by-name terrorist threats. Nothing. Once Carter lowered the hammer, Bob had to go home and break the unbelievable news to Naomi. That bothered him far more than the idiot XO's egomaniacal actions. He actually cared about her. And she cared about the Army. She had always been involved in the wives' activities supporting the troops and now felt "abandoned" by the entire organization. Being relieved of command, no matter what the reason, was a career death knell.

****

Just a few years later, it all came to a career head. Regulations allowed just 90 days between being passed over for promotion by the Board in D.C. and involuntary separation. Out-processing at Ft. Ord was the final step in getting clear of the service. It was a four hour round trip to Ft. Ord and a full afternoon of pencil necks with rubber stamps. First stop was the S-4, supply office. Although he had already turned all his tactical gear in to the company supply Sergeant, Ft. Ord regulations required a face to face check of the paperwork. It's the kind of bureaucratic idiocy he had endured his whole career. Too many folks checking too many other folks for things that had no real meaning or importance to anything. It's the kind of real-life lunacy that was easy fodder for shows like McHale's Navy,

MASH, and Catch 22. Fortunately, it would all be over in a couple of hours.

Another stop on the out-processing train was the debriefing for his Top Secret clearance. Again, the real work had been done at Hunter Liggett, but the Ord boys had to cross the i's and dot the t's. Vehicle tag, housing clearance, medical and dental clearance, physical security debrief. One stop after another, one form after another, one rubber stamp after another. Bob carried the form from one desk to the next, and got his rubber stamp and initials from each pencil neck.

And then, the final stop: Finance. This is the only one anyone really cared about. This is where the checks were cut for any remaining pay and allowances, TDY (Temporary duty), advance PCS (Permanent Change of Station), and, in his case, separation pay at ETS (Expiration Term of Service). His last Army check.

He took a seat on the ass-hard oak chair that had to be sixty years old. Scratched and lacking sheen, but sturdy still after decades of wear it reminded him of the chairs back in the library at St. Alphonse. He flipped through some of the paperwork he had already received, mostly to pass the time. The finance clerk was busy with another soldier. This fellow was a lean, but not well worn E-7 out-processing on his way to Germany. He eavesdropped on the conversation without much effort since the acoustics of the old wooden building broadcast every spoken word in the room. The only challenge was to keep track of the one conversation of interest.

The E-7 had been posted to the 7th Infantry for at Ord for a little over three years. He was hoping to retire as an E-8 in Germany, his wife's native country. The CPT didn't hear where he was headed in Germany, but that didn't seem to matter to the Sergeant. Germany was a small enough place that he and his wife could visit her hometown in Bavaria in just a couple of hours. And finally settling there was only a matter of more paperwork. Schreiben, Bitte!

After a final signature, the clerk handed the E-7 his PCS check. He thanked her and promptly picked up his Army issue black briefcase to store the paperwork and check. As he turned to the exit, he gave a nod to the CPT, who nodded in return with "Auf Wiedersehen, Sgt."

The clerk was about to say next when she realized the CPT was the only one waiting. She glanced quickly at the standard-issue black and white clock on the wall above the chairs, and exhaled quietly, deliberately. It was 1615. She knew the CPT was the last for today.

"ID and paperwork, please", she stated with neither care nor concern. The CPT was ready, as always, and handed her the items. The clerk was in her early fifties. Her hair mostly the original light brown with just the start of gray. Light crow's feet gave her away, despite her makeup. With her pleasant face and faded lipstick near-smile, he expected the next few minutes would go without friction.

"OK, CPT, I need just two more signatures and you"ll be done." She handed him a DD 214 form that showed all the active and reserve service, and any unused leave days. Dollars and cents were determined by backroom clerks cranking out a formula based upon the Form 214 and who knows what else. Luckily, the total severance numbers agreed with his own calculation. He wasn't about to stand there and second guess the clerks, even though he knew through his earlier failed payroll experiences that mistakes are made every day, especially with numbers.

It was while he was stationed in Augsburg, serving as Company Commander, that his personal checks started to bounce. Check bouncing was a chargeable violation of the UCMJ and not acceptable for an officer. It took nearly a month of phone calls and official requests before the problem was resolved. It seems Bob's bank back in CT had a name very similar to another bank in the same town. When the DoD decide to go with "electronic direct deposit" Bob's paycheck ended up going to the wrong town bank! Such is the typical screw-up in the military for which the guilty party is never held accountable. In the end, Bob ended up paying the bounced check fees even though someone else made the error. That's the kind of apathetic bull that always pissed him off. He took full responsibility for his actions, good or bad, and expected everyone else to do the same. What a life disappointment it became when he finally realized that personal responsibility and integrity were rare.

The clerk added the final form which calculated the dollars and cents due. His eyes went directly to the bottom line. From there he worked upward through the column of numbers, trying to understand how the bean counters arrived at the final sum. At first glance, it just didn't appear correct. It looked about NINE THOUSAND dollars short!

'Do you have a question, CPT?

"Yes, Ma"am. I was trying to follow the calculations to understand the final check amount. It seems short."

"Well, Sir, you are probably not deducting the taxes on your severance. Congress authorizes a final severance for someone of your rank and time in service of thirty thousand dollars. However, the IRS gets the usual percentages that come out of your monthly paycheck. That's why the final sum seems so short."

Despite his reputation, he was speechless. He couldn't fathom that taxes on that amount would be nearly a third of the check. He also knew there was no mistake. He simply had not calculated such a deep cut from his final check.

"OK, I see that now," he finally said, nearly under his breath. "I had no idea the taxman would take such a huge chunk."

She gave him a few moments to gather his thoughts.

'That's not all, Sir. I have one more item to cover" she added, as she pointed her pen to the last paragraph. "You see, as a Reserve Officer separating from active duty, you have the option of finishing out your career to retirement in a Reserve unit."

She knew he knew that, but she paused just to let it sink in. Then, she lowered the hammer. "You need to know, however, that if you retire from the Reserves and receive a pension, the government will take back your severance."

He knew, generally, that was correct, but never looked into the details. Retirement of any kind was now more than twenty years away.

'So, if I retire from the Reserves down the road, the government will take back this amount?" he asked, pointing the after-tax amount on the sheet.

Now she hesitated with caution. He could tell she did not like this part of her job. She enjoyed dispensing money. That makes people smile and feel good about their service. But not this time.

"No, Sir. They take back the entire thirty thousand."

"'The entire amount before taxes?" He repeated, knowing full-well the answer wouldn't change.

"Yes, Sir. The entire amount."

At that point, his greatest challenge was to finish the process while remaining an officer and a gentleman. The fury welling up inside was the evil that he had fought, and internalized, his entire career. Now he was faced with one more insane bureaucratic load of bull that served no real purpose but to put a feather in the hat of some lackey in Congress who insisted on the repayment clause before he'd vote for whatever pissant bill happened to include severance payments to service members.

He stood there, just staring at the form, almost shaking in disgust and anger. He dared not make eye contact with the clerk, or anyone for that matter. The beast within needed to be put down before he could continue.

"I see," he finally capitulated, "what else do you need from me?.

She had seen this anger before. For some she had processed, it made no impression on her or her work. It was her job and she did it well. But, there were some she processed that she recognized, by experience and instinct, had already been horribly screwed by the Army in one way or another. She recognized the CPT as one of them.

"I'm sorry, Sir. I just need one more signature on this form verifying that you have read and understand what we just discussed."

All clear thinking was out he door. He said nothing, again, so out of character. And then he made his last official signature. He realized he was using the gold Cross pen his father had given him when he went to college. It was engraved "M.A.V.", Michael Anthony Vitti. He was better able to put things in perspective with the sight of the pen. Dad's life was much, much harder than his.

The clerk gathered up her paperwork and his in separate neat stacks. On top of his stack, she carefully clipped the check. As she handed him his stack, her eyes connected with his. With all sincerity, she said, quietly, "Thank you Sir. I wish you the best of luck in the future." He put the package in his black briefcase, nodded to the clerk a "Thank you", and headed out the door, his shiny black shoes making almost no sound as he walked across the now empty room.

His Accord was parked over by the row of Eucalyptus trees which stood between the edge of the parking lot and the ocean. The smell from these "cat pee" trees is one that is never forgotten. They were such an odd tree. Tall, flowing, very malodorous and dropping huge brown seed pods. The cool ocean breeze carried the odor to him across the parking lot, as if calling him to the car.

He jumped into the driver seat and tossed the black briefcase on the passenger side with his head cover. There he cranked down the windows and sat for a while. Just looking at the Pacific and enjoying the cool breeze. He contemplated his thirteen years of service. Instead of a monthly retirement check for the rest of his life, he got less than a year's pay. And the government took back almost a third of that for taxes! He took the time to let the breeze cool his temper before driving the two hours home.

His thoughts wandered from one to the next. Some forced him to question his decisions, while others just engendered disgust with people and circumstance.

He thought back to Connecticut when he made the agonizing decision to re-join the service so he could properly support his family. The TDY trip where he slept on the floor after the MPs knocked on his door at 2am to warn him that him name was on the Red Army Faction assassination list. The unending weeks on maneuvers in Hitler's former caves on the French border. The time he found himself placing the CSM in alcohol rehab against his will. The moment he learned his promotion to Major was not going to happen had him grinding his teeth. One moment after another, some enjoyable, like commanding his troops, others not so much, like dealing with Major Carter, the nefarious leader of the unofficial Black Officers group.

He tried to close his eyes and clear up all the anger. That took a while. For the first time since he was a child, he noticed a tear forming in the corner of his eye. Eventually, a bit more settled, he turned the key and headed toward the back gate. He never exceeded the posted limit on post. It was the easiest excuse for the MPs to ruin his day even more. He crept along at 25 as he rounded the corner toward Post Headquarters. He hadn't realized what time it was until he noticed two cars stopped closer to the HQ, both drivers standing at attention. His dash clock clicked over to 1631.

He pulled over, turned off the radio and got out. He put on his cover, stood at attention, faced HQ and rendered a proper salute.

He stood there at attention throughout the sounding of retreat. He couldn't see the flag being lowered at the far side of the parade field and blocked by the HQ building, but had seen it hundreds of times before. Following retreat, the single canon salute, and then The Star Spangled Banner. The whole daily ceremony didn't last more than two minutes. But this time, it seemed to last forever. The entirety of his career was summed up in just two short minutes. The end of a day. Then end of a career.

One last time.

One last salute.

Chapter 19~History Repeats Itself

A month had gone by since the Texas Governor had removed the lock-down and mask mandates. However, most of the retail establishments and all of the government buildings were still playing the sheeple routine; masks and social distancing. It was enough to make Bob puke. He didn't so much care that masks were still in play, or that getting the vaccine was now in vogue. His concern was for the future. Today's children were being abused by ignorant, fearful adults. He wondered with great concern, what this meant for the future. More critically, he felt that no one else, and absolutely no one with the courage and leverage to fix it would ever come out of hiding. Where the children go, so goes the future. It was looking very, very bad! The only saving grace was that Bob was on the downside of this life and would probably never become a true victim of the maniacal ploy to control everything and everyone, should it turn out that the conspiracy nuts were right all along.

Everything You Need to Know About Communism was Bob's introduction to the subject back in 7th grade. While stomping his shoe at the UN and promising to make American a communist country drip by drip, a very young Bob was reading about the absolute Godless nastiness of communism. He was both scared and amazed learning how life could be that bad, compared to the freedom guaranteed by the Constitution. No free speech, no right to ask questions, jail for political opponents, and other punishing and nefarious rules to control otherwise free men.

Now, he was starting to see some of the same nastiness in the U.S. Social media sites on the internet were being censored by self-appointed mindless minions. If a comment violated the site's arbitrary and capricious "guidelines", it would be removed and eventually the account would be blocked. However, they were not censoring merely for foul language and hate speech (however they defined that), but merely for opinions contrary to their political stance. They went so far as to label anything they didn't agree with as mis-information and dis-information, and often, racism! A full-scale culture war was in progress. The greater concern was that it appeared all the social media sites and most the "Main Street Media" were controlled by left-wing socialists. They were the same types that attempted to coerce the University of Dayton newspaper into becoming their commie mouthpiece back in his college days. History was, indeed, repeating itself. This time the weapons were far more powerful than the paper and ink of a campus weekly. The entire world was connected electronically and controlled by those who wanted to destroy America and Capitalism, by any means necessary.

Why write about this now, especially in a story about growing up in the last century? It reveals the endless distractions Bob endured as he tried to pen his first work of fiction. Unlike Thoreau, his adolescent literary mentor, Bob couldn't just grab his pencil and his notebook and go live in a cabin in the woods until it was finished. He wished he could. But, he managed to forge on with more (hopefully) entertaining stories.

So, here sat, decades later, trying to finish his Great American Novel. Fifty years of work, kids, grandkids, foster kids, financial disaster, careers success and career failure, loyalty and betrayal, love found and love lost had transpired since the start of his book. All the stuff needed for the great American novel.

His first draft was on New Year's Eve, 50 years earlier, His life kept him so busy that he never had the time or energy to go back to writing.

That didn't mean he didn't think about his novel. He wrote it in his mind many times over the decades. But he never put it in writing, and never shared it. He was a bit superstitious about anyone, other than his wife, reading it. Sometime after the turn of the century, he made time to start actually writing, again. When he queried some of his friends and family, they agreed to review the pages he's finished. The feedback was varied and interesting. Everything from "too much detail about a house" to "where are the girls?" Obviously not Pulitzer Prize stuff, at least not yet.

After he retired to Texas, his mind was just not into writing. Bogarting old murder mystery reruns, yes, Reading, yes. Golf, yes. Writing, not so much. He had outlined all the topics he wanted to cover, and reviewed them over an over, often adding to the list. But, he was still only writing in his head. He had read recently that the bigger part of stress was the direct result of things left undone. That made sense, but didn't motivate him to write.

He often asked himself what it would take to get fully involved in it? A quiet place to work? Some really positive feedback? A nice advance from a yet, unknown publisher? But he wasn't in it for the money. That would be just some welcome icing. Alas, he just needed to motivate himself to get off his ass and make it happen. Despite 50 years of delays and procrastination, the mere fact that it had been 50 years (and he wasn't getting any younger) was just the motivation he needed. But now, on the eve of a new decade and a full two decades into the 21st century, with the clunky Olivetti rusting in a dump somewhere, he set his Apple Mac on his lap, in front of the TV, and began typing. What a wonder, he thought! This just may get done after all! After a couple of pages, he went to bed. At his "advanced" age, he no longer had the energy of youth to keep working into the wee hours. There's always tomorrow, he hoped.

So, while he thought his novel would be a tribute to growing up in the twentieth century, the twenty first century was turning out to be a tour through Dante's inferno. America had gone from a country of laws, loyalties, family and tradition to a cesspool of character assassination, entitlement claims, cancel culture, and "underserved" nonsense!

All the principles he lived by and which formed the very basis of life and opportunity in America were being destroyed by a very small, but vocal and violent faction of the population. These folks were firmly supported by the main stream media, referred to as MSM, not because of any principles being challenged, but merely for profit. The more conflict the MSM puked out into the airwaves, the more money they made from greed-drunk advertisers and their lame-brain viewers. The car, drug, ambulance chasers and fast food industries continued to pour billions into advertising, pursuing the holy grail of eyeball count. This happened despite the growing social media outlets that were grasping for the very same ad dollars. They had totally lost sight of the fact that the pie hadn't been growing much, but the slices had been getting smaller. But they still grappled for their holy grail, and changed the game by eliminating all integrity in media. Sensational stories were pimped just for the sake of voyeurism, profit and controlling the message. After all, the decades-long motto of all news outlets was still intact:

"If it bleeds, it leads!" They had turned their reporters into street whores, and their news reports into British fish and chip wrappers pushing stories about heroic three-legged dogs and immoral Hollywood celebrities.

The American political system had become a victim of all the constant, nasty media stories. So much for the American dream that Bob had set as the basis for his novel! The very fabric of the dream was being torn away from within. High profile people were being "suicided" because of what they knew or who they associated with. Statues of war heroes that had been displayed for decades were being torn down because they were suddenly "racist." Streets, schools and sports team were renamed to meet this new demand for cultural destruction. It got so bad, that the majority of MSM outlets took on a campaign to destroy a sitting President! This had all the marking of a coup, without the guns.

Conspiracy theories were becoming more and more popular, with the disconcerting but unidentifiable "deep state" boogie man being the greatest of them. Some believe there was always a deep state; a global group of billionaires whose self-assigned mission was to control everything and everyone they could.

They started and ended wars, funded and defunded financial institutions. They stole huge contracts from the government, railroads and oil being the early examples. And, they controlled global news distribution. Control the narrative, control the people. It was all so Orwellian that any comments that contradicted the MSM were quickly and permanently erased. Conveniently, there was absolutely no way of proving or disproving the theory. After all, a man can hang himself in a jail cell with a paper robe where the guards were missing and the cameras were conveniently turned off, and there were no repercussions. That story, one that might have saved hundreds of children from a life of human trafficking and child porn, fell by the wayside and was ignored by the MSM as quickly as the three-legged dog story. The child sex trade continued full force, and nobody was sent to jail or the gallows. Mission of cover up, complete. "Pay no attention to the man behind the curtain!"

But these things were happening every day! Doctors were urging their patients to stop watching the news or risk the physical and mental consequences. The President resorted to calling out the "fake news", which just pissed them off more and engendering a response never, ever seen in the country before: destroy the sitting President by any means available. The war for the hearts and minds of Americans was on! The war to destroy America had come to us. Yet, not a single shot had been fired.

Then, along came a global pandemic. As if the whole thing was planned by Hollywood and the timing perfected. Communist China had grown a bat virus that had supposed deadly effects on humans and was now able to spread from human to human. You no longer had to eat an infected bat to get sick. The scientists then replicated the virus and it quickly spread all over the globe. In a matter of weeks, there were cases popping up on remote Pacific islands! It just didn't seem to be a natural phenomenon to those with common sense. How in the hell does a virus go from a "highly secure" Wuhan, China lab to a remote Pacific island in a matter of weeks without human intent and intervention?

Some suspected it was all deliberate and planned. Why? Global domination? Revenge for getting their commie assess kicked in the trade war with the US President? Were the global billionaires trying to change the balance of power? If anyone knew, they weren't saying. This was excellent fodder for the likes of Michael Crichton or Stephen King.

The virus spread like a high school rumor, and millions were infected. Tens of thousands died, mostly due to advanced age and weakened immune systems. But, alas, those nasty left-wing politicians had a motto, "never pass up a good crisis." So while they pretended, as always, to be concerned for the people, they stepped up the fear game and damn near destroyed the economy.

Tens of millions were put out of work, thousands of mom and pop businesses had to close their businesses permanently, and in "an abundance of caution", children were ripped out of school and sent home to be taught "remotely." The number of people who died of overdose, drunkenness, suicide or simply because they were deathly afraid of going to their doctor, and draconian measures that locked them in their houses will never be known.

That wasn't the lead story. The number of "cases," "tests," "deaths" and "overwhelmed" hospitals led the daily news. It felt a lot like the media coverage of the Vietnam war, where "body count" was more important than any other factor and it was thrust in your face 24/7. It was the 21st century version of McNamera's whiz kids. Unfortunately, this time around, it was designed to keep people scared enough to obey. Nothing more. Just do what you're told!

This evil was further supported by the dearth of real, scientifically backed, information about the virus. Americans were obviously too stupid to understand and make their own decisions. Governors were locking down entire states and mandating citizens to wear unproven face diapers to supposedly "control the spread" although, once again, there was absolutely no science behind their claims.

Churches were closed, but football stadiums were open. You could get infected from a doorknob, but not from a fast food container or the mail. The level of absurdity could not be measured. The democratic, leftist agenda was entering a new phase. Absolute control over the people with the goal of submission of the masses through fear.

A greater part of the problem was the incompetence of the CDC and WHO. Their penchant for pimping half-truths with nebulous and confusing language guaranteed that no one would really ever understand the issue. It was all about compliance under force of government. In one state, hair salons were forced to close, while in another state one salon was being used by the CDC as the best example on how well masks work! Absurdity on steroids.

To make things even more insidious, neither the WHO nor the CDC was sharing any real science. Even the mandates or "recommendations" were based mostly on theory, assumption and conjecture. For each and every recommendation, you could insert "we think" before or after the statement, since that was what they were really saying. Despite their best recommendations, all interpretation was left up to the most scientifically ignorant state and local officials, most of whom had an agenda of their own.

For many, shutting down the economy would strengthen their position in the new world order. Hungry, homeless, desperate people are always easier to control. A new plantation was being established, with slogans such as "we are all in this together" and "wash your hands." That allowed the Chicken Littles of society to bully free-thinkers that if they didn't strictly obey the arbitrary and capricious mandates, they were killing grandma! And they would challenge and vilify anyone with a differing opinion. It was reminiscent of all the so-called "religions" that make up and enforce idiotic "rules." For example, the Catholic Church prohibited cremation until 1963, but the ashes still had to be buried so that folks don't forget who you are? Huh? So your deeds and accomplishments over your entire lifetime mean nothing, but how you discard your lifeless sack of ashes is somehow important to your salvation? The progeny you leave behind are going to somehow forget you if you don't have a thousand-dollar headstone in some creepy, church-approved cemetery? Lest he be thought a heretic in the 21st century, he didn't discuss such things with others.

This "death ray virus" mandate frenzy turned out to be very much the same. Old farts were walking their dogs and driving alone in their cars wearing a mask! This outlandish new cult, fed on a daily basis by the bullshit media, had taken on a life of its own. Self-appointed holier-than-thou morons were badgering and bullying those who chose to think and act differently. They even got their own label: "Karen." All these Karens were convinced that someone outside, without a mask, did not care about anyone else. They totally disavowed the CDC guidance that keeping 6 feet separation was enough! If asked why the mask was needed if 6 feet separation works, they often went on a mumbling rampage of "you just don't care!" "Well, you ignorant old fart, if you care so much, shut your mouth and keep your distance!" Problem solved. The fact that they were OUTDOORS was just meaningless to them. They incoherently thought that the virus floated in the air like seasonal pollen just waiting to kill them! Bob often wondered "just how many idiots can one world take?" Then, again, if the government had been more honest and forthcoming with scientific facts, or at least answers based in science, the so-called "pandemic" would never have gotten the attention (and fear) that it did.

And, just like that, a miracle vaccine appeared! Although the average time to market for any drug historically stood at about 10 years, this vaccine, which modified human DNA, was cooked up, tested and produced in a mere 4 months! He felt that was just insane. But, what bothered him more, was that so, so many folks were just fine taking this unproven drug and, in fact, were clamoring for the shot! Apparently, the unknown risks were just another "conspiracy", ignoring the fact that all drugs have side effects. But, somehow, in the minds of the sheep, none of that mattered. He wondered where so much blind trust in the government came from. Despite his 30 years of working in Federal government, it actually scared him some.

The very "American Dream" that formed the basis of Bob's novel was being destroyed right in front of his blurry eyes. But Bob persevered in writing, motivated, perhaps by the evil actors who were determined to destroy everything he believed in. He went into a stream of consciousness and the sentences just fell out, as if giving a lecture to a class of college kids on his views of life, love and politics. He felt it important to codify what was happening in the country and world that the media and their deep-state pimps might destroy. He was convinced that he was one of only a few folks who understood and discussed the gravity of the situation and the potential horrible outcomes for the next generations of Americans. He felt a bit like Voltaire, who was vilified and exiled for expressing thoughts deemed to contradict the king. His only vindication was that he was allowed back in France with just enough time to die.

All this nonsense infuriated him to no end. Dealing with people who acted more like sheep than free-willed humans was quite depressing, in societal terms. Worse was the fact that there was absolutely nothing he could do about it. Nothing. He had already written to the Governor, the County Judge, the Chair of the CDC and other lesser-important individuals. Not one of them had the common courtesy to reply. Not one! It appeared all communication was deliberately one way! No questioning the authorities. No feedback loops. Zero interest in what the average citizen might have to say about all these arbitrary and capricious decisions that were destroying the country. It was a lockdown of two-way communications. He felt he was endlessly cueing the mike but getting nothing but dead air as a response. It made him feel a lot like being abandoned at a World's Fair, or being unceremoniously separated from his livelihood. So, going back to writing would hopefully be a healing force.

Chapter 20~You Can Call Me Nigger!

Bob and Marshall Bessemer arrived at their first duty station, Ft. Leonard Wood, Mo. on the same clear September day. While Bob graduated UD with an ROTC commission as a Signal Officer, Marshall was fresh out of the U.S. Military Academy at West Point. West Point grads all earn an Engineering degree, although their Army assignments spanned all Combat and Combat support roles, the most common was an Engineer Battalion.

They first got to know each other, briefly, during the New Officer Orientation. But, their real friendship came out of evenings at the Officers" Club. Although officers were "allowed" to eat in the mess halls as long as they paid their own way, most single officers took some meals in the O Club, as it was called. While dinner was served in the ballroom on certain evenings, most meals were consumed in the bar. Tilma, the cook, was a pro at grilling anything and everything. The ribeye steak was her speciality. Like most bars, it was a cordial and smoky place, with a jukebox and pool table. You could also have your food served in one of the activity rooms, usually hosting a semi-serious 25-50 poker game. Since the options for restaurants at Ft. Leonard Wood or the nearby town of St. Roberts were somewhere south of nil, the Officers" Club was more than adequate and no more than a fifteen-minute ride from anywhere on post.

The ballroom hosted music, sometimes live, usually not, on most weekend nights. It drew a sizable crowd on live music nights, and perhaps, half as much when the the vinyl records or tapes were the only source of tunes. The central focus of each evening was, of course, drinking and dancing. However, since men didn't dance with men, the evening was hopeless unless some of the local school teachers and their friends made a showing. Female officers were not abundant at an Engineering post, and fraternization regulations put the kibosh on most female officers making a showing at the club.

Turns out that Marshall was not your run-of-the-mill Academy graduate. He played first string on the Army football team, had a Black Belt in Karate, and worked the weights and heavy bag almost daily. He was also the first Black Officer Bob met. Despite four years of ROTC at Dayton, and several months in Officer Basic School at Fort Gordon, Bob had not met a single Black Officer. Black NCOs and troops were plentiful, but not officers.

Bob had not met many Blacks at all in his short life. There was Jeremy, who was on Chuck's Little League team. Nobody made any fuss over his pigmentation. He was a great catcher, but not such a great hitter. Otherwise, he was one of the team.

There was one Black student in his high school, Willy. He had a good sense of humor and kept everyone smiling with his trumpet cheers at the basketball games. He was an adequate student, otherwise, just another seminary student.

The third Black person he met was Davie, the foul-mouth machinist who maintained the presses at the Advertiser. He was a Vietnam Veteran that didn't seem to have been too shaken by his combat experience. But he had a vocabulary that would make a sailor blush. That was Bob's first tutorial in the world of nasty language. Davie lived in one the the limited number of taxpayer subsidized houses down by Mill Pond, which he never talked about.

In short, Bob's experience with folks of other cultures was seriously limited growing up in Northfield. While there was no obvious racism in the town, what prejudice there was, was directed equally toward all persons of "lower class." The Italian kids were treated no better or worse than the Black kids. That was evident when the one and only Black kid, who called himself "Rev," showed up to caddy at the country club and was treated no differently than the Italian caddies. They were all treated equally as servant class.

Ironically, Bob had seen plenty of racism on the TV news. The sixties was all about racial equality, highlighted with church burnings, riots, and keen media photographers that were sure to get the most heart-wrenching violent pics they could. Cue the attack dogs. But, still, none of it had any visible effect on the townsfolk of Northfield. It was a peaceful, clean, respite from the harsh violence of the big city, just a 40 minute train ride away. New York City, where a young Northfield girl named Kitty had been stabbed to death in the street while dozens of people just watched it happen.

Northfield was also protected by wealth. Not formally, of course. There were no concrete barriers with armed guards at the parkway exits. But it was understood that any violence, for whatever noble reason, would not be tolerated there.

Another race-centric experience was during Bob's first year of college. He had been voted into the position of President and General Manager for the campus AM radio station. One Monday evening, he was holding an interest meeting on the second floor of the former women's gym. The meeting was open to all interested students. About ten minutes into the meeting, a tall, wiry Black fellow with a huge Afro with a pick sticking out wandered in and immediately started a discussion of what type of music the station would play. He was told the format was "free form", and not dependent on any single genre, the fellow started to get agitated. He claimed that the station should play mostly Black music, if not all Black music. That statement managed to quickly piss off a couple of the country boys, and a loud argument ensued. Bob intervened and settled things down, but the Black fellow stomped out and down the stairs, cussing all the way. They all looked at each other with the thought " Well, that was interesting."

About 20 minutes later the fellow returned with a brass bar about a foot long, ready to "crack some honky heads." While tempers flared and threats were exchanged, Bob managed to call the campus police, who arrived in mere minutes to escort the fellow off campus. Turns out, he was not an enrolled student and was just agitating for Black Power. Not a great introduction to the "racism" issue, by any measure. They managed to productively finish the meeting, even with frayed nerves.

So, when it came right down to it, Marshall was Bob's first real insight into the true Black culture. As a West Point grad, Marshall had already extricated himself from the bonds of the "shuck and jive" of psychological slavery. At age 22, he had seen more success than any of his ancestors, some of whom were slaves in the deep south 150 years earlier. He never showed a hint of self-subjugation or step-and-fetch-it mentality.

Strangely, the topic of ancestry only came up once in a conversation at the club, when another Black officer pressed Marshall for an answer. It was clear it was not something Marshall cared to discuss or even remember. He might be called an Oreo by some Black racists, but certainly not to his face. Nobody dare poke that bear. About three months after their assignment to Leonard Wood, Bob and Marshall were sitting at a table in the ballroom, just listening to the music and waiting for some others to show up. Neither of them drank alcohol, so two cokes sat on the table between them. After some discussion of their new jobs, and a deliberate pause, Marshall leaned on the table toward Bob and quietly stated, "You can call me nigger." Bob pushed back in his chair in disbelief. "What?" Was all he could utter in response.

"Listen, Bob", he replied, "You are a squared-away guy, despite not being from the Academy and I respect you." It won't bother me for you to use that name with me."

"You know damn well I would never say that, Marshall." Bob stammered. "Why would you even think I would use that word?"

"I didn't." I just wanted to know that it's no big deal between us." Marshall replied.

Dazed and confused, Bob got up to get a couple more Cokes. Nothing more was said. Ever. And Bob would never understand why Marshall said that. It was beyond absurdity and well into the realm of surrealism, like a Dali painting Scotch taped to a Manet in the Men's room at the Guggenheim. Just ridiculous.

Luckily, that odd conversation didn't change their relationship. They continued to come to the club every

Friday night, drink Coke, and dance with the local girls. The only similar conversation had to do with Bob's dancing. Marshall called across the dance floor, for all to hear, "Damn, Bob, you are the only white guy who can dance!"

Both their assignments were planned to last three years, typical for Army officer assignments outside a combat zone. However, about two years into their tour, Marshall became conspicuously absent. Bob new he was dating a local teacher who just happened to be the daughter of the white Post Commanding General. They had been coming to the club together for months. Then, out of the blue, "poof!" Marshall was gone and never seen again. A few weeks went by before her fellow teacher spilled the beans. The General was not at all happy about his bright, beautiful daughter dating a Negro, West Point Graduate or not. After a few desperate conversations, Marshall was given orders for a recruiting position in Los Angeles. Not a bad assignment for a young officer, but not a career-maker for a West Point graduate. The gang at the club never saw either of them again. End of a story of a character not soon forgotten.

Chapter 21~The Vacation of a Lifetime

One of the true highlights of his teen years was Bob's school trip through Canada. He gathered just enough money to make the trip with about 30 other schoolmates on the "Bluebird," the school's one and only bus. Wynn Darington was the school's baseball coach, janitor and bus driver. He had a marine buzzcut to match his stout stature, although he was never admitted to being a Marine. He was also the school's mascot handler. King was a Purebred German Shepard from the American gene pool. He made the entire trip sitting in the first seat behind Wynn. The kids were accompanied by several of the teachers, including the Principle, Father Gilbride. He was a tall, lanky basketballer chock full of intelligence and goodwill. It was a real kick to watch him fold his 6 foot 4 frame into his tiny Karman Ghia. Nobody ever figured out how he managed to push the seat far enough back to actually operate the pedals.

The trip started out calmly enough. A bunch of hormone-depressed seminarians bouncing up the New York Thruway, north toward Niagara Falls. Wynn stopped frequently enough for the boys to take their breaks and buy some food. At one moment, the bus was as noisy as a locker room, the next, as quiet as the school chapel. The scenery was mostly farmland, since the small towns had been bypassed long ago by the interstate highway system.

By mid-afternoon, they had arrived at a campground on the southeast side of Lake Erie The school had reserved a large bunkhouse with an adjacent picnic and barbecue area. The northeast corner of the building faced a bit of old forest that hugged the lake for a mile or so. Almost before their feet hit the ground, a couple of the seniors had a fire going hot enough to cook dogs and burgers quickly. That suited the boys just fine, since they all claimed they were "starving" from the long ride. About the same time, a game of nickel-dime poker broke out. Bob was amazed to see some of the teachers jump right in! It wasn't long before Wynn brought out a six pack of Schlitz, and passed them around to the adults. They were strict about that, although Bob was convinced he saw one senior take a slug once or twice from a momentarily unattended beer.

As the bellies were filled and the embers faded down, the games continued. Someone was fiddling with an AM/FM transistor radio, looking dutifully for a decent music station. Bob and a couple other of the younger students went inside to claim a rack for the night. There was no contention in that endeavor, so they went out on the porch overlooking the forest.

Bob found an old chair and sat it facing the lake as the sun began to set. The other boys quickly wandered off to explore until dark. After about ten minutes, a rather cute, red-headed girl showed up at the foot of the stairs. She introduced herself a Marsha Smithfield from Santa Monica, CA. She was a high school freshman camping in the park with her parents and younger brother on summer vacation.

They chatted about the usual nothing for quite a while, as the sun broke the horizon on its way to the west. Nonetheless, they were far too involved in their conversation to take much notice.

"How about we go for a walk?", she asked Bob. "Our camp site is just about a half mile through the woods. He, being the consummate Catholic, had to weigh the invitation and couldn't just take her up on her offer without considering the ten commandments. She, standing on the stairs by then, reached up to Bob to grab his hand. At that very moment, Father Palmer, showed up out of absolutely nowhere and announced that "It's past sunset and everyone needs to be inside." Decision made, opportunity lost?

"Nice talking to you, California! Maybe we will meet again." The first time any girl, outside of his family, took an interest in him, and poof! Gone.

And that, as they say was that. He spent the rest of the evening and most of the night imagining what might have happened if they had taken that walk. Needless to say, he dreamt well.

The next morning, they headed to Niagara and spent most the day touring the falls and the Skylon Tower overlooking the falls from on high! It made for great pictures.   Unfortunately, John Z. lost his wallet somewhere in the tower. They went back in to take a look, but didn't have the money to go back up into the tower. They checked with Lost and Found, to no avail. John spent the rest of the trip asking for a few coins now and then, mostly to eat. It didn't spoil the trip. They made their way down into the tunnel to the Horseshoe Falls viewing area, getting soaking wet in the process. Fortunately, the fairly warm summer air and slight breeze dried them out quickly.

The afternoon was spent finding their way to Expo '67 in Montreal, the Canadian World's Fair and 100th Birthday Celebration! They were scheduled to spend the whole next day in the park.

On the following morning, after spending the night at a nondescript campground, the bus pulled into the massive parking lot at the Expo. The Expo had been built on man-made islands, a feat in itself even before considering the technology and architecture of the park. The total estimated attendance from late April to October was projected to be about 26 million visitors from around the world. Once the Expo was over the final count revealed a gate of over 50 million visitors!

Right after they passed through the turnstiles, mostly in one group, Bob decide he needed to buy some film when his eye caught the familiar gold and black Kodak sign. He and one other schoolmate got in line and were to the counter in two minutes. The other fellow bought his film and was gone to catch up with the group. Bob's purchase took just another 30 seconds to complete, but by time he left the kiosk, all the classmates were gone! All 30 of them had vanished, as if taken by the great wave of people. Bob doubled his pace into the crowd, looking for just one familiar face, or jacket or hat. Nothing. Another hundred yards, and nothing. He began to panic a bit, but noticed the overhead tram was only a few yards away. He quickly got in the line for the cars, hoping he could spot his crew from the air.

After a few round trips on the tram, his effort failed him. He got a great view of the park, but there were far too many humans down there to discern a mere handful. It was at that point that he fully realized he'd been unintentionally abandoned. He was alone in a foreign land at a World's Fair! Luckily, he had noted the location of the school bus and knew that he had to be back at the bus by 4pm. Beyond that, he was on his own to explore the massive exhibits and pavilions. But when he went into a pavilion, he was always looking for a familiar face. He'd long remember the Kodak pavilion, of course, with its color palette bordering the circular building. The US pavilion was mostly a display of the space race, with a hanging satellite, and the burnt remains of a flight capsule, showing the damage it took re-entering the atmosphere.

After a while, it got real tedious, trying to enjoy the phenomenal displays alone while trying to find just one familiar face. He resigned himself to the fact that he could do whatever he cared, as long as he was back on the bus at 4.

He spotted a pay phone by the AT&T pavilion and decided to call a girl he'd recently met back home, mostly to commiserate. It was a very short call, since the operator kept asking for money. Bob just didn't have much in the way of coins, Canadian or American, so the "hello-I'm in Canada, alone-goodbye" story was much abbreviated. But, at least she was a familiar voice.

Bob saw less than half of what he might have otherwise. Between the crowds and the constant search for schoolmates, his interest waned as the day wore on. He took the monorail around the park, but mostly saw water. After all, the place was built on an island!

He made his way to the bus before the deadline, and found a seat. Alone, again. But not for long. All the other boys trickled in two, three and four at a time. George was the only one to ask where Bob went. It was a short answer that nobody really heard. Ba-dee, ba-dee, ba-dee, that's all folks! On to the campground, once again.

The drudgery and disappointment of the day wore off gradually as he lay in the sack listening to the noise of the card-playing rabble and his radio. Nobody spoke of the missing student incident, figuring they dodged a bullet.

The next few days they worked their way around Lake Ontario, stopping each evening in a different campground. A few had shelter, but most were just out under the stars. One in particular was just a wide open field with dozens of others camping in nearly neat rows of tents and fire pits. That was quite odd to Bob, as he thought back to all his past campouts. Most of them were in the woods, with each campsite separate from the others. This one site in Canada was more a "commune" atmosphere. To add intrigue to mystery, many of the campers were celebrating America's Fourth of July, complete with hot dogs, hamburgers and firecrackers. That, he felt, was somewhat surreal. There must have been plenty of Americans touring Canada on that weekend.

Another evening, they were camped on a small river near a wooden bridge. Bob walked out on the bridge with a couple other students to have a smoke. While smoking wasn't prohibited by the school and several of the teachers smoked, it was still better for the students to keep a low profile. The bridge was very European in design. Heavy horizontal beams were balanced on both vertical and angled supports. All the joints were wood, not steel. The boys stayed quite a while, just smoking and passing the time with the BS of the day. While it was not really secluded, it was quiet and felt a bit separated from the rest of the world and very comforting. A far cry from the stress of the Expo fiasco.

The following night, now on the north shore of Lake Ontario, was more interesting. After setting up camp and eating, cleaning, and reading, they were once again snoring. For no particular reason, Bob awoke around 6am. The sun was just about to crack the horizon in the east. Bob made his way to the edge of the lake for a better look, where he found a rowboat tied to a tree. There were no non-school campers in the area, so he was perplexed as to who's boat it was.

Then, Bob did something he'd not done before. He "borrowed" a stranger's property, the unclaimed boat, and headed out on his own toward a breaker about a quarter mile away. The water was calm, the sun was rising, and the Canadian air was cool and fresh. He pulled on the oars at a steady pace, glancing behind him occasionally to measure his progress.

When he got within a few yards of the breaker, he could clearly hear water slashing the rocks. He searched up and down, but the water was still as calm as a preacher's demeanor. He wedged the small boat between to rocks, confident it wouldn't be encouraged to move in this calm. He jumped out onto the first rock, which was a big as a Volkswagen. He climbed, confidently, yet carefully from one rock to the next until his head barely poked above the berm. At that instant, he was nearly blown back into the boat by gust of wind from the other side of the berm. Undaunted, he climbed onto the berm, staying low into the wind, where he found the rusty remnants of a railroad line. He scoured up and down he line to make sure it was truly a defunct line, then brought himself upright to view the other side. Not only was the wind relentless, but the water on the other side had two and three foot waves with noticeable whitecaps. He glanced back where he came from, fighting the wind to stay upright. He could barely make out the edge of the lake with the campground, since his eyes were starting to water from the wind and the noticeably colder temperature beating on his back.

It was surreal. On the one side, absolute calm and peace. On the other, a brutal chaos of wind and surf, beating up the rocks. It was truly nuts. He would never forget that morning boat excursion, as long as he lived. The stark and riveting contrast of two worlds just a few yards from each other was both confusing and amazing. He carefully climbed back down the granite boulders and into the boat. His energy to row had peaked from the adrenaline rush of his discovery. It was a much shorter trip back to the camp.

As he tied up the boat, he noticed that most the boys were still in the sack. Only two grills had been lit up for breakfast. One of the guys asked him where he'd been.

Bob replied with a simple "Out on the lake." End of another long conversation. But he was OK with that, since he didn't feel like sharing that special experience with everyone. Just another shiny gem of exploration to tuck into his backpack for his enjoyment, alone.

There were only two days left before they were due back at the school. They crossed the border and made it into New York the following day. There, they toured the Ausable Chasm, an unassuming and unexciting tourist trap, and made camp at Green Lake State Park.

Of course, the first order of business was to visit the lake to determine why it was green. The first and simplest answer was algae. However, it turned out that it was a little more chemically complex than that. Its green color is a result of high levels of calcium carbonate and not phytoplankton or algae. The density of calcium carbonate reflects, rather than absorbs, the green wavelength, making the lake look green. It's just an optical illusion, fooling human perception!

It was safe to swim in and quite a scene; green all the way across to the other side. Funny how nobody wanted to swim that day. As they were walking along the shore, Bob's eye caught a slight glimmer in the sand. He reached down and retrieved a women's watch. Amazing, the second buried watch he'd found in his short life. Since there was no lost and found office, and absolutely no one in sight, he buried it deep in his pocket for later investigation. Was this actually some good luck, he thought?

The final day of travel, actually about 5 hours, was anti-climactic. Some were asleep while others shared what they had acquired on the trip. Bob had purchased a souvenir cigarette lighter at Ausable Chasm, but it came without fuel. There wasn't much to show off there. Some of the other kids had tourist trinkets, others bought snacks. To each his own.

The Bluebird rolled into the school parking lot around 3 pm, leaving plenty of time to unload, check everything and return home. Bob grabbed his camping gear and headed over to this '60 Saab. It was a clear, warm New England day in July, so he slid open the canvas "sun roof" and headed out toward the parkway. He'd be home in 20 minutes, in no hurry.

Mom greeted him with her usual droll humor. "Did you have a good time or did the Mounties throw you out?" He didn't even acknowledge the "joke" and said "Everything was good." "Maybe it was both," he though to himself. He figured he would share the trip highlights later, after some food.

The next morning, Saturday, he was up early to try and catch a morning loop at the Country Club. He managed to get two loops, morning and afternoon, which helped refill the piggy bank after the vacation.

As expected, nobody at the caddy shack was the least bit interested in where he'd been for two potentially profitable summer weeks or what he'd experienced. They were there for one purpose only. Make money. They couldn't care a ruddy rat's ass about Canada.

Chapter 22~Childhood Dreams and Powerless Minions

ob never had those reality show dreams of greatness. His dreams were limited to not getting beat up in school, or doing well on the Algebra quiz. While he had been somewhat prodded to make an attempt at professional golf, he took a hard pass on that once he entered college. There had been some quiet interest among a few members of the country club along the lines of "sponsoring" Bob on the PGA Tour. Sure, Bob was a good golfer, but pro-level? Even with daily workouts and practice, that would still be years in the making. The Military Draft wasn't waiting and the PGA didn't constitute an exemption to conscription. Another opportunity lost, however unrealistic.

Bob's dreams were a bit more esoteric. Not cars, motorcycles or anything material. His dreams were more along the line of the Man of La Mancha; a beaten and battered, self-appointed crusader for the underdog. Of course, there was the shading of Superman, Batman and the Green Hornet. And throwing in the Bonanza Cartwrights and John Wayne in the mix would be OK, too. The influence of television in the '60s was overwhelming.

While many kids in the '60s were slobbering over the Beatles and Elvis, Bob was taking on the subconscious aura of an unknown hero. No mask, no cape. Just intent on helping others even if he didn't yet know how. But, like a good Boy Scout, he would always be prepared to help the old lady cross the street.

While that hinted of romanticism, much of his motivation was pragmatism. If he wanted a new pair of sunglasses, he would have to earn the money. The same mantra followed him his whole life and he managed to instill it in his kids and grandkids: There is no free lunch. You eat what you kill, in contracting jargon.

Some things you learn subconsciously. At the top of the list is "Misery loves company." There are innumerable literary examples of "making do" in abject poverty. Over the centuries, it has become almost a blood sport to see who can best cope with misery. "Mister, can I have more?" From the Dickens novel reflects the ingrained mentality of "knowing your place" in the world. The wringing of hands and constant worrying of the underlings were becoming perfected through each generation as a non-productive mantra intended to show deep concern for people and unfortunate life circumstances. "If life gives you lemons, make lemonade." Not exactly a positive life plan.

It was no different for Bob's family. While they had shoes on their feet, adequate nourishment and a place to sleep, they were part of the "servant" class of the 20th century. The Industrial Revolution mentality was alive and well in the 20th century. Get up early, eat a good breakfast, report to your station at the first horn, and on and on. Chuck was a mechanic and estate gardener, his father, Antonio, was a stone mason and an estate gardener. Antonio, a young Italian immigrant at the time, dutifully served in the Army of his new country in World War I. Chuck followed suit in WWII where he learned his blue collar skills. Chuck's oldest brother served in WWII also, as a mail clerk and spent his post-war career in the United States Post Office. Meeting society's expectations for the working poor, even though they were not factory workers, the revolution mentality still drove the economy. The expectation for most was wage slave. It was obvious to some that the public school system was still designed to turn out "workers." all the while getting the rich kids to college. In fact, if you came from a wage slave family, the schools would channel you into the "trades." If you came from the estates, you were shuttled into other academic side of the house. Crossing over the dividing line was difficult, at best. "They knew" where you should be directed, not you, and certainly not your wage slave parents. Getting out of this socioeconomic rut would take courage, creativity, and generations of hard work.

Each of the family war veterans had to take at least one second paying job to minimally support their families. That was the expectation in those times. It wasn't until much later in the 20th century that wives started to work outside the home for a paycheck. While Angie worked before getting married, which she proudly referenced from time to times as her "time working at the Gristede's market." With eight eventual children, working outside the home soon became a non-starter. She would take some menial jobs once the kids were out of the house, but that never amounted to a financial windfall by any measure, just some extra money for the bills or an emergency.

While each of these jobs and skills had some value, they did not provide sufficient income to "step up" in the world. While there was absolutely no thought of climbing the social ladder, especially in the predominantly white and prosperous village of Northfield, there was thought and some discussion of giving the children a "leg up" in life. The simple act of putting the children in the local Catholic school was a good start, but that did not work out for all eight. Only Mike, Tony and Bob completed all eight years at St. Alphonse. Once again, the money had run out for private school tuition, as did the generosity of others.

But, you always had bitching, moaning and laughing away your trials and tribulations. Bob didn't really recognize until later in life that laughing at everything, laughing after every statement, funny or not, was a cultural behavior. "I'm sorry, I just ran over your dog. Ha, ha, ha!" Or "It's just a little blood, you'll be fine. Ha, ha, ha." It was never an intentional "in your face" laugh, but more a nervous laugh brought on by insecurity, like the court jester who knew he'd be sent to the dungeon if he didn't make the king laugh! It's very similar to the "shuck and jive" behavior of other cultures.

So each kid was on his or her own to work their way out of poverty. Thankfully, they were all brilliant students and had great work ethic, or all might not have turned out as well as it did. The first step for most young folks trying to get out of poverty is to get the hell out of town! There was no career opportunity in Northfield that rose above the working poor class. Northfield wealth was a closed shop and invitations to join were never issued to working class types. The town needed cops and firefighters, teachers, garbage men and, of course, estate landscapers. They didn't need any more lawyers, brokers, politicians or Real Estate Agents. Those careers were all booked in town, generationally.

The primary option for poor kids was defense of country; more military expendables. Made out to be a great and noble cause by the politicians for every peon to accept, there were few options. Mike joined the Air Force out of high school and Tony was drafted into the

Army. That was not the first or only time Bob was glad to not be first! The snippets of news he got from Mike and Tony, added to the Kronkite news from Vietnam, convinced Bob that, if he had to join up, it would not be as an enlisted man. They were the real expendables! But he had also learned that the life expectancy for a 2LT in Vietnam was 30 seconds. There's always risk.

Grandpa Antonio Vitti worked his knuckles raw as a stone mason for decades. He worked the dams, bridges, berms, and buildings for the construction contractors, supplementing his meager immigrant salary with landscape work on the Failer estate.

The kids never really knew Antonio in any meaningful way. He smoked a pipe, tended a huge Italian garden, and enjoyed his whiskey. The most revealing incident Bob remembered was one Sunday evening when Grampa got a bit snockered and ended up on the dining room table, ranting and raving at what? Nobody really knew. The only revealing word was the President's name mentioned more than once. It might have been taxes, the war, treatment of immigrants. Beyond that, it was anyone's guess. But, it was easy to see he had a fiery temper and was quite opinionated.

But that freedom of opinion was widespread in the family. Mom was always passing judgment on others, starting with "those damn rich people." She had an opinion on everything and never hesitated to voice it.

From the weather to the lady down the street, whose grown son still lived with her. Most of the kids picked up at least some of that need to give everyone a "piece of her mind." However, that unintentional nurturing almost always had negative results. Having opinions without power to change something or fix the problem is hopelessly frustrating throughout life. Bob spent his whole career learning that if you're not the lead dog, the scenery never changes.

Ironically, "Keep you opinion to yourself," was another of Angie's nuggets of advice.

❧❧❧❧

Minor conflicts of siblings were common in the family. Since valuable possessions were scarce, when one was obtained, it is was guarded like the Crown Jewels. One Christmas present Rick got when he was 15 was a stereo record player, a first for the family. So Bob made his first music record purchase, under the erroneous assumption that the record player would be available to him, as well. He bought the Deep Purple album that was actually purple vinyl with some of his Christmas money and made the mistake of playing it on Rick's record player without asking. As soon as Rick heard it from the bedroom he flew down the stairs in a rage screaming at Bob to turn it off and take the record off. A loud argument ensued, in the effort to establish rights of ownership. Bob got so incensed at Rick's selfishness that he took his brand new album and smashed it over Rick's head! That was a quick waste of five dollars. While the argument was short and mildly violent, no one was injured. The act of busting the record did, however, engender a bit of short-lived laughter and even mild satisfaction.

The only other "violent" incident was when Tony wouldn't stop calling Bob "bones." Bob was at his limit and took the opportunity to punch Tony square in the nose. Once again, there was no lasting harm done, but the message was sent and received.

Such arguments did not happen on a regular basis, since the kids were taught to keep their hands to themselves. Fun wrestling was the most "grabby" activity that was tolerated. It was almost a miracle that all eight kids made it to adulthood without too many scars.

But the real measure of success was success, itself. While none of the Vitti kids would make it to Wall St or the halls of Congress, or even to professional sports, they all played their seemingly minuscule but expected roles raising kids, working one or more jobs, serving the country and the community and buying that 3 bedroom, two bath "investment of a lifetime." All according to society's expectations. If that sufficed as "life success", then all is well. However managing and controlling the "unwashed masses" requires the constant management of their expectations. Kids with big dreams are oblivious to others' plans to shape their lives. They just chase their dreams without regard to the sometimes harsh realities of life. The non-dreamers were mostly realists and practical planners. They knew by time they graduated high school the barriers to climbing the income or social ladders were clear. Harvard? Dream on. UCONN? Now that's more your speed.

That whole sense of "class society," hardly discussed in the press or in school, was a harsh reality for those who were born on the "wrong side of the tracks." "You get what you get and you don't throw a fit" was a common retort for those kids who's expectations far exceeded their parent's resources.

And from that mentality and social norm came the working class. Very few ever born into the working class ever make an upward move. Even then, it's never more than one rung on the ladder.

While the TV folk would have everyone believe that the house with the white picket fence, a new car in the driveway and "a chicken in every pot'" as the "American Dream," to most immigrants it was the hope of a better future for the children and grandchildren. If the house and car came along, fine, but it was really the education and opportunity to escape the "poor working class" they were chasing. Simply put, Antonio Vitti and Michael Carchia came to America so that Bob and his siblings could have a future they could never have in Italy, even though it would be decades before they were even born! Some of the Vitti clan did struggle their way to the next level on the socioeconomic ladder, but not all. Their success wasn't stratospheric, but measurable. Just being able to quit working before death was an admirable goal that was attained by a couple siblings. No yachts, no Rolls Royce, no mansion on Martha's Vineyard, but enough to retire and maybe even leave a few bucks for the next generation. Grandpa Antonio would be proud.

Chapter 23~The Payroll Thief

One of the many "extra duties" assigned to young officers was that of payroll officer. Monthly pay for the soldiers was made in cash at that time. It was a long-standing Army tradition to pay the troops directly. The popularity of direct deposit was still a few years off. Collecting, counting, dispersing and reconciling the money was a duty every young officer endured.

The first step for the Payroll Officer was to head over to the finance office, count the money and sign for it. Once the pay officer was settled in at the pay site, usually the gym, each soldier in turn would approach the table, present his ID and witness the counting of his pay on the table. He was free to go after that, since payday afternoon was always free time. After a couple of barracks burglaries were reported, the Commanding General decided that no soldier could leave the pay site with more than 100 dollars in cash. Each soldier was directed across the gym to where a sales agent of the local bank would gladly sell them money orders! Mandatory! Supposedly to minimize the thefts. "For their own good." All it managed to do was focus the thieves on other items in the barracks and make a ton of money for the bank. It was just another great example of an egomaniacal "leader" having a solution to "everything."

One Payroll afternoon, when everyone was "off duty," Bob was out playing golf, his usual custom for payday afternoons. Around the second hole, two Military Police approached him and said he had to go with them. No explanation other than an "irregularity" complaint from the payroll office. Bob was taken, unceremoniously in the back of the sedan, to MP HQ, where he was treated like a common criminal. After the mugshot, fingerprints and rights warnings, the MP officer finally filled him in on the issue. It seemed another payroll officer was robbed, tied to a tree far out on the rifle range and left to his own demise. A "witness" had reported that the lead culprit "looked like Lt. Vitti."   After making sufficient alibi to the investigator, (uh duh, I was taking care of my own payroll at the time and I have 120 witnesses) he was released without further action. The fact that he was now permanently "in the system", was no cause for concern for anyone else. Mistakes happen, right?

As it turned out, the culprit was another payroll officer, who just happened to live across the street from Bob, and was desperate to pay his gambling debts to the local mafia. He had engaged a couple of civilian co-conspirators who followed his instructions to the letter. Unfortunately, once they got their cut of the payroll, they dashed east on the highway toward St. Louis, spending at every stop like they had just won the lottery. One of the local cops alerted the Military Police, and the culprits were quickly in handcuffs on their way back to Ft. Leonard Wood. All three of the thieves were taken to jail to await trial.

While Bob was released with no charges, there was not enough time before dark to finish his round. He headed home to relay the saga to his wife, who got a real kick out of it. She also referred to "that idiot across the street," who was "destined to get himself in trouble someday." Turns out the criminal's failed career was just the least of his problems after that day. He still owed the local mafia.

Chapter 24~Cheating Death

Although the law in Connecticut did not require motorcycle helmets, Bob and his friends were raised to know better. They never rode without one, long before the federal government spent millions on TV and other ads to convince everyone riding on two wheels to wear them. That campaign was similar to the "cigarettes will kill you" campaign, but on a much lower profile (and much cheaper to the taxpayer). After all, it just made sense to protect your noggin while riding. They really didn't need the government to tell them that. That's why God made parents and common sense!

While most of Bob's excursions on his motorcycle were fun and safe, he did learn a hard lesson about watching where he's going on two wheels. As he pulled into the gas station at a common sense speed, the front tire hit a small patch of oil and began to slide sideways. The bike started to fall to the right just as the front tire struck the island with the pumps. In an instant, the rear of the bike bucked like a rodeo bull tossing Bob over the handlebars. He had the agility to get his feet under him before hitting the concrete, but the momentum of the bike was transferred to him. As his feet hit the ground he had no choice but to immediately start clumsily running, or fall on his face. The momentum carried him all the way to the far end of the parking lot, a good 25 feet. At that point, still on his feet, Bob stood face to face with with a few locals smoking cigarettes. Always the comedian in the face of jeopardy, he looked them straight in the eye and casually said, "Guess I'm gonna have to get those brakes fixed," and strutted back to inspect his fallen horse. Once again, he dodged a bullet. He was reminded that life is messy, and only made more so by older cars with oil leaks!

❧❧❧

Probably the scariest and most unbelievable story Bob every heard was from his good high school buddy, Jim S. Jim was a big time New York lawyer who often shuttled by helicopter from NY to their New Jersey offices, about a 15 minute flight. As it was later told in the New York Times, a routine morning flight in mid March turned into instant disaster when the copter carrying Jim and two others plus the pilot, crashed into the frigid East River on takeoff. The craft quickly sunk to the bottom with all on board. The Pilot managed to escape to the surface, but because of the not-so-brilliant design of the aircraft, those in the rear were trapped. As it turned out, there were no handles on the inside of the passenger compartment! It was probably sold as an early "safety" feature so that passengers couldn't open the doors during flight, "for your safety"! Jim rode the copter all the way to the bottom, all the while desperately trying to find a way out. He was submerged at the bottom of the near-freezing river for a full 18 minutes, until the water rescue team extricated him, barely alive, and evacuated him to the nearest hospital.

It was at that hospital that the impossible happened! The staff immediately started pumping warm fluids through Jim any way they could. The risky process gradually warmed him up until further treatment could be made. Bob had lunch with Jim a good 10 years after the incident, and was surprised there were no long term issues. The man was drowned near death, but was revived to finish out his years without missing a beat! Now that's a miracle!

❋❋❋❋

On April 3rd, 1974, about two weeks before his graduation from UD, Bob attended a School of Education reception held on the top floor of the Admin building, the tallest on the campus. As the grads sucked down the cafeteria snacks and the President made his remarks, he noticed the skies getting disturbingly dark and ominous. It wasn't until the reception was over and Bob was walking through the Student Center that some of the news was trickling in from Xenia, Ohio, just a short drive east from Dayton. He was quick to learn that Xenia had been decimated by a massive tornado with extensive death and damage. Had that tornado wandered just twenty miles west, it might have devastated the Dayton campus and surrounding areas.

He walked away from the TV screen thankful that he'd dodged yet another bullet

❖❖❖❖

Chuck only once told a war story from his tour in the mountains of China during the Second World War. The story of his Jeep sliding off the icy dirt road while driving down the mountain to base camp was indelible, being the one and only war story he ever told.

Almost 50 years later, Bob had a similar experience while assigned to the evaluator force for a 7th Infantry exercise at Fort Hunter Liggett. During night maneuvers, with nothing but a ground guide wielding his red lens flashlight and blackout lights on a vintage Willys Jeep, his driver dutifully followed the ground guide right off the side of the dirt road as they descended from the highest hill in the tactical area. The Jeep skidded sideways for what seemed like an eternity, finally stopping some distance from the road.

There were four in the Jeep, including the driver, Bob, a Butter Bar in the back left seat and an overweight Reserve Major in the right passenger seat, on the uphill side."Nobody move!' Bob ordered. He wanted to make sure the Jeep was fully hung up before attempting an escape. They had no idea what was awaiting them in the darkness below. The ground guide, who had tripped on a rock and tumbled off the road was picking himself up from the dirt a few feet downhill from the Jeep. He scanned the scene with his red-lens flashlight, not seeing much of anything. However, Bob's eyes had fully adjusted to the dark, making it much easer to evaluate the situation. All four wheels were still in the desert sand and a rucksack-size rock was the only thing keeping the Jeep from sliding further into the darkness.

Bob was quick to action. He ordered the driver out first, to climb out over the fat Major, who made great ballast. The left passenger was next, using the same tactic. Finally, the Major made his clumsy move, out over the radio and Bob jumped out at the same time. They watched in stunned silence as the Jeep didn't move an inch even though it was leaning at least 45 degrees. It was well secured against the rock. After checking that everyone was OK, the memory of Chuck's Jeep accident in China hit Bob like a bold of lighting, stunning him into silence for a moment and sending a chill up his spine followed by a silent chuckle. Having no time to reminisce, Bob ordered the LT to get on the horn and call for recovery.

Bob passed by the same spot in the daylight next morning. He was a bit unnerved to see that the Jeep was still there, and the rock had kept the four of them from sliding another 50 yards to the bottom of the ravine. Oh, but for the Grace of God.

❈❈❈

So, so many times when the kids skinned a knee or cut themselves, out came the Mecurochrome; Mercury and Iodine! With the approval of the family doctor and the infamous FDA, mothers everywhere were dabbing every kid's slightest skin damage with this poison. A favorite phrase when applying to a small child was: "Quit your crying, you won't die!" Which was phrase generously used by parents of small children for generations. Its companion was "Just blow on it, Bobby. It won't sting as much."

Applying the phrase "You won't die" to the kids' most hated food was also somewhat effective. "Eat your broccoli, you won't die!"

On the far side of that coin were phrases meant to scare the kid into "looking both ways," or "No running with those scissors!" These became catch phrases uttered by parents to remind the kids that the world is not always a safe and kind place.

Unfortunately, Grandma Carchia took caution to extremes. One fun Saturday, two of the boys were climbing a Maple tree in Grandma's yard. When she saw them, she sprang out onto the porch waving her ever-present dish towel and shouting "You boys come down out of that tree before you hurt yourselves." While they were only about 12 feet off the ground, they obediently scurried down rather than suffer the wrath of Grandma any further. They would have many other opportunities to take the risk of getting hurt for an adventure or something exciting and new. And it certainly would not be the last tree they climbed. Far from it.

❈❈❈❈❈

Into every life some rain must fall. Fortunately, the rain is sometimes dodged, especially when the rain is metaphorical and the real threat is tons of locomotive with brake failure

Bob had arrived a bit early for the 5:10 from NYC. He took a seat on the park bench at the end of the railhead, on the outside of the chain link fence and facing town, his back to the train. He checked his watch to find out it was only 5:05. A moment later he heard the warning horn from the approaching train. Normally, the last blast heard was as the train approached the final crossing at Grove St. just a hundred yards from the station. Not this time. This warning horn was persistent and got your attention.

Something was wrong, seriously wrong. Bob instinctually turned to the sound only to see the train coming directly at him and not slowing at all. More horn. Close and loud. Bob grabbed his bag and dashed out of the way, off the bench and down the hill toward the Post Office. He noticed that there was no sound of brakes. None of the normal screeching, sparking, grinding of steel on steel bringing the beast to an eventual stop.

Not this time. There were no brake sounds as the runaway pushed the huge iron stop block though the fence, then through the park bench and out into the center of the intersection as the train bounded forward, now off the tracks and digging into the concrete and asphalt. The noise was unbearable. The grinding of steel on concrete and asphalt was a totally new and horrible sound, ending only once the lead car came to a precarious stop just feet short of the curb on the opposite side of the intersection, missing its front wheel truck! It was exactly 5:10. Amazingly, not a single auto or pedestrian was injured which was a miracle in itself. Once again, Bob had dodged a bullet. This time actually dodging an out of control train.

Bob was walking cautiously back up toward the train wreck when he saw what had to be an impossible sight. There it was, the 5:10 from New York, sitting out under the traffic light in the middle of the intersection! He unconsciously hurried his pace to get a closer look before the fire department arrived. There was little to see, since the smoke and steam of belching locomotives of the past had long been replaced with all-electric engines. But, just seeing the how the train had pushed the heavy stop block through the fence, destroying Bob's favorite "wait for the train" bench on its way to the stop light was enough to make him cringe.

The few injuries reported from train passenger were all minor bumps and bruises from the disorderly stop.

Getting the train out of the street and back on the track was the real challenge. It took several days and lots of heavy equipment for the New Haven Railroad to get service up and running again to NYC.

A few years later, another NH Railroad train derailed on the final curve coming into the station, right behind Grandma Carchia's house. The first on the scene that time were brother Rick and his wife Cyndi, who just happened to live in Grandma's second floor apartment. They did their best to clear debris from the lower side of a derailed car in an attempt to pull some injured passengers free. They had just barely cleared a path to the leaning car when the Police and Fire Departments arrive and sent the young heroes packing. The Advertiser got the shot of the two in the middle of the debris field, the derailed train in the background for the Thursday edition. Unfortunately, there was one death and several severe injuries in this accident, a major story for the little town.

Chapter 25~Unsafe at any speed - Pimping Fear

Part and parcel of the post-war generation was a love for cars and driving. Bob was no exception. He got his driver permit at 15 and Chuck bought Bob his first car, a used 1960 Swedish Saab, for sixty bucks! The Buick dealership he worked for also had a SAAB sales and service department, and Chuck had a good relationship with Tony, the only Saab mechanic in the area. This phenomenal car was designed as basic transportation with safety and economy features well ahead of its time. The "Big Three" auto manufacturers were selling sexy, large muscle cars and showed total disregard for features later models would include as standard equipment. A Swedish engineer invented the three-point restraint system, and made the design and patent available to anyone. The overall design of the car was anything but sexy, unless you consider a sliding canvas sunroof as sexy! Angie described it as a "little gray mouse" running down the street, and Grandma Carchia said she alway knew when Bob was coming to visit because the Saab sounded like her old percolator coffee pot!

The Saab was unique in other ways, also. In a world of six-cylinder and eight-cylinder Chevy, Oldsmobile and Ford monsters, it had just a three cylinder, two cycle engine, a bit like a lawn mower. Every time he filled up with gas, Bob had to put a pint of motor oil in with the gas. That was something no other car required. Another Swedish design, but this one didn't have any longevity in the design department. Most probably because the car smoked all the time, as the engine burned the oil-laden fuel. But it saved on oil changes!

The greatest design feature of the old Saab was something called "free-wheeling." There was a push-pull lever next to the gas peddle. If you pull out the lever, the engine and transmission would be continuously engaged, like any other car. However, if you push the lever to the floor, the engine would disengage from the transmission any time you decelerated or took your foot off the gas. In effect, the car would be coasting! Of course, this was a great way to save gas. Bob calculated that he actually made it all the way to 50 miles per gallon in a 1960 model car! It would be decades before other car companies managed to get to a measly 30 mpg.

Unfortunately, there's always those detractors who apparently knew diddly squat about auto design and safety. They claimed, without any real-world proof, that once the engine and transmission were disengaged, the driver could lose control as they tried to stop the vehicle with just the brakes! WOW, could you get any dumber than that? Did they really believe that this innovative Swedish car company, a company that made its bones building fighter jets, engineered a car that wouldn't stop?

While Saab went on to make continuous improvements to it's vehicles, at once being labeled the "safest" cars on the road, it was decades before the Big Three caught up to things like seatbelts, airbags, anti-lock brakes and traction control and only after Saab had those on the showroom floor!

A young Harvard lawyer who made his notoriety and career criticizing cars and car companies chose one of Bob's all time favorite cars, the Chevrolet Corvair. This car was so unique it was considered "esoteric" by some and "Unsafe at any Speed" by others. Bob's used "Monza" model was a two-door convertible with automatic on the dash, the standard six cylinder engine with four carbs, wooden steering wheel and leather interior. It was the kind of used exotic car you could find cheap in a place like Northfield, where Wall Street went to bed every night.

The problem the ambulance-chasing, opportunistic media pantywaists had with the Corvair was its "floating rear axle" design which they falsely believed to be a "one car accident" waiting to happen. In their faulty logic, the rear axle could collapse on sharp, high speed turns when the wheel came back to the ground after lifting off the road! Bob proved, quite unintentionally, that that was load of bull! He drove the hell out of that car on all those nasty Connecticut roads and never once did any wheel collapse even if it left the road surface! In fact, Bob got his first speeding ticket in his Corvair coming down the NY Thruway more than a bit over the limit. The media "proof" of the imaginary fault was one "test" video where the axle failed when the car LEFT THE ROAD on a high speed turn!   Of course that's the 5 second clip the media wet their pants over and showed time after time after time! Not once did they consider the fact that A PRODUCTION CAR ISN'T DESIGNED TO LEAVE THE ROAD AT JUST ANY SPEED! Yet, the campaign claimed the Corvair was "unsafe at any speed" so effectively that it engendered a Congressional hearing. Imagine making a living by destroying technology you know nothing about. Or attempting to tilt the marketing tables by pushing fear, based on nothing but theory and one questionable film clip. One detractor had written a book based upon lawsuits filed against GM, not one of which were won by the complainant! Not one. Bob was convinced it was all kabuki theater to somehow warp the American driver's attitude toward certain cars, and to make a shitload of money screaming "Timmy's in the well, Timmy's in the well!" But folks like the lead critics would confidently and continuously preach that it's "for your own good." They considered themselves heroes of the people. Bob thought them all to be self-appointed know-it-alls who actually knew nothing about cars or engineering. But, Bob had practical experience and drove the hell out of that Corvair for an entire summer and had a boatload of fun.

In all the blather, there was little, if any discussion of operator error, that is, shitty drivers. And no discussion of road conditions attributing to the accidents. As Bob would later learn as an Operational Test Engineering Analyst in the Army, the "investigations" of GM appeared haphazard and amateurish, at best.

The long-lasting unintended consequence of this fiasco was the institutionalization of always blaming others, which only made the lawyers wealthier as consumer lawsuits piled up trying to place blame on someone else, anyone else!

Bob didn't see the Corvair critics as any kind of heroes. His Corvair was a prize and an absolute pleasure to drive, at any speed. If only the critics had actually done any real engineering research and testing. Hell, there was no evidence that they ever even sat in a Corvair. Besides, there weren't any write-ups addressing the potential faults and failures of a six cylinder air cooled engine and the special attention it might need to keep it from melting down. That might have actually been some value to potential Corvair buyers. Bob eventually blew his engine after the fan belt failed and Angie sold it to the junk dealer for $50 when Bob went back to college.

A few years later Texas A&M published a safety study on the Corvair and determined that the critics were wrong about the Corvair being "Unsafe at any Speed." Case closed, but so was the assembly line for one of the coolest "pony" cars ever built.

As it turned out, both of Bob's first two cars were "unsafe" according to the self-proclaimed experts. Yet, Bob managed to drive the crap out of both of them and survive without a single incident or accident.

Bob would go on to own 50 cars over the next 50 years, some as a single guy, but most as a married man. From the huge and highly reliable '66 Chevy Impala, to the highly competitive '75 Ford LTD and the '67 Mercedes 230 tank they brought back from Germany, and on and on and on. Bob had made a list of all the cars they had owned over a 30 year period, and was surprised at the number and variety. Interestingly, all but three were used cars. The only new ones were the '73 Ford Maverick Bob bought in college, the '89 Chrysler Accord, which smoked its way into oblivion within three years and the '98 Chrysler Concorde, which was the most unreliable car they ever drove.

The car that brought the most fun and great memories was the 1973 Porsche 914. Bob found it in the local Oldsmobile dealership where it had been traded in for a "grocery getter." He paid a fair price for it, and soon discovered why the near "fire sale" price. The car almost caught fire. Even though the Germans were great engineers, something can always slip by. In this case, the fuel hoses that fed the injectors were the braided type. But their short tight turn from the main fuel line to the injectors, combined with the constant heat of the air-cooled engine, resulted in fuel leaks right over the manifold, the hottest part of the engine. Bob found reports of 914s burning up with nearly instantaneous combustion. He made the necessary repairs quickly, replacing each little braided hose with a sturdy rubber piece. His repairs averted a potential disaster down the road.

That wasn't the only time Bob averted a fire in the Porsche. On the way back from a grocery run with all three kids in the car and the food in the passenger foot well, smoke began to pour out from under the glove compartment. Bob and Nye basically tossed the kids out of the car, followed by several bags of groceries. Upon further inspection, Bob found that a positive wire from the 8-track player had grounded out on a piece of metalwork, causing the smoke. Luckily, a fire never started and, once again, he dodged bullet. So, just how do you fit three kids and five bags of groceries in a Porsche 914? Very, very carefully.

❖❖❖❖

The long and winding road along the river and around the Ft. Leonard Wood golf course was irresistible. He would take a couple of laps whenever he could, hoping the MPs were busy somewhere else that day. He'd get the little 914 up to 80, which made it one hell of a ride when he came up off a little rise, but the tires never left the road. He also soon learned what a sports car was designed for: handling. The most challenging turn in that circuit was the nearly 90 degree right-hander on the way back to the golf shop. It was a bit hairy all the time, but so much more hazardous when a bit of winter sand was present.

Bob could never recall how many trips he made around that loop with no accidents, no incidents, no MPs. He had finally realized a whole different aspect of driving fun: speed and handling combined!

❉❉❉

On one late summer afternoon, Bob went up to Cheryl's house for a visit. He parked his Saab in the usual place, toward the back of the oversized drive, but not blocking the two car garage. Some time later, Cheryl's dad backed out of the garage, hitting the Saab and sending it down the steep embankment and into the woods. It actually jumped over a small stone wall to finally get hung up on a sawed-off stump of a birch tree.

It was such an unusual site, that Syd, photographer for the Advertiser, somehow got word and came out to document the mishap.

As a tribute to the hearty design of the 1960 Saab, once a few of the teens managed to free it from the stump, Bob climbed in, started her up, and backed her up the steep hill to the house. After studying the damage, he eventually drove it home, albeit missing 3rd and 4th gear!

Dad managed to salvage the car by buying another one just like it, initially as a parts car. But '61 he bought was actually in better shape than the '60, so Bob made it his own.

Mattered not, since the only thing missing was the ten-inch speaker Bob had wired into the original car for his own, personal sound and some actual base. He had salvaged the speaker from an old console TV, where it had served for years, putting out rich, wide-range sound with excellent fidelity.

The first Saab ended up in the junkyard once any usable parts were removed. The speaker was not one of them. Heck, he thought he might be able to find another speaker, but did he want to put out all the effort to rewire the second Saab? It never got done.

Chapter 26~A Litany of Unfortunate Incidents

He was acting the adventurous ten-year old when he wandered into the neighbor's driveway and was immediately attacked by a short, ugly dog. The Beagle-devil chomped onto Bob's right leg, leaving four distinct bright, red holes. After extricating himself from the situation, evidently with the dog as shocked as he was, he took a seat on the "boundary rock" that designated property lines along the road (there really wasn't much of a sidewalk to speak of.). Not five minutes passed before Angie was on the front porch asking Bobby "what's wrong?" She always knew when something was wrong with her kids and she was spot on, once again. After spending a couple of minutes denying everything, Bob finally admitted he rode into the neighbor's yard and got bit by the dog. Angie quickly jumped into action, retrieving Bobby and taking up to the doctor for wound inspection and tetanus shot, always that damn tetanus shot!

✽✽✽✽

On one warm spring afternoon, Bob had just climbed the steps to the front porch when he heard someone shout, "Hey Vitti!" As soon as Bob turned to the shouting, a rock the size of a baby's fist hit him square in the nose. Blood gushed immediately, but Bob was able to get look at the perpetrator, he was a public middle school kid name Ruggio or Riggio or whatever. He was one of those kids that were always in trouble and referred to as "Nasty Bastards from that part of Italy." Bob was bleeding and his nose was throbbing. His only recourse was to go find Mom and get some first aid. There wouldn't be any chasing down and beating the crap out of the fat kid. He would have to garner some patience for another time. Fortunately, that opportunity never arose. Ruggio out-sized Bob by at least four inches and thirty pounds. And he later learned that this nasty subculture of Italy never fought fair. Bob was glad that opportunity to defend his honor never occurred. Bob learned a lot about unwarranted cultural prejudice and unwarranted violence that day. There was no logic to be uncovered. It was just that subculture of Italians that were the "badasses of Italy" and proud of it.

❖❖❖❖

On a nearly routine, monotonous trip to the bus stop one morning, the Buick wagon threw a shoe! The front right wheel actually departed the car on a right turn on a broken axle. Fortunately Chuck was never speeding, or he'd hear about it from Angie. The wheel noisily dug into the road tar and then into the grass, bringing the green monster to a smooth, gradual stop. Unfortunately, this was not just a normal school day, when missing the bus was easily remedied. No. On this fine October morning, the entire class was boarding a charter bus to NYC for a show on Broadway, The Man Of La Mancha. This musical was about a nutty Spanish fellow who goes on a quest, with his unwitting, yet wise wingman Sancho Panza, to right wrongs but ends up fighting windmills (dragons) in defense of a local prostitute he believes is a noblewoman! Oh, the Unbeatable Foe, that Unreachable Star!

Chuck talked a neighbor into borrowing his phone to call for help and a ride for Bob to the bus station. It all worked out when his boss showed up and rescued the big day. That was Bob's first foray into professional theater, but by far not his last. He enjoyed the theater, but soon realized that the "big city" was not his forté.

❖❖❖❖❖

It was also not the only time Bob was in a car accident and survived. When he was about 8, Mom was stopped at a red light on Rt. 123 when a Chevy came up from behind them seemingly unaware that the light was red. The real horror was that their old Buick had a rear-facing third seat with Bob and two siblings in it. After a bit of frantic but unproductive screaming, the Chevy driver managed to stomp his brakes enough to make the collision somewhat less than a "fender bender." In fact, it was more like a "bumper thumper" with no injuries, fortunately, and no damage to the Buick (they really were built like tanks in the '50s!)

Bob's most un-memorable car accident was the day he was born! Chuck got the call at work that Bob was about to make his grand entrance, and backed his Buick out of its space and smack into a customer's Electra awaiting service! He notified the boss of what happened headed home to pick up Angie and sped off to Stamford Catholic Hospital. Fortunately, Bob was undamaged when he emerged from his ten month prison sentence (he started life out stubborn.) Of course, he never heard the story until he was much older, but never figured it would be "one for the books." A more significant car accident happened when he was driving home from college in his new '73 Ford Maverick. His bud, Jim, was in the passenger seat on the ride home. As they traveled east on the relatively long stretch of Route 80 in Pennsylvania at about 80 miles per hour, a Volkswagen bus pulled out of the median strip, against all common sense and the law, and pulled directly into Bob's path. Of course, the bus struggled to get up to 20 mph with a boatload of what appeared to be very well-fed church-goers, forcing Bob to take immediate evasive action. The bus pulled into the passing lane, where Bob was after passing two tractor-trailers, so Bob moved over to the travel lane, all the while slowing down. Suddenly without warning, the bus pulled all the way across into the travel lane, which forced Bob to go left into the passing lane. Unfortunately, his momentum carried the car all the way onto the left shoulder, clipping one or more delineator poles in the process. Bob's next action was to find the relative safety of the right shoulder, now that the bus had made it up to speed. Unfortunately, the two tractor-trailers were now approaching from behind in the travel lane. Bob managed to quickly bleed more speed without fishtailing in the sand, and came to a dusty stop on the opposite   shoulder. Within a few seconds, both trucks blew by, at speed, apparently oblivious to the emergency.

When they finally came to a halt, Jim found himself, out of sheer fight or flight, down in the wheel well in front of the passenger seat. He was a bit shaken, but not injured in any way. In fact, within a few seconds he was laughing and yelled to Bob, "that was some damn good driving, asshole!" "Glad you enjoyed the ride." Bob fired back.

They got out to inspect the damage, not even realizing there was any at first. They quickly found that the driver side moulding was gone, as was the side view mirror. Otherwise, the car was fine. Since they were curious where the mirror ended up, they drove back to where they were forced into the median strip. After about a 10 minute search of the tall grass, they drove on to find the nearest State Trooper station.

Once they arrived, they explained to the duty officer what had transpired, but to no avail. The trooper told them that "since there was no contact with the other vehicle, they couldn't place any charges at all." That didn't seem fair, and Bob offered to take the trooper out to the spot where it all happened, but the trooper stood firm that nothing could be done. "No injury, no damage, no accident," was what Bob heard.

Bob and Jim went on their way to Connecticut, but when they stopped to take a leak at a rest stop down the highway, Bob reached into the back seat to get something. He was more than a bit surprised to find the missing side-view mirror! It had flown through Bob's open window past his head, nearly embedding itself into the back deck before tumbling into the seat with Jim's bags. They reckoned that had to be a close call and they were fortunate that that potential second rider didn't make the trip. That could have been real ugly.

Further discussion of the incident convinced them both that spending the extra money for the optional "wide stance" tires for the Maverick might just have saved their lives. Idle speculation. They'd never know.

❈❈❈

Of the many rites of passage that Bob endured, claiming the Grand Union as a newspaper boy was one of the most memorable. It was the first time he had gotten "tough" on a personal basis. He had already made financial arrangements with the paper boy who had "owned" the Grand Union as a selling spot and it went unchallenged for weeks. Out of the blue, a new kid, about Bob's age and stature showed up trying to sell papers. Bob wasted no time in confronting the new kid and educating him on the unwritten turf rules. After a brief, non-violent "discussion," the new kid went on his way to find another spot. But the brief encounter with "the competition" had its own lasting effect. While he was ready for a dust up, it didn't happen, which was a real surprise. He was so, so glad that the other kid wasn't big enough to wipe the sidewalk with him. Bob had already survived some altercations as a caddy, where the guys were much tougher and usually larger.

While Bob had his unfortunate dog incident when he was ten, he wasn't the only in the the family history that was attacked by a dog. His son Carl was mauled by a bloodhound that he was trying to catch for the owner as it ran wild through the park across the street. Ten year old son, Carl, received bites to his face that required over 100 stitches! But they were able to save his eye! The lawsuit that followed was, as expected, a farce, as the dog's owner tried to push the blame on Carl because "he should have never tried to catch the dog." The final settlement was put in trust until Carl's 21st birthday, and, in the end, wasn't enough to buy him a decent used car. A typical outcome for the New Jersey justice system.

Bob's first trip as a company commander to the field in Germany was a convoy to Massweiller caves on the French-German border. This complex still showed the signs Hitler's occupation, where the eagles had been removed from over the entryways, but their "shadows" in the concrete remained.

While there were several levels dug into the mountain, only the first level was accessible. All the others were deliberately flooded and said to be booby-trapped. The common theory, based on the size of the defunct industrial conveyor that could still be seen running between the first and second floor darkness, was that this was formerly an underground manufacturing facility.

It was a chilly wet November when they left Augsburg by convoy. As company commander and convoy leader Bob rode in a vintage Willys Jeep with a simple canvas top and, of course, no heat. He spent the entire four hour trip sucking diesel fumes from the many trucks in the convoy and ended up getting pneumonia the first day in the field. He went to see the medic who told him that he had to go back home to Augsburg. Bob, of course, refused since he was in charge of the entire comms center operation, which included 120 soldiers and almost 150 pieces of equipment. The medic then capitulated and directed Bob to eat everything in sight, drink constantly, and

"Oh by the way, while you're at it quit smoking," he added.

Bob followed these directions to the letter taking the cold pack decongestants and aspirin, drinking all the water and juice he could find, and constantly eating. He even forced himself to sneak stuff out of the mess hall so he had some snacks. On top of that, he quit smoking, cold turkey.

The following Friday the company had an opportunity to take a break from operations and go down to the local Gasthaus for some brew and chew. Bob's troops, with their usual sense of humor, purchased a pack of German L&M cigarettes. They all signed a beer coaster with "best of luck" and "we'll see what happens" and presented it to their Captain at the bar. The challenge of not lighting up in a German Gasthaus was a real one, since they are always full of smoke. Bob got a real chuckle out of the "gift" and packed it back home after the operation was completed.

Many years later that same pack of cigarettes ended up in his Army trunk and stashed in the basement. He had gone down to the basement one afternoon to look for something in the trunk and noticed that the cigarettes had been opened and a few were missing. Since Naomi was still a smoker, he didn't have to go far to find the culprit. On a prior occasion when Bob was out of town, Naomi ran out of cigarettes and was unable to get to the store. So she got into the trunk pulled out the old nasty, dried up, stale German cigarettes and decided they were good enough. He noticed that she never smoked more than two.

❖❖❖❖

For reasons Bob could never recall, he pledged a fraternity as a Freshman in college. He had been subjected to the "hard sell" during orientation, but never really knew why he chose THAT fraternity. Probably had something to do with academic "help" or some such promise. He managed to complete all the assigned tasks, humiliating and otherwise, right up until the Friday of Hell Week. Then they dropped the hammer. One Friday afternoon of "hell week,"a senior member of the fraternity tracked Bob down in his dorm room and asked him out into the stairwell for a "chat."

"Well, Bob," the fellow started, "We are not going to pledge you into the fraternity. It's nothing specific. We all think you're a nice guy, but we voted that you just don't fit in with our group." Bob was more relieved than disappointed. He knew exactly what "didn't fit in" meant. Bob didn't drink or smoke dope and many of the activities of the past weeks were based upon those vices. So, if he didn't fit in with a bunch of drunks and stoners, so be it. No regrets. As things turned out, he never did have time for the antics of a fraternity.

❖❖❖❖

One of the worst feelings Bob experienced was the day Cheryl revealed that she had a neighbor down the street that would be going to Alfred University with her. Bob had never met the fellow, but knew he was a local drug addict. Cheryl told Bob that she was going to "help" him. As Bob pulled away from Cheryl's house one late afternoon, he saw in his rear view this addict fellow headed into Cheryl's house. Bob was devastated. Things were going south just way too fast. "What the hell was he doing going in as Bob was just leaving?" As Bob coasted to the stop sign, Cecilia came on the car radio. His 10 inch speaker behind the back seat was vibrating with the base.

"THUMP, THUMP, THUMP"

Some lyrics about breaking my heart
THUMP, THUMP, THUMP.

Some more lyrics about coming home.
THUMP, THUMP, THUMP,"

By now Bob had made the 90 degree turn half way down the hillside without flipping the Saab, although it was close. He dared to accelerate down to the bottom of the hill, until he realized that his ability to stop at the end of the street was now very questionable. The music continued to drive him and the Saab.

More lyrics about breaking my heart and my confidence.....

THUMP, THUMP, THUMP.

The lumpy, bumpy Connecticut roads didn't make stopping the car any easier. Bob floored the brake pedal all the way to the firewall and put the car in second, forgetting that the car was in "freewheeling" mode, meaning no engine braking available. The little gray mouse bumped, skidded, slid and finally came to a halt about ten feet past the stop sign. Bob was highly pissed at himself. He reached up and turned off the radio. The big rear speaker immediately stopped vibrating. No more THUMP, THUMp, thump…. He took just a minute to settle himself, realizing that flying down that road the way he did was just plain stupid and not in his character or best interest.

He cranked the engine over, put it in first and crossed over 123 to Forest St. Just two turns from there and he'd be on Hoyt St., less than a few minutes left to totally calm his emotions before getting the third degree from Mom. While he managed to get past the Mom gauntlet, Bob couldn't stop thinking about what he saw. While Cheryl wouldn't kick him to the curb for another couple of months, he saw the handwriting on the wall. Cheryl was on a mission to fix a drug addict, so to speak. Nothing would detract her from her mission, especially since they would see each other every day on campus. He pulled out his best optimism card and convinced himself that this would all blow over.

Chapter 27~Just Building Fun Memories

Bob's memories of the big barn on the Failer estate were some he never shared. While he didn't have may opportunities to play in the barn because it was off-limits to the kids, he clearly remembers sneaking behind the wheel of a big green Ford Woody wagon and later, finding old toys on the second floor (definitely off limits), including some toy clay bricks and tubes of oil paints. The excursion can be described as both a day of fun discovery and of "pushing the limits" at a very young age.

Another fond memory made at a very young age was Bob's "Banana chews" excursion. At about age 9, Bob took off down Hoyt St across the very busy Maple Ave and up about a quarter mile to the Mars convenience store (or what passed for convenience store in the '60s). He had heard that they were selling banana and mint chews at two for a penny! He had just twenty-five cents to his name, but that got him a bagful of tooth-destroying taffy squares, which he, of course, promptly bit into on his way back home, Mom was right there to greet him when he bounded up the front steps.

"Just where have you been, young man?" She asked with that "look" every mother learns from the start. She always knew when something was up. It was almost mystical.

"I just went to the store to get some banana chews. They were just two for a penny," he replied, thinking that is "great deal" would garner a more relaxed response from Mom.

"You mean to tell me that you crossed Maple Avenue just to get candy? Have I taught you nothing about these roads and the crazy drivers around here?"

He hesitated to answer, knowing no answer was good enough at this juncture. "Sorry, Mom, but I did listen to all your instruction about crossing the street and I did it right." He finally replied.

It took him nearly two weeks to chew through all fifty hard taffy pieces, but longer to chew on Mom's disappointment and anger. In the end, it was just an early adventure, excursion, experience. Nobody was harmed in the filming of this episode.

❧❦❧

When Bob was about 11, he went down to Cosgrave's to play. There were several kids there he didn't know. When they decided to go explore the neighbor's back yard, which was an overgrown mess, Bob tagged along just out of curiosity. After a few minutes looking around, two of the older kids came up with the odd idea of an "initiation" of the younger kids. They never did say what they'd be initiated into. They managed to sucker one of the young kids into dropping his pants and running the full fence line of the overgrown yard. The kid even took off in his tighty-whities to meet the challenge. Once he got to the back part of the yard, he started screaming and crying. He managed to struggle his way back to the group. That's when they all noticed that the kid was being chased by a rather large swarm of yellow jackets.

Within seconds, there was the nightmarish scene of half a dozen young kids screaming, running and tearing off clothes as they tried to escape the angry stingers. By the time the first kid made it out of the yard and across the stream, he was down to his birthday suit, and somehow, his shoes. As each kid passed through the hole in the fence, fewer and fewer bees were swarming, as if to say "keep out and we won't bother you."

Bob had hung back observing the whole episode from the hole in the fence, so he fortunately had no stings. There would have been no way to explain that to Mom.

When the coast was clear, each boy quietly retrieved their clothing, not wasting any time. While it was going to be a funny anecdote later in life, we were just glad none of the boys were allergic. So much for trespassing and silly initiations.

❊❊❊

One of the greatest non-career accomplishments of the Vitti family was brother John's hand-painted mural of the Beatles Yellow Submarine Album cover on the bedroom wall. It took him an entire summer while home from UCONN to complete. When done, it was an absolute masterpiece, worthy of the Museum of Modern Art. But true to Vitti karma, the wall was unceremoniously destroyed when Mom's house was sold to pay the nursing home and soon torn down to make room for a larger house. There was a great deal of artistic ability in the family. But the display of that talent was rare.

❖❖❖

The best caddy lunch Bob ever had was on a dreary, rainy day in a temporary trailer serving as the pro shop when the original hundred-year old pro shop and caddy shack were being rebuilt. Pete handed Bob a 20 and told him to go downtown to the Grimaldi deli. There he was to get two orders of lamb stew and some French bread. Being the dutiful servant, Bob got in his Saab and made his way down to Elm St in town. He had never been in this deli before, but from his many years of delivering newspapers, he knew where it was. In a matter of minutes, he was headed back up Smith Ridge with a rainy day lunch for two. This was so out of character for Salitti, not only to invite Bob to chow, but to pay for it, Bob was a bit confused. However, just one taste of the stew and Bob forgot anything else he might have been thinking. This was a small reward for Bob from his otherwise gruff boss. Partake and enjoy!

After lunch, Bob brewed two cups of fresh Maxwell House coffee. He would aways remember the keen taste of the coffee at the caddy shack and attributed it to the iron content of the Connecticut well water. Just fantastic! And Bob really wasn't a coffee drinker. He liked his bottled coke and the occasional Nehi Grape or Root Beer, but coffee was a bit too mature for him. But he thoroughly enjoyed the caddy shack coffee that day!

He didn't realize it at the time, but that day was sort of an unannounced "right of passage." A recognition and acceptance of who he was. Indeed, there was a new sense of mutual acceptance after that rainy day lunch.

❖❖❖❖

A popular pastime to occupy the caddies time between loops was gambling. While 21 and Acey Deucey were the most popular ways for the older guys to take the leaches' money, pitching pennies was a game that required some actual skill. Of course, only sissies actually tossed pennies. Nickels, dimes or quarters were most often the buy-in.

The game was simple. Pick a wall and mark a toss line some distance away and toss the coins, one at a time. Whoever got theirs closest to the wall took them all. Unless someone tossed a "leaner." Then all the others had to pay them double. While there were often arguments about who was actually closer, there was always an older caddy hanging around to settle the squabble.

Nobody ever lost much in the coin tossing. Not like the card games, where 10-15-20 bucks could be in the pot in any given hand. The younger kids always backed away from those games. Except Bob, of course. He was never afraid to jump into a game. It took him a while to realize that the older guys were strangely winning way too many hands. It was his good sense telling him that he was up agains a little caddy "mafia" and he would never win more than a couple paltry hands.

✻✻✻

Another fun contest was car coasting. Country Club Road was conveniently downhill for about half a mile, but the drivers had to hang a right on Indian Rock Road to finish the route, twisting and turning around the back of the golf course past some of the biggest homes in town. The contest was simple. Start at the top of the road where it left Rt 123 and without starting the car, roll down the hill as fast as your dare to see who could coast the farthest. Their skill and risk were challenged as the roads in rural CT in the '60s wavy, bumpy and pothole plagued. Knowing where all the bad spots were and avoiding them became the tougher part of the challenge.

While Bob's free-wheeling Saab transmission made it a pure coaster, cousin Jimmy's '59 Chevy was much heavier, often taking him out nearly to the end of Indian Rock Road.

Despite the inherent risk in this type of "soapbox derby," there was never a wreck or injury. Interestingly, the derby was not continued when the younger kids advanced to senior caddies. No guts, no glory?

❄❖❄❖❄

Despite some ugly incidents, Bob's four-year tour of Germany had been both wonderful and awful. It was the first time in Europe for himself and his family. His first encounter with a German was a total language disaster. He had taken the train to the port on the north coast where the soldiers' cars were delivered. Once he arrived at Bremerhaven, he had to take a cab to the dock. "Bitte, ich muss mein Auto am Dock absholem." He knew he had butchered the German language. But, before he could give it another try, the driver asked, "so you need to go pick up your car?" in educated English.

Bob was more surprised than mortified, but it was close.

"Yes, I've just been transferred to Augsburg."

"What kind of car do you drive?" The driver asked.

"A Porsche."

"Excellent! He replied. Then, after a slight pause, "You know you could have bought one here, right?"

Everybody's a comedian.

The process of picking up the car was well rehearsed and simple. The vehicle had been searched for contraband, per SOP. Bob was handed a damage inspection sheet to conduct his own walk-around. Nothing was out of sorts. No harm done. He handed the sheet back to the agent, who tore off the yellow copy and handed it back. The agent then asked to see the LT's European insurance card, and took a copy. He then handed over the keys and said, "It's ready to go, drive carefully. Weather's coming in."

The LT pulled out into the massive parking lot to review his map. He knew the major highway back to Augsburg in the south, but signage was much different in Germany. Highway signs showed what major cities or areas were "down the road." Signs displaying "north, south, east, and west" were pretty much nonexistent. He knew what major highway he had to find, but asking directions in a foreign country was iffy, at best. Fortunately, his cab driver was idling at the far end of the parking lot, waiting for a fare. Bob pulled up beside the cab and the driver kindly showed him the way to the highway. A moment later, it began to rain. He checked his wipers and all was well. He turned on the headlights, and they worked just fine. Now for the defroster. It took a few minutes for the air-cooled engine to produce anything resembling warm air, especially since it was about 35 degrees out! It was also getting a bit dark with the weather coming in.

When everything checked out, he headed for the highway. The cab driver's instructions were perfect and he was headed south on the autobahn in about ten minutes. By then, the rain has turned to frozen rain. Despite the lack of warmth from the air cooled engine, he had a driving confidence and competence that kept him safely on the road. Despite faster Porsches and Mercedes running past him at 100 kilometers per hour, he managed to stay "straight and level" for the next 6 hours.

✳✳✳✳

One of the most enjoyable pastimes for Bob and the crew was bowling and pizza. Bob, Jim and Greg, along with one or two of the girls that hung around from time to time, would roll a few games at Rip Van Winkle lanes and then head over to Springfield Pizza for a couple of slices and some juke box tunes. The regular standard was Steppenwolf's <u>Born to Be Wild</u>. They spun it up even before ordering their pizza on most nights. The pizza was always excellent and the tunes even better. Which almost made up for the fact that none of them could bowl worth a damn. Bob's best was 205 and the others around the same. But, it was a boatload of fun and kept them off the streets.

✳✳✳✳

Another funny bowling story surrounds Bob's first date with a redhead he met at the library. They both spend endless hours in the town library sometimes perusing the racks for topics of interest, or just sitting by the large window reading. He decided to take her bowling to get better acquainted, but got quite a surprise once they started the game. He couldn't help but notice a scar on each of her thumbs. She noticed that he noticed and explained that she was born with four thumbs and had two removed as a baby. She bowled just fine, but Bob had a bit of a challenge getting his head around being born with four thumbs. There never was a second date, for no thumb reason.

One of teenage Bob's newfound passions was pinball. The Corner Cigar Store had the only game in town. A single dime got the lights flashing and the bells ringing. It was mesmerizing. Then again, so was the store. It was owned and operated by an old, gray couple that keep the place clean and tidy. The odor of fresh cigars hung like moss on an old southern oak. He might have eventually bought a car with all the dimes he stuffed into that pinball machine. Like any addiction, the more he won, the more he played.

On one lazy afternoon, as Bob was trying to beat the high score once again, in strolled a fellow in a leather jacket and Army boots. The two eventually struck up a conversation about mostly nothing. However, in a later discussion, this much older George fellow talked about his time in the jungles of Vietnam as a sniper. The details he shared with Bob were both shocking and intriguing. The conversation seemed to never end. This otherwise nice guy was a trained killer. He never bragged about his "kills," but it was obvious he was good at his job. He talked about vantage points, cover and concealment, tying himself to trees, light discipline, fields of fire and knowing the enemy, especially enemy snipers. He disappeared from the pinball scene as quickly as he had appeared. Bob later wondered if, just maybe, he had imagined the whole thing. He never saw the sniper again. But he always remembered the story.

Chapter 28~It's the Flashes, Not the Photos

ost folks have never stopped to consider things that they witness every day that have a sneaky impact on how we think. For example, near the end of his senior year in college, Bob was hired by Professional Golfer Jack Nicklaus' management team to photograph the Boy Scout breakfast at the Dayton Convention Center. The event was both publicity for Jack's new Muirfield Village golf course in Columbus and for the co-located Six Flags amusement park. Bob went about his business doing his best to capture the event, all the while a bit enamored and distracted by the very presence of the greatest golfer of his day! However, when it came time to actually buy some pictures, not a single photo was purchased! Bob was beside himself, second-guessing his product and quality. He had never been shut out by any customer until then. After all, the whole idea was to capture the event in photographs to publish or share within the Nicklaus organization and the press. The Boy Scout Council might have purchased a few for their own publicity.

However, it didn't go that way. Many years intervened before the lesson was learned through the catch phrase "Sell the sizzle, not the steak." In other words, Bob had been hired to provide a sense of "importance," a perception of great things going on, similar to the carnival barker shouting "Just two bits to see the man eating chicken!"   For the first time, he understood that for most, "perception is reality." They probably never had any intention of actually buying photos, but just wanted the presence of a "photographer" to give credibility to the event. As you go back in history, the drums, the elephants, the trumpets and the strumpets, the cameras, the large, noisy flash bulbs of the 20th century all just to build the false perception of something important going on.

Had he any idea of this farcical approach to building perception, Bob just may have doubled his appearance fee for the breakfast. Unfortunately, he never charged an "appearance" fee. Live and learn.

❈❈❈

As a Freshman in college, Bob learned a powerful lesson on the importance of attention to detail. He was just starting to look for ways make money through photography. He decided to borrow an idea he'd seen around: Photographing martial arts, like Tai Kwan Do, Karate and Judo. Despite the fact that he had no experience photographing in this area, he paid to have some business cards printed up and started posting them around on bulletin boards.

One Monday after classes, Bob returned to the dorm to find a note from the chaplain to "come see me." Turned out that a simple typo had the priest spinning in his collar with concern. The business card he pulled off the board in the Student Center was advertising "marital arts," instead of "martial arts." And despite the fact that there was no <u>Funk and Wagnalls</u> definition for "marital arts," the priest had made his own interpretation and decided it was the work of the devil. Nasty idea to photograph couples in the act. The priest should have researched a bit more.

In the end, though, it amounted to nothing more than hard-earned money wasted on business cards. Bob should have triple-checked the spelling. Lesson learned, again, at little cost.

Chapter 29~Barefoot and Pregnant

The study of Anthropology has confirmed that all species require a hierarchical structure to survive in the long term. Humans are no different. It would have been quite helpful, however, had someone in the nurturing and teaching chain, be it the parents, nuns, priests, or teachers had actually revealed the truth of the class system to the kids. The only glimmer Bob ever got was from Angie's repeatedly saying that "Those rich people are no better than you," and alternately, "Those damn rich people!" That only served to convince the kids, Bob included, that they were poor! In turn, that put proper emphasis on the non-productive whining and complaining by all poor classes. To reinforce the mantra, social studies experts have long determined that "misery loves company." Phrases like " You'll have to live without it" and "We can't afford that" were commonplace in poor homes.

While there never was a known "official policy" on keeping the country's workers poor, it didn't take a genius to figure it out. Throughout history, the peasants were fed crumbs, while the elites ate pheasant. And it doesn't take a cynic to soon believe that it is all intentional, at least "behind the scenes," a bit like the secret handshakes of those mysterious community service clubs. There were rules and customs that were adhered to, but rarely spoken of and never, ever written down.

Keeping the peasants distracted worked well. From harvest festivals to fish on Fridays, the lower class was easily distracted through entertainment when force was not practical. In the 20th century, it was music, movies and TV, especially TV, that was used "en masse" not only to distract through entertainment, but to also condition through the mesmerization of repetition.

One major theme pushed by the rich and powerful was "knowing your place." If you were born to poverty, then deal with it. It's your lot to be poor and hungry. If you want more, go work for it. One of Bob's Commanders in Germany had a plaque on his desk stating: Nichts ist kostenlos/*Nothing is Free.* Unfortunately, for most, it's nearly impossible to escape poverty, regardless of race or ethnicity. But the elusive carrot was always there. In the meantime, just know your place. Strangely enough, this oppressive mentality was passed from generation to generation, maintaining a death grip century after century, primarily through long-standing traditions and peer pressure acceptance. After all, if just anyone was granted access to the great gilded halls of business and politics, who would be left to collect the garbage and fight the wars? There has to be a class system to preserve not just the "order of things," but to ensure the survival of the culture. "Just who do you think you are coming into a fine establishment like this?" Was not only aimed at Blacks.

All human subjects are expendable. That concept of "expiration of human usefulness" wasn't limited to Army troops and German Jews. It was prevalent in every society. Throughout history, peasants were needed to do all the "lesser" jobs for the king. They were allowed to eke out a living on the land, as long as the king always got the best of everything. As the Industrial Revolution kicked into gear, the same peasant class was the human backbone of the factories. While the power had been spread a bit beyond the grasp of the royalty, a new industrial power gentry was born, including Carnegie, Rockefeller, Morgan and a host of other great industrialists. The peasant class, however, gained little. They considered themselves fortunate to have enough income to put food on the table, if not heat the hovel. Those fortunate to have a sellable skill and some hustle, like Michael and Antonio, had the advantage over their peers. They were able to obtain positions with the wealthy elite of that New York or Connecticut and build a solid foundation from which their descendants could launch a decent life.

If only to confirm his suspicions, Bob later learned that the high schools, especially in the wealthier towns, had an undocumented process of channeling students into either "academic" or "trade" career paths, "for their own good," of course. That served well to reinforce the hierarchical class system that nobody appeared to openly acknowledge or discuss. The poor constantly bitched about the wealthy, and the wealthy tolerated the existence of the poor. A balance of power, so to speak. After all, what's a war without soldiers?

A more philosophically interesting and intriguing revelation came slowly to Bob. That is, some religions prefer that their followers be poor generation after generation. That mentality further ensures workers for the fields and factories. The Catholic Church was famous for this. For centuries the Church promoted large families, even if that meant living in poverty. Misery loves company, right? The Baptists, on the other hand, had no issue with wealthy worshipers. The richer your followers, the more money flowed into church coffers. That translated into more and bigger churches, more "missions" to other countries and bigger, better cars for the preachers. That message came across loud and clear when Bob was hired to videotape a Baptist revival. The guest preacher expounded upon wealth and poverty and claimed outright that "Nowhere in the Bible does it say that pious men cannot be wealthy." That hit Bob like a sandbag dropped from the catwalk. Just think, God does not require you to be poor! That was only for Catholic priests, he thought. It's called the vow of poverty, which, incidentally, he never observed in the Northfield parish. Huh.

Chapter 30~Surprises and Awakenings

On the rare occasion that some of the guys piled into one of their cars and went into town to get lunch at the Italian Deli by the firehouse, Bob would always hear "Whadya wan on you sangawish Vitti?" as he entered the door. The short but stout owner, Nicoletti, still had a thick Italian accent even though he'd been in the country for decades. But everyone knew what he was saying and he rarely had to repeat himself.

The front door to the deli was spring-tethered screen door with a "Pepsi' push bar that closed with a noticeable "screech-thump." Nicoletti always knew when someone came or left. The store was small, with sturdy oak and glass coolers, each with it's own large chrome handle which opened with some effort, but closed with authority.

For sixty cents, Nicoletti would make him a simple bologna and cheese on a hard roll with mustard, but for a buck he could get a half-loaf Italian with the works! Roast beef, ham, capicola, prosciutto, cheese, lettuce, tomato with oil and vinegar! The fresh-baked Italian bread, alone, was worth the trip. Not even the older, bigger caddies were hungry after a half-loaf! Bob stuck to the smaller hard roll sandwich, sometimes bologna, sometimes ham. It filled the bill. But, it was not an every day feed, or he'd risk running out of lunch money.

Every guy in history most likely got a "Dear John" letter at some point, abruptly ending a relationship with his girl. It was a very common occurrence during wartime, as uncertainty mixed with loneliness to sway girls from their promises.

Bob's came in the form of a letter in the mail from Cheryl, who wrote, ad nauseam, how it just wasn't looking good for them after just a few months apart at different colleges. More fodder for those who believe that long distance relationships just don't work.

He wasn't at first convinced that it was all bad. His immediate reaction was in the range of expected rage. Another student had just received a wood-crated stereo straight from Japan and left the empty crate in the hallway. Bob asked one of the other students to hold it out so that Bob could beat the crap out of it. It worked great to relieve some of the anger quite quickly and his knuckles only bled for a bit.

The other thought Bob had was the guilt of being free from the shackles of a young relationship. It was both liberating and frustrating. Another of life's initiations better experienced early in life. He was back out on campus checking out the girls the next day. No drunken fits. No driving the car like bat out of hell to nowhere. Just one phone call to see if the relationship could be recovered. No go.

❈❈❈

He sat there in his uncomfortable easy chair and took a couple of laps around his his cerebellum in search of the next jump-off point. He decided he needed to clear up some details of his early life.

He struggled to get a grip on writing more of this hopefully great story. He wandered into the kitchen to make a cup of tea. Tea had always been his drink of choice since high school. He made a bit of a ritual of his evening tea in his off-campus apartment, often with an un-toasted cinnamon Pop-Tart, since he didn't have a toaster. The caffeine never affected his sleep and didn't become any concern until he was in his 60s.

Over the decades, a cup of tea became a simple escape from whatever was bugging him at the time, be it bad bosses, unruly children, hormonal teens, or greedy contractors. His wife, Naomi, also grew up on tea. Her Grandma Rose would put the pot on the wood stove before breakfast, and they would draw from that same pot well into the evening. By that time, that pot of tea was well brewed.

While Bob was always thin, he certainly had no eating disorders, unless you consider his addiction to sugar. He spend all too much of hard-earned money on candy, pastries and ice cream. All the kids got their share of Mom's grub on a regular basis, but all grew at their own rate. Bob remained a lightweight until he was a couple of years in the military and finally made it to 150 pounds. He was still 150 on his 70th birthday. Beyond the basics, Bob had no real favorites when if came to food other than sweets. He wasn't born with a sweet tooth, he was born with 32 sweet teeth, half of which were eventually pulled when they rotted out.

He learned early what he could get for 25 cents at any store in Northfield. He might get five candy bars, two Ding Dongs, an ice cream sandwich, or some of the best jelly beans on the planet at the Swiss Chalet confectionary.

He never tired of sugar. Much later in life, Bob even tried to find those same uniquely fantastic jelly beans through extensive searches of the internet, but failed.

❖❖❖❖

Bob's earliest memory of being disappointed by an adult was the Nu-V vitamin bar incident. One of Dad's customers found out that he was also a Scout Leader and asked him to conduct an informal survey of the new Nu-V vitamin snack bar. Dad handed Bob a case of the product and instructed him to make sure all the scouts got one.

Well, Bob thought he would have time to sample one, himself. He thought wrong. Although he managed to lug the case into the campground, along with his backpack and other camp gear, it seemed Dad wasn't happy that the case of goodies ended up, unopened, in Bob's tent until the next morning. Dad located and took the case when the guys were at breakfast, not telling Bob anything.

When the guys returned from breakfast, there was Dad handing out a bar to each guy and saying "Let me know what you think." Bob was more than devastated that Dad didn't trust him to do the job and that Dad didn't bother to tell him what he was doing.

On the one hand, Bob though he'd hit it rich with all this food product. On the other, he kinda knew that he was enacting his first "power play" of sorts in holding on the whole case just a bit longer. But he learned what it was like to he given a responsibility only to have the rug pulled out from under him even before he made his play. It was the first time, but it wouldn't be the last, for sure.

As far as the product survey went, it was a total bust. The attempt to cover up the nasty taste of vitamins with a coating of chocolate was a real miss! It would be another decade before any company successfully conjured up a vitamin bar that met the taste test. This one, however, was a big fail. At least it didn't give anyone the "turkey trots."

Chapter 31~The Search for Leaders

One of the individuals who impressed Bob early in his career was the E8 that ran the Field Wire Course, Bob's first assignment as Office in Charge. Chief Bazaan, as he was called, was a former tribal Chief, and completely looked the part. Dark-skinned, barrel chested, huge smile. He looked like the old Cigar Store Indian on steroids. He knew his job inside and out, got along with his peers and superiors, who respected him without question, and ran the school without breaking a sweat. He had done a tour or two in Vietnam, but didn't speak of it. The daily operation went so well, that the Chief spent his lunch hours playing Spades with the female E4 clerk assigned to the front office. If there was a spark of romance between the two, Bob didn't notice and didn't go looking for it. They worked extremely well together and that's all that mattered.

Part of taking over as Officer In Charge was completing an inventory of all government equipment. Anything missing was usually charged to the outgoing officer.

Because it was a communications school, there was a lot of expensive equipment to manage and secure. Before the first inventory day got started, the Chief pulled Bob aside and whispered to him "Make sure you check inside the SB 86 battery box." Nothing more. The

Chief knew that the very expensive batteries were missing, and, for whatever reason, he made sure that Bob, an officer he just met, wouldn't take the hit for it. They got along famously for the duration of the tour and Bob never forgot that unexpected kindness.

As Chief Bazaan walked the LT around the school facilities, they came across a class in session on pole climbing. Every 36K Field Wireman had to be able to climb utility poles as part of their tactical training. As the LT stood there observing the lesson, the Lead Instructor, who the LT had not yet met, motioned for the LT to come closer to the pole. The SGT introduced himself and then introduced the LT to the class of 20 or so trainees.

"Gentlemen, this is your new OIC, LT Vitti."

"LT, have you ever climbed a utility pole before?"

"No, SGT, never."

"Trainees, I realize that some of you are convinced that climbing this 30 foot pole is an impossible task. However, I will show you just how simple it is by teaching our new OIC how it's done and sending him to the top and back down."

There was a bit of huff and guffaw from the trainees and more than a bit of disbelief from the class.

In the next five minutes, the instructor explained the process and suited up the LT to climb.

"All I want you to do, LT, is climb the pole the way I just showed you, and ring the bell at the top. Beware, that most guys who burn the pole do it on the way down. Please, LT, don't burn the pole. You'll make me look bad." He said with a chuckle. The class responded in kind.

The LT shoved his first gaff in with just a bit too much force, making it hard to remove and relocate higher. But he managed. Hand over hand, foot over foot, one step at at time and before his nerves shattered, he was ringing the bell. But only after he almost crashed and burned when his lead hand went right over the pole before he knew he had reached the top.

After ringing the bell and getting a cheer from the class, below, he carefully went into descent mode, foot under foot, hand under hand, until he was finally reunited with terra firm. Applause from the class, along with the usual trainee wise cracks tempered for an Officer's ears.

"That, Ladies and Gentlemen, is how it is done!" declared the Instructor. Just a few minutes ago, this young Lieutenant had never climbed a pole. After 5 minutes of instruction, which is far, far less than you will receive, he clambered up this pole and back home without even a single splinter. Congratulations, Sir, and thank you for your help. You did a great job."

They exchanged a salute and the LT left the pole farm with the Chief.

"Did you put them up to that, Chief?" Asked the LT.

"Me, Sir? Well, I would never do anything like that, Sir." Chief protested.

But the smile on Chief's face betrayed his answer.

"So, this is how it's going to be, eh?" The LT asked himself. "Hell, I can deal with this." He assured himself, as the Chief took him into the next classroom. "This might just be fun."

❖❖❖

Bob was elected President of the Catholic Youth Organization as a high school freshman. The duties were simple, and didn't take a lot of his time, except for trip planning. The group decided to put together a ski trip, which Bob balked at since he'd never touched a ski. But he put the trip together with the eager help of some of the parents.

A few weeks later, the group jumped on a bus and rode up to a ski area in Vermont. Bob was a bit enamored by all the young ski bunnies he encountered for the first time.

He managed a couple of snow-plow trips down the lower part of the slopes without killing himself or anyone else. But, he was way, way out of his element. From the clothes to his inability to show any skill, whatsoever, on the rented skis, Bob learned that not everything comes easy.

But, alas, the ski trip was a rousing success and the reviews from the parents were plentiful and sincere. As President of the CYO, Bob had pulled off a successful and safe ski trip for a couple of dozen hormonal teens without incident. The next time he would put skis on was while on Army tactical winter survival training in the Bavarian Alps! But, that's a story for another day.

❖❖❖❖❖

"Get these fatsos out out of my comms center!", was the order Bob got from the Division commander who was inspecting the communications center in support of the annual REFORGER exercises. There had been a major push in recent months to slim down the Army, physically. New health and fitness programs were instituted across the forces to lose the fat and get the troops in fighting condition. While Infantry and other combat units were usually in excellent shape, the Intelligence and other support entities ("rear echelon MFs") were regularly out of shape. And while recent efforts led by the Sergeant Major were having some success, many overweight "lifers" were just not making any progress.

The primary measure of fitness was the annual physical fitness test every troop had to pass. While there were always a few who were ordered into remedial fitness programs, the vast majority would do the requisite pushups, sit-ups and complete the two mile run in the prescribed time. But the PT test had no direct correlation to body fat. Dietary guidelines were slow to be implemented and always voluntary. But there was always at least one field grade officer who would make it his personal mission to "remove the fatties."

The General in the comms van had a valid point, but an unproductive approach. Bob escorted the two Sergeants off the site and told them to keep themselves busy but out of sight. There would be no punitive action taken, since being reprimanded by the General in front of the troops was punishment enough for senior NCOs. Message sent and received, General.

✵✵✵✵✵

Bob's first assignment out of Signal Officer Basic School, was to the 21st Replacement Depot in Fort Hood, Texas, a unit he knew nothing about. He tapped a few of the local personnel resources and discovered that, if he ended up at Ft. Hood with the Vietnam war still going on, the odds were better than 50/50 that he would end up in the combat zone within a few months. The mission of that unit was to assign troops to combat units and train them up for deployment. Bob wasn't having anything to do with that, if at all possible. The only thing that bothered him more than dying for his country, was killing for his country!

Bob knew he had to find a way out of these orders. Vietnam was not in his future, if he had anything to do with it. He contacted Officer Assignment Branch in Washington, D.C.. After a long and "educational" discussion with LTC in charge of new officer assignments, Bob struck a deal to get his orders changed in exchange for one extra year of obligated service. His new orders would read Ft. Leonard Wood, MO. Saved from war, at least for now.

✹✹✹✹✹

A few months earlier, Bob had another odd opportunity to get out of his service obligation. Every officer was required to pass a complete physical before being commissioned. For cadets coming out of University of Dayton, the recruitment center in Cincinnati was the assigned clinic.

Once the physical was complete and Bob was awaiting results, the Warrant Officer in charge came by to chat.

The first thing out of his mouth was: "I can get you out."

"Out? Out of what?" Asked Bob.

"Your service commitment," the Warrant replied, seriously stone-faced.

"How can you do that?" Bob asked.

"You have a protein disorder. All I need is the clinic commander's signature, and your are free to return to whatever you want. No commission, no service commitment. Certainly, no Vietnam."

Bob sat back in his chair, eyes wide open, trying to understand that this was not a joke. Somewhere in the regs, the Warrant had found a reference to Protenuria as grounds for release for medical reasons.

"But you have to decide right here, right now." The Warrant added. " Once the Colonel signs your health report, the option disappears.

Time never passed so quickly, except during a Calculus test. And it was just as stressful. He had learned plenty about decision analysis and making hard decisions, but not under these conditions. Many years later, he wrote a graduate paper on the dilemma of making decisions with less than perfect data. But, just how do you make a life-altering decision in just a "few minutes?"

You call on your heroes. What would they do? Cowards don't run. Challenge and adversity are the lifeblood of all heroes, real or TV phonies. Besides, this was the only plan Bob had. If he took the "out," he'd be back in his apartment in Dayton, trying to plan his future with just a few bucks in the bank. It just didn't sit well from any perspective. After all, he was raised to keep his commitments, regardless. That was a decision that made itself.

The conversation with the Warrant when he returned was short and to the point.
"Thanks, but I'm going to keep my commitment."

The Warrant just shrugged his shoulders and returned to the commander's office to get the physical signed adding "temporary" to the description of the condition. That one word changed his career before it even began.

Managing 120 troops and even more pieces of construction equipment can require a big pair of stones, and more than a few good NCOs. Bob's most challenging convoy was from Picatinny Arsenal in New Jersey to Camp Edwards in western Cape Cod, Massachusetts. In 1978, He was assigned as an Engineer Platoon Leader in a Reserve Unit even though he was Communications Officer. (Beggars can't be choosers.)

The road trip was to complete the two week summer training required by all Reservists every year. Their mission was to build two road drainage culverts and prepare ground for a ball field. There were also a couple of other other building tasks to be completed in the two week period.

The convoy began uneventful enough, but got very sketchy very quickly as the vehicles moved through NYC. One of the fuel tankers holding 5,000 gallons of gasoline took the wrong exit off the GW bridge and ended up in a not so nice neighborhood. The recovery was unnerving, but successful. They didn't spill a drop or get involved with the locals. Taking a wrong turn was a mistake none of them ever wanted to make again.

Once successfully in place at Camp Edwards, with camp set up before dark, they were ready to start building the following morning. The culverts under the main road went in quickly and without great effort. The ball field project, which everyone wanted to work on, was a bit more involved and took the better part of the first week before it met the established standards.

The four outbuildings were tackled the second week, but not before an unheard of "beer run" on Saturday afternoon. Bob was taken aback by the adamant way the New Jersey Reservists demanded they take the 2 1/2 ton truck to the local market for "supplies." After Bob queried the Company Commander for his approval, two senior NCOs and a driver took off on their supply run. While the whole effort seemed absurdly against regulations, it was more like routine for this unit. The "beer run" was a thing. It supported morale. And since there were no drunken brawls for the duration, all's well that ends well.

The two-week mission was a total success and Bob learned a valuable lesson: Flexibility in command.

Chapter 32~The Politics of Apathy

Bob had, of course, experienced a great deal of apathy and incompetence over the years. In fact, some of his first writing assignments addressed the abject apathy of students at UD. There was always a handful of greasy long-hairs pissing on Nixon and giving childish speeches on the front steps of the Kennedy Student Center. Agitating for more power over the administration, these anarchist wannabes had no future and were just hoping to get their face on the cover of the campus newspaper. And the newspaper too often obliged. With ideas like courses on getting laid and other sex-infested course ideas. Sure. On a Catholic campus. Good luck with that, hippie! The Student Council was a prime mover in the attempt to command attention and make "change." But, once past the newspaper articles, there was no substance. Perhaps it was the lesson for the apathetic. Nothing works "right" when you are not in charge. And these left-wing nut jobs were not in charge of the college, and never would be. The otherwise preoccupied and apathetic student body was not supporting their anarchy.

At one point, they threatened to burn down the ROTC building and advocate for the total removal of all military from the campus and the curriculum. During the Vietnam war, the military was an easy target, even if nothing positive could possibly come from dismissing the program from campus. The administration put a stop to that almost immediately, with the ready help of the Pentagon. Unfortunately, it was a bit risky to go about campus in uniform. But that, too, was long gone in a few weeks. The anarchists had no power, but they didn't come to that conclusion until they were the ones being shut down and finally escorted off campus. A conservative Christian school had only so much tolerance for such Godless subversive nonsense.

The football team continued to lose season after season. The University of Dayton (UD) players continued with their plays and variety shows, classes continued and the band played on. Ironically, common sense won the day against the nasty bastards of the anarchist underworld. At least this time.

Incompetence, on the other had, was pervasive no matter where you looked.

A great example of incompetence and self-importance occurred during Bob's time at the Signal Officer Advanced Course at Ft. Gordon, GA. Every officer in every school was pulled out of class for a presentation in the central auditorium on the newest electronic position location system. While it was interesting enough in terms of technology, Bob realized the system would not be available for the field for probably ten years. The very next morning, the students were ordered back to the auditorium for a repeat performance of the same presentation. Word through the grapevine revealed that "some generals" were flying in to see the presentation and they didn't dare have an empty auditorium! So, like a Hollywood movie, they took the bums off the street, dressed them up, and paid them five bucks to act as "extras." The only difference is that the officers didn't get the five bucks. But, like so, so many times in history, the officers "followed orders" and filled the seats so the Generals wouldn't have to see an empty auditorium. True leadership at its best.

When assigned to the computer center at Ft. Hunter Liggett, Bob returned from travel to find a half dozen new, shrink-wrapped mid-frame computers sitting in the hall. Turned out, some Congressman forced the higher headquarters to purchase these systems "for the field," although he had no business force feeding technology to the troops. This is the raging ego and money driven incompetence Bob witnessed throughout his career. These useless computers ended up in Bob's computer center because the higher headquarters had an upcoming inspection and had to "get rid of" the unwanted, unusable hardware. So they were dumped at the computer center at Hunter Liggett, and other test sites, with no instructions, no mission and no support. Just deal with it, Captain.

Chapter 33~Why is Life so Hard?

As Bob looked back on what he'd already written, he noticed a consistent theme of poverty, hard work and tough times. And forever being cold. He contemplated how it measured up to any average life in the world, but lacked any meaningful point of comparison.

Another less-than-fond memory involved a "new student' at St. Alphonse with more than a couple of screws loose. He was the cousin to one of the girls in the class, who was one of the best and brightest. It was a revelation to see that two such different characters could come out of the same gene pool. The Principal decided that the new kid, Darrel, needed a constant companion from first bell to last. Bob was volunteered for the position. Bob spent the rest of the year shadowing Darell so he wouldn't get into trouble before climbing back into his mommy's car at the end of the day. This batshit crazy kid was what society later tagged as "Special Needs" child. Alas, it was a good lesson in reality for Bob.

It had to suffice that life is messy, it's hard. You have to take it as it comes and manage the ups and downs, unless you are a third world dictator or the Queen, herself. Then, all your challenges are met and handled by your staff. While the life of millionaires and billionaires seems to be so much easier than the average

Joe, he felt walking a mile in their shoes would be necessary to fully resolve the question: "Can the life of a millionaire be as hard as that of a worker drone?" For now, Bob could only imagine an answer.

But for the commoner, the drones, the minions, putting food on the table was the essential challenge, not what helicopter to buy for the yacht.

G. Micheal Hopf wrote in his poem <u>Those Who Remain</u> about the endless cycle of civilizations where hard men create easy times and easy times create weak men, or something to that effect. Bob didn't need the actual quote to weave the meaning into his theory of failing civilizations.

Bob once saw a short news clip embedded into a video on communism in the '60s. There was an old lady leaning out her second story window somewhere in the Soviet Union and answering the reporter who had asked her a simple question: "Why aren't you out helping your neighbors pick the crops before the rains come and ruin everything?" Her answer: "I'm 70 years old. Sure, I could go help, but why should I? I have a roof over my head, clothes on my back and food in my belly. It's always been that way. Why should that change because one old lady doesn't go out into the muddy fields to help harvest the beets?"

Bob would never forget that short exchange. It was the purest illustration of Communism. No work ethic. No concern for the welfare of others. As long as I have what I need, why should I ever work? Weak men and women are the behind the downfall of all civilizations.

Bob sensed that what was going on in his country at the moment looked and smelled a lot like the approach of Communism via the weak sister, Socialism. He only hoped that his simple novel painted a picture of American life as it was a few decades earlier, and this picture would resonate with his readers. Life is hard. Sure. But life under any form of Socialism or Communism is more than most people can handle.

That was the message, if there ever was one, that Bob was addressing. Take responsibility for yourself. Don't count on others to harvest your beets. Make it on your own merits, your own sweat, blood and tears. It will be far more rewarding than any other option.

Chapter 34~Bob's Passion for Golf

Bob's golf career didn't come to an end when he left for college. While he had caddied and played for seven years and served as Caddymaster at 17, he never lost the passion for the game. He played competitively as a young teen, winning several trophies along with a set of socket wrenches, believe it or not, in a "closest to the pin" contest, But, without the time or the money, he only played one or two casual rounds in his four years at UD. However, he lit it back up once he was in the Army. Every Army post had a golf course, sometimes a cranky little 9-holer, other times a competition-level Robert Trent Jones course. He found time at Signal Basic school at Ft. Gordon to play some golf on the Robert Trent Jones course, which was a real treat at Army rates. Annual membership was less than a hundred bucks for unlimited golf. He didn't play competitive golf at Ft. Gordon, but managed to get his game back in shape in just 4 months. This was also when he taught Naomi to play, and she took to it quite readily.

Bob played a lot more golf once he got to his first assignment at Ft. Leonard Wood, MO. The course there wasn't as upscale as Trent-Jones, but it had a well-organized Mens Golf Association, which sponsored regular tournaments as well as the annual club championship. Every Saturday a fairly regular group of members played a serious "skins" game where the pot could grow upwards of 50 dollars! Bob had played plenty of rounds for bets, but this was a serious chunk of change.

For the next three seasons, Bob kept his head above water, not making a fortune, but not losing his shirt, either. Along the way, he qualified for the Major Command Championship Team, which sent him to tourneys in Indiana and Alabama to face other Major Command teams. While he didn't come back with any trophies, his team always placed in the top 5 or 6. More importantly, getting his game to the next level was more valuable than a trophy.

Bob managed to win the FLW Club Championship in 1975, but lose to the '75 runner up in 1976. His game had really matured over recent years and he finally found the money to buy a new set of clubs. He had been playing the same clubs since 1969.

Bob's later assignments did not have golf courses on site. He did manage to play a local muni in San Luis Obispo, and had the pleasure of playing the Blackhorse and Bayonet courses at Ft. Ord in California. Since he had not been playing on a regular basis, the scenery overlooking the Pacific was far better than his performance on those tough courses.

There was neither time nor money to play once he left the Army in '77. It was an everyday challenge just to stay above board financially for about three years. Certainly, no golf.

Once he arrived for the Advance Course at Ft. Gordon, the Trent-Jones course easily sucked him back in. Almost every weekend and class breaks, Bob could be found at the golf course. Once assigned to Augsburg, Germany, he joined the only course in the area, The Bavarian Golf Club, which was only a ten minute drive from post and patronized mostly by Army personnel.

The tournaments at Bavarian were not as plentiful as other posts, and the skins games were rare. But it was still a golf course, albeit a 9 hole course that was played twice around from different tees. Golf is golf and passion is passion.

One of Bob's most disastrous rounds was the greatest example of choking at the finish line. Bob was four strokes ahead of the competition as he stepped up to the last tee. Unfortunately, he let his confidence morph into cockiness and push-sliced his first drive out of bounds right (Elvis has left the golf course.). He teed up his second ball, and as usual, overcorrected with a pull-hook out of bounds on the left (Elvis has left the golf course, again!). He finished the hole with a disastrous eight, and lost the tournament by one stroke! How's that for passion?

There was another great break in the golf game when Bob left the service for the second time, involuntarily. He didn't pick up the sticks until he relocated to Northern Virginia and a job with a "Beltway Bandit" as government contractors were called. He soon learned that both his boss and his boss and his boss (the President of the company) were avid golfers. Whenever the company needed a team for a tournament, Bob was invited as the "fourth." They did manage to win a few, but results were inconsistent over the years. It was, however, a boatload of fun and great networking!

Throughout this period, Bob's passion for golf outpaced his fun money, so he played far fewer rounds than he would have liked. But, once again, beggars can't be choosers. His game quickly faded, as it's known to do, but not his passion.

Once his final job ceased to exist, he took a totally different track. He went to school to become a certified Golf Professional, an Instructor. He quickly picked up a teaching position at a golf facility just a mile from home. He thought he was in golf heaven. He was able to make his own schedule, book his own clients including last-minute bookings because of his proximity to the golf facility. That facility shut its doors less than a year later, to make room for more luxury housing.

He picked up a job for the Head Pro at a Regional Course in the next county. He had to change the way he did business a bit, since now he had a 40 minute commute and a very involved boss. His boss was also the Head Coach of the golf team at the high school across the street from the 6th hole. Very convenient.

Bob was asked by some of the team Moms if he wanted to coach the team. They had observed him teaching a class of little kids on the putting green and liked what they saw. Bob decided to give it a go, but needed the Head Pro's permission. Bob managed to convince the Head Pro that he would make a good coach, and applied for the position with the school's Athletic Director. Thanks to the parents, the offer was quickly made and accepted. Less than a month later, he was the Falcon's Head Golf Coach.

For the next 5 years, Bob enjoyed the hell out of coaching high school golf. Not only did he have excellent golfers and students, the parents were an absolute pleasure to deal with. There were no "helicopter Moms" or Dads who were convinced their kid was going to the PGA!

The Falcons managed to qualify for the State Championships in his first year of coaching. While they didn't excel at the tournament, they were the first team in the school to go undefeated in the regular season and have a run at states ! All in Bob's first year! The football and baseball teams were a bit peeved at that! He always believed that he melded the team's talent with his own passion for the game to get them that far that fast. But, it didn't hurt that the Falcons were the only team in the county and, perhaps the state and country with a certified Golf Pro as their coach. Of course, that didn't hurt matters.

As a new coach, Bob didn't realize what an impact he had and connection he made very quickly with these young minds. It wasn't until Bob's Mom passed and he had to travel back to Connecticut the same week as the Regional competition that he recognized the connection. While the basketball coach stepped up to take the golf team to the tournament, they didn't do well. When Bob queried the team at their next practice, they told him that, while the basketball coach was a "nice guy" and knew the game, "he just wasn't you, Coach. He didn't do the things you do or the way you do them!"

Bob accepted both the testimonial and the lesson learned, but the team didn't make it to the State Championship that year!

Regardless of their performance, Bob made it his mission to make sure every team member played at least one contest in regular season. No bench warmers. He also made it his mission to recruit some girls to the team without lowering the bar or making exceptions. Luckily, he had a young lady as a student in his private lesson book who had never touched a club until she started 8th grade, but worked to become good enough to make the team by time she entered high school. She went on to become the number two player on the

Falcons team before graduation. From zero to sixty in less than four years! Bob also recruited a second young female golfer with great talent. She played on the team until her senior year, when other priorities took over.

Two of Bob's Falcons went on to play college golf. Bob was amused and a little bit jealous, when his best former Falcon called to tell him that "they gave me a whole new set of Titliest clubs, Coach!" What breeds success? Hard work and perseverance? This young fellow had everything needed to go on the PGA Tour, but his father forbade it. "Career was more important than golf."Can't argue with that, Dad.

Bob went on to coach the Falcons for five years, until the commute became ridiculously difficult with all the new home construction. It was a great run and memorable experience to coach these young folks. He was selected as Loudon County Coach of the Year in his first coaching season. That was mostly due to the excellence of his golfers. But it was the parents that made it easy. Their unwavering support for their kids, discipline and the decorum of the game were invaluable to the success of the adventure.

Soon after, Bob took a teaching position at a county course in Fairfax, where he taught both individuals and groups, including kids' summer camps, for a couple of years. When his golf school had an opening at another county course, they asked him to teach there, at Burke Lake Park. It was there that Bob was tapped to be the golf coach for Special Olympics Area 26. It was both a challenge and a joy to coach this group of energetic golf students. Bob also learned what it was like to be a parent of a special needs child (even though many were not children). He spent several years as their coach and enjoyed every minute with them. Once again, the support of the parents was tantamount to the success of the effort. Bob tossed out all his golf trophies when he retired, but he kept the one plaque he received from the Special Olympics golfers.

Bob checked off a bucket list item (not that he ever really had them) when he attempted to qualify for the USGA Senior Open at the Homestead, in Hot Springs, VA, Sam Snead's old birdie hunting grounds. What Bob didn't realize before submitting his application, is just how bad a physical shape he was in. The course was near the border of Virginia and West Virginia, a very hilly area. Simply walking the course with a caddy became difficult and tiring. After all, he was now in his mid 50s and not in horrible shape, but not in great shape. His legs got very tired after the first nine and his game got tired as well. He finished just a few strokes out of the "alternate" scores, but it was a great experience just to try. Ironically, that was the first time Bob had his own caddy. That was a nice treat, but very expensive. His caddy got a great chuckle when Bob told him he caddied for two dollars a bag in the '60s! Bob was out almost $100 when the day was over, not including the entry fee or travel and hotel. For that, he got to play one of the oldest and most famous courses in the country and canned another great memory.

Bob quit teaching in 2016, when he and Naomi decided to retire to Texas. Although he was offered a position to teach at a local retail golf establishment, he turned it down. He had exceeded his expectations as a Professional Golf Instructor and decided to focus on playing. He started playing with some groups in their retirement community, where the wager was never more than five dollars! But he enjoyed the game more than ever, despite the failure of his aging body to keep up.

Hundreds of books and articles have been written over the decades either about great golfers or by great golfers. Nicklaus, Palmer, Snead, and dozens of others wrote about their golf careers. Some were just stories from the road, while others were highly instructional. Bob's favorite was the Ben Hogan's <u>Five Lessons: Modern Fundamentals of Golf</u>, published in 1957. That was the book Bob used to build his golf swing and he kept that book in his library forever.

But golf is more than just a sport and leisure pastime. It serves as an analogy to life, if you are paying attention. The first rule is to "play the ball as you find it." Some folks are born to wealth others to poverty. Quit whining and play your life as you find it. There are a multitude of other Rules of Golf that few folks can digest in one sitting. Life is the same. You learn the rules as you go along. Golf is also the only game where you are expected to call your own fouls and assign the punishment. If your ball moves as a result of your action, that's on you. Replace the ball and take your penalty. Nobody else may have seen it, but you did. Take your penalty and play on!

We see lots of rude noise on TV during a pro tournament broadcast. It's unnecessary and runs counter to the traditional refinement of golf. Some shallow-minded minion yells "mashed potatoes" or "get in the hole!" just so someone can hear his loud mouth on TV? How pathetic! What's worse, is that this horrible behavior is becoming acceptable, even by the broadcasters who could easily cut off a few microphones and deny the idiots.

If the long-standing traditions and courtesies of golf could be papered across society, the world would be a far more enjoyable place to live. From simple things, like not stepping on another golfer's putting line and staying quiet when others are swinging to more complex ideas, like helping an opponent properly identify his ball in the leaves, golf blends rules with common courtesies. The contest is not finished until the ball lies at the bottom of the cup. A metaphor for life, if only life were so simple.

Show up, shut up, and keep up! Words to live by?

Chapter 35~And Miles to Go Before I Sleep (All Credit to Robert Frost)

Bob took a break from writing and made a second attempt to use the new software application to dictate his story rather than typing and typing and re-typing. Unfortunately, this software, like most other software produced at the time was absolute and total nonsense, not ready for prime time! It was coming up with words and sentences that were nowhere near correct. But as a stubborn Italian he wasn't ready to give up on it so he gave it another stab. "Maybe it's my voice," he mumbled to himself. "Maybe I should use my radio voice" he said hoping the software will recognize every word properly, he turned back to the story. The whole idea of describing the house in such detail was to put in place a good setting for the entire story and reveal an impeccable attention to detail in storytelling. Nye just thought he was complaining, like most stubborn Italians.

But, Bob knew he wasn't done writing. He had been bitten by the creativity bug and, while it was sometimes tedious, it was rewarding. Part of his problem was selecting the most interesting topics and events. He never identified his "target audience" that other authors and reviewers insisted was necessary. Since it was all fiction, that was an open door through which he passed over and over again on his quest to finish the "Great American Novel" and become a "Paperback Writer." His audience was anyone who liked a good, humorous, maybe even educational story, or series of stories, as it turned out. Beyond that, it was anyone bored enough to read a new writer. It really didn't seem so complicated as others were making it out to be.

So, he would move ahead, if only one yard at at time. By the fall of 2022, he knew he was close to the goal line, and just moved on. Perhaps another game of inches to the finish line. He had originally speculated, with no real-world experience, that about 90,000 words was a good goal. One of his friends and published author suggested that I might consider writing two books, since there was so much material. As he continued to press on, that goal seemed to keep moving further and further away. He was now thinking compromise, shorten the distance to the goal post, do an end run around his original, arbitrary word count. Why not? The work was his to do whatever tickled his fancy as a writer. It was just that simple.

So being the stubborn ass he was, he pressed on. He knew some of his stories would have to wait. He was no spring chicken, and had already lived longer than his father. But pessimism was not his preferred life companion, so he just assumed he would continue to write.

After all, he hadn't fully developed the characters of the siblings. He had yet to write about raising step-kids, grandkids and a Foster kid. He hadn't written about working in the Silicon Valley. There were so many more stories and, just maybe, a few lessons yet to be shared with the readers. He wasn't done. Not by a long shot.

We shall see.

Never stop drumming and stay warm!

Acknowledgements

In any meaningful endeavor, there are a multitude of folks providing assistance to completion. I extend my sincere gratitude to all the great minds who helped me bring this book to fruition.

First, of course, my dear wife, Naomi, who is an avid reader and pulls no punches in her commentary. I'm glad she was also one of the final reviewers and caught a few "uglies" in the pre-production draft. This novel would be far less enjoyable, and much more snarky without her input.

LTC(R) Wesley Riddle, a published author and reviewer, Oxford Student and West Point graduate, was an early reviewer of this work and helped me get going in the right direction.

Lynn Griesemer, the author of several books on various subjects, provided meaningful and productive feedback on all aspects of writing and publishing my work. Her husband, Bob, another published author of technical publications, offered a pair of focused eyes and sharp mind providing needed feedback.

Hank Haliasz a retired Air Force Officer and published novelist of several "edunovellas", acted as a mentor in the realm of story telling and self-publishing. Sharing his successful experience in this world of digital publishing is greatly appreciated.

Brothers Tony and Rick both provided valuable feedback in the early days. Their words of encouragement are greatly appreciated.

Finally, I must thank my youngest daughter, Sharon and her man, Mark, for reviewing the final product for publication. Reading the entire novel while working full time was, I'm sure, a challenge, but they persevered and helped me put this "masterpiece"to bed!

About the Author

R.J.Vitti graduated the University of Dayton in 1974 with B.S. English Education. He earned a Master of Systems Engineering in 2001 from the George Washington University in Washington, D.C. In his varied and remarkable life, Bob experienced things that few others, if any, ever come across. His professional career spans over 50 years, including the jobs he had as a young man.   Paperboy, caddy, photographer,   Cable TV installer, Army Signal Corps Officer, Communications and Computer Systems Analysis, Systems Engineering Manager, Golf Pro, High School Head Golf Coach, Special Olympics Golf Coach, and others.   And now, Novelist! Who woulda thunk?

Bob is retired in Texas with his wife, Naomi Rose and their two fur babies.

The Book Title, <u>Lock it Up, Don't Burn it Down,</u> was suggested by his youngest daughter, Sharon. It was the phrase she heard constantly over the years from Dad, which served as a reminder that life comes with risk.

Living an interesting and meaningful life requires you to go out, manage the risks, and live in the real world.

Life is Good

9 798218 100056